The Abandoned Woman

NOVELS BY RICHARD CONDON

The Abandoned Woman
The Whisper of the Axe
Money Is Love
The Star Spangled Crunch
Winter Kills
Arigato
The Vertical Smile
Mile High
The Ecstasy Business
Any God Will Do
An Infinity of Mirrors
A Talent for Loving
Some Angry Angel
The Manchurian Candidate
The Oldest Confession

OTHER BOOKS

And Then We Moved to Rossenarra
The Mexican Stove

The Abandoned Woman

RICHARD CONDON

The Dial Press
New York

Published by
The Dial Press
1 Dag Hammarskjold Plaza
New York, New York 10017

Manufactured in the United States of America

First printing

Designed by James L. McGuire

Library of Congress Cataloging in Publication Data

Condon, Richard.
   The abandoned woman.

   1. Caroline Amelia Elizabeth, consort of George IV,
1768–1821—Fiction. I. Title.
PZ4.C746Ab   [PS3553.0487]   813'.5'4   76–56240
ISBN 0–8037–0283–3

For
The London Library

Author's Note:

This is not a history. It is a novel
in which Caroline of Brunswick, later
Princess of Wales, later Queen of
England, is a central character.

Ne'er read a tale for historical facts;
Read tales for historical truth,
Why take a woman who's all chips and cracks?
You can have one in passionate youth.
History, a mirror which facets ten mirrors
Concealed in a mummy propped up in a booth,
Or, 'tis also a woman, abandoned and naked
Who pants on a divan to embrace the right sleuth.

—The Keeners' Manual

The Abandoned Woman

book one
marriage
(1794-1795)

TORY PARTY IN POWER
PRIME MINISTER: *William Pitt, the Younger*

Her passions are so strong that even her father, himself, said she was not to be allowed to go from one room to another without her governess, and when she dances this lady is obliged to follow her around and across the floor for all of the dance, moving like a games referee or a hasty crab, or both, to prevent her from making an exhibition of herself by indecent "conversations" (spoken from her hips and hands) with men, and that all amusements have been forbidden her because of her immodest conduct. There, dear brother, is a woman I do not recommend at all. All these charges must be true. If it is an invention then he must be more than the Devil who has invented such a pretty tale.

—Letter from the Queen of
England to her German brother,
the Duke of Mecklenburg-Strelitz,
October 1794

1

Caroline, wearing a yellow dress, sits in her boudoir in her father's palace at Brunswick, staring into her mirror. She is a pretty woman of albuminous simplicity. She speaks aloud to the mirror in labored English: "But is Captain Manning's way the best way to make to learn a language?" Images of herself as she takes sexual instruction from Captain Manning, ex-Irish Guards, in contraposition to him; nude or wearing an Army greatcoat; standing, sitting, or sprawling, make her laugh in star-bursting shapes: sagital, bicorne and infundibular. The power of the noise of her laughter creates a temporary vacuum around her, causing her to gasp after each aria.

Brushing her cheese-colored hair, she sings a rude barracks song, in English, which Captain Manning has taught her. She thinks of how all the other princesses in Germany probably want to hang themselves this morning because they have wasted a year learning to speak English. She, of all of them, is going to marry the Prince of Wales, the handsomest man in Europe. A delicious shiver goes through her. She will be bedded by her own first cousin. Incest!

The handsomest man in Europe has sent her a miniature portrait of himself. She takes it into bed with her, presses it into her most intimate places, and almost faints with pleasure. She knows the handsomest man in Europe must have many mistresses. He must know more ways

than Manning. After years in bed with him she will get fat
and old, like Mama, and one day reign as Queen of England. She bursts into another raucous song, her voice as
tuneful as a turkey's: *When after all is said and done/'Tis better
to be married.*

Mama says that twenty-six is already very old for a girl
to be chosen to marry such a Prince. He is thirty-two. He
wants her. Right at that moment, she imagines, he is probably deep in a piggy-pile of lewd mistresses and as he does
it to them and they do it to him, he is thinking of his little
Caroline and when they will be together.

She giggles into the mirror, producing outstanding
new sounds. Perhaps Lord Dickie Adler, or the Thuringian banker who spends so much time in London, Er-
minius Levin, have told the Prince a thing or two about her
already. She has to stuff a stocking into her mouth to stifle
the laughter. It is not true that twenty-six is already old.
How will she become a proper, wise Queen of England
unless she knows life? Even as it is she does not know it
enough. Papa and Fräulein Rosensweig, her governess, see
to that. Still she has had mad little moments with Bocca,
the war historian; and with Vicomte Bertie Caen, who
made her sit with him afterward while he wrote down
every detail in his private chronicle; with Sidney Smith,
the admiral; and with Franz Heller, the mercenary; but
most of all with Captain Manning, the master, whom Papa
himself decorated in the field of battle with three berib-
boned orders ripped from his own uniform. She giggles
again. She does not count tossings by peasant boys in the
fields or even the unknown visiting Englishmen who have
slipped into her bed at night. It is still not a lot of living,
she is certain, but Papa is a very strict man who struggles
daily to live up to what Pitt the Elder has said of him: "His

days are precious to Europe." But to have enjoyed even so few men is a wonderful thing. She sighs with pleasure.

The Brunswick court is far pleasanter than Versailles ever was. Its immorality is by no means on so grand a scale, while its freedom from courtly restraint is much greater. All foreign travelers of good birth are welcome here. It is popular with wandering mercenary soldiers having no money and fewer scruples. Between wars the Duke supervises strings of masked balls, banquets, garden fêtes, operas. The social occasions inspire constant copulation. In all the years Caroline is at Brunswick, active, vigorous sex is in the air as if it were a form of national entertainment or a component of the local atmosphere.

During her twenty-six years there has been no lack of formal suitors for Caroline's hand. Her father is the glorious Duke of Brunswick. Her mother is the sister of the King of England. But as possible husbands step forward, something always happens, causing their suits to fall through. Aside from these formal courtships and informal liaisons Caroline has had two quite serious love affairs; serious at least in intensity and duration. The first was with the (then) Major Franz Heller of His Britannic Majesty's German Legion; the second was with Sidney Smith, Royal Navy, at the time attached to the Duke's military staff, a man destined to distinguish himself gallantly with his marines and seamen against Napoleon's Egyptian army corps at the siege of Acre. His jolly tar style of conducting a love affair is endearing, based upon friendship and common feelings for amorous uses. Major Heller's style is more grossly sentimental, loudly and self-pityingly lachrymose; possessive and violent; a grotesquely complicated man, capable of total loyalty to three or more quite opposite forces; a quintuple agent; a man in waiting. Caroline last beds Major Heller at Brunswick when she is sixteen; Captain Smith when she is twenty-two. She vows that, if possible, she will never forget them.

Caroline has other skills. She invents and builds ingenious mechanical toys which she distributes delightedly among the children of Brunswick cottagers. The toys are so good they are copied by commercial manufacturers. She is passionately fond of children; sponsors a dozen at a time to play at the palace, among them one or two "little mistakes" of her own. She is a good student. She is acclaimed as best royal performer on the harpsichord in Europe. She is a fine sculptress. Her religious upbringing is consciously scanty by family plan because, as her father noted, she would have to marry a Prince, but it was impossible to know whether he would be Catholic or Protestant.

Someone knocks at the Princess's boudoir door. It opens without her permission, so she knows it is Papa. She turns away from the mirror and stands to greet him in English. "Guten Morning, Papa," she says.

"Good! You must say good morning."

She smiles at him and shrugs.

"I shall be receiving the British envoy in a few moments," her father reminds her.

"I observed him at dinner, Papa."

Papa is Charles William Ferdinand, Duke of Brunswick. He has passed along all his bland coloring to his children. His large ears have missed the Princess and so has the syphilis and also, hopefully, that nudge toward insanity conferred on some of the other children. The Duke, while syphilitic, is not mad. The madness comes from Mama's side of the family, the English royals. The Duke knows that with the match the bride and groom will be sharing some decidedly irregular blood entangled in the chains of some very old diseases, but such things go with the royals' trade.

"Tell me your observations."

"I was impressed, Papa. Lord Malmesbury is the most British object, including their flag, I have ever seen."

"Yes. Amazing! Not one un-British sound or move. Yet the man has lived all over Europe. It is negative magic, really."

The Duke is wearing a dress uniform, with the starburst of a Marshal of the Prussian Army, at ten-twenty in the morning. His indefectibly rigid posture informs all that he is the greatest of the condottieri of Europe; defender of kings if the price is right. He speaks French in the palace because he knows there are always servants at the keyholes. "You make me content that you have observed Lord Malmesbury so acutely. There is hope."

"I have made you happy!"

"Lord Malmesbury is to be your model."

"Yes, Papa?"

"There are only five people whom you may see alone from this moment. Hm? Five. Nummer eins: Lord Malmesbury, who will demonstrate England to you. Hm? Two—your aunt, my sister, the Abbess. Trois: my good friend, Mademoiselle von Hertzberg. Quatre: your governess, Fräulein Rosensweig. Fünf: your mother, because there is no way we can prevent that. Four women, one man. Do you understand?"

"Yes, Papa."

"You are not so much as to *stand* near any other person. Particularly I refer to Captain Manning. *Verstehen?*"

Caroline begins to weep. It will encourage her father to leave before he can think of other terrible rules. Tears run down like crystal fudge upon her red-on-white cheeks, furrowing the carmine candy and pure white cream underneath. Her eyes become pink. "Oh, Papa," she wails. "I love you dearly. Better nor anny oder pairson."

He lifts her chin with two fingers to kiss her lightly on the cheek. He whirls in a perfectly executed military about-face. He marches out of the room.

Before Caroline can return to her visit with the mirror, her mother comes shuffling into the room wearing a purple peignoir and laden down with jewels. The arrival alarms Caroline. Her mother does not leave the comforts of her own apartments for anything less than a fête. They speak in sloppily constructed German make-shifted out of her mother's laziness.

"Mama! What happened?"

"Where?"

"Why are you here?"

"Why not?"

"Why *not*?"

"My own daughter has been called to my homeland across the seas to become the future Queen of England; why shouldn't I counsel her? No one understands my heart. In God's truth, I have nothing to love and no one loves me."

"What counsel, Mama? I can hardly wait."

"Not counsel, a warning. Take it or leave it, I couldn't care less, and it is very chilly in here. Your father is always warm from some woman's bed, so he doesn't care if anyone else is warm."

"Offer the warning, please, Mama."

"Beware of the Prince's confidential counsellor. Franz Heller. Formerly of my brother the King's German Legion."

"*Hel*ler?"

"A blackguard. He does the Prince's dirty work. I hate to say this about anyone, but Heller is a bad German."

"Are you saying that the Prince would allow this man to damage his own little bride, Mama?"

"Puzzle it out. But the Prince is much less than he seems from seven hundred miles away. Up close he is his mother's son, a nothing without a heart, but with four mirrors."

"You walked all the way over here from your wing to tell me things like this about the man I'm going to marry?"

"No, you little idiot," the Duchess says, "I came to warn you about Heller." She shuffles out of the room. Caroline understands that her mother was only telling her, in her own insistently detached way, that Caroline must not take any chances by renewing her past with Colonel Heller. Caroline hates all advice, anyone's advice, unless she is giving it. She knows far better than her mother that Franz Heller is a monster.

Lord Malmesbury backs out of the apartments of Lady Maria fFletcher, Marchioness of Horne, so that, if he is observed, it will be seen that he is actually going in. In a stately manner he hastens to the Duke's study. Malmesbury is a compact Scotsman (lightly scented with vetiver root) whose court clothing makes it appear that he is wearing a large codpiece. ("It has to be a codpiece" more than 700 aristocratic women have wondered, bemused in six European capitals.) Malmesbury is not wearing a codpiece. Also, he has a fleshy, definitely formed nose under watchful eyes. He is forty-two. He was Secretary of the Embassy at Madrid in 1770; was Minister at Berlin in 1772; ran British counter-spying behind the lines of the Continental Army in North America from 1775 until 1778; and after that was at St. Petersburg, then at the Hague until 1784. Were he three inches taller, he would have been a general; three inches stouter, a bishop. He is intelligent; greatly experienced of life; keen about his work.

The Duke reaches his study twenty-four seconds before Malmesbury knocks; is deeply into state papers when the Earl enters. He greets and seats the ambassador absent-mindedly; he stays on his feet. He paces and dominates the interview by elevation and his great prestige. To get the talk started he speaks of an account he has written to the King of Prussia suggesting a union of English and Austrian armies against Napoleon. He says flatly he will not command this force but will gladly supervise the execution of any plan for the defense of Holland. He deprecates the Austrians. "The men are good but the officers are radically inclined. The Emperor is weak. Rollin is corrupted. Ferrari is a democrat and, I fear, the ridiculous Illuminés have taken root and govern everywhere."

What Malmesbury understands all this to mean, and correctly, is that the amount of money offered to the Duke to take command is not yet right. Malmesbury makes no counter-offer on behalf of his government, so the Duke dismisses politics.

"I ask your opinion of the Princess in relation to the Prince of Wales."

"My orders are flat, Your Grace," Malmesbury replies. "His Majesty has withheld my discretionary powers to comment or interpret in this matter—to him or anyone else."

"Why?"

"There is to be no discussion. He has chosen the Princess for his son. He wants no further recommendations from me—or through his son from me—nor will he grant the existence of my thoughts and opinions in this matter. I am here to arrange the marriage. I have no other existence in the matter where the King and the court are concerned. It is a firm order."

"I do not ask about the marriage," the Duke says, in French. (He fears that French is a dying language, that some strange Napoleonic argot may spring up as had the new French calendar.) Malmesbury enjoys speaking French as very little else seems to be spoken in Europe by those people who have something to say.

"I will tell you about the marriage," the Duke says. "Politically—excellent. Also your Queen is a mortal enemy of my wife's and she is greatly upset that our daughter has been chosen for the Prince, so there is that in its favor. The Prince chose her; the King endorses. Two against one on the home front. Physically, it is a bad marriage for them and for their children. I know all this. I want your impressions of the Princess, please. I want the English view of her."

"Ah! I see. Then I would say—a pretty face not overly expressive of softness. The figure—substantial. *Fine* eyes. *Good* hands. *Wondrous* amiability. A universal reputation for genuine kindness. Tolerable teeth but perhaps going. A *good* bust. She is short but she has impertinent shoulders."

"Saucy?"

"Yes, frankly. But only the shoulders."

"And that is the English impression."

"Well! I would say that is a very *favorable* impression."

"She is not stupid," the Duke says slowly, "but she has no judgment. She has been strictly brought up because that was necessary." He sighs a baffled father's sigh. "The King is my brother-in-law. I want you and the King to know I am perfectly sensible of the facts of the character of the Prince. I am aware of the inconveniences which would result from his liking my daughter either too much or too little. We both know the character of the Queen, so we look for no help for the Princess from that side of the palace." The Duke does his best to soften his arrogant eyes. "But you can help her, Malmesbury."

"And so I shall, Your Grace. That is—insofar as I am permitted to help."

"By the Princess?"

"By my government. To pinpoint, by the Prince."

"I see. Very well. Nonetheless, the Princess likes you. *No, no!* Forget that. Never mind that. She *trusts* you. Already she has been told—that is to say she has told *me*—that she will depend on you to learn what is right in all things English."

"You see, Your Grace," Malmesbury says, "I am a professional diplomat. My Foreign Office—or the King—the same thing really—moves me from place to place. I have no way of knowing how long I will be on this assignment, but as long as I am with your daughter, you may know that I will do anything and everything to ease her way in England."

"Thank you, Malmesbury. I do depend upon you to counsel her. You must tell her not to be free in giving out her opinions of persons and things aloud. Her mother is a *reck*less talker, which is where the child learned it. The Princess believes this is how her own conduct should be modeled because her mother is English. Nothing could be further from the truth as we all know. You must try to make everyone in London keenly aware that a German court is much, *much* less formal than an English court." The Duke tightened up his own court the previous week by sending back to Egypt his young Coptic mistress and restricting himself for the duration of Malmesbury's visit to only two mistresses; Mademoiselle von Hertzberg, who came to Brunswick with her husband, a professional courtier, from Paris, and a young Italian girl who didn't get out of bed very often to show herself.

The Duke says fervently, "I implore you to advise the Princess rigorously never to show any jealousy of the Prince and to drill her on the reality that, if he has any moods, she must not notice them."

"I shall apply myself earnestly to that task."

"But I understand your professional demands. You cannot remain with her forever, like a chamberlain. Will you do this for her? Will you think with all your mind for someone as massively English and as utterly trustworthy as yourself to replace you when you must go on to your next assignment?"

"Perhaps a woman, Your Grace. The right woman of knowledge, experience, breeding and integrity could be closer to the Princess than I will ever be."

"Yes. A really formidable English noblewoman. Do you think you can come up with precisely the woman in the next few days?"

"I think so. Yes. Why so soon?"

"Because I want to be sure that my daughter's right to request by name not less than one lady-in-waiting is written into the marriage contract so that, if the Prince should oppose this person who will be my daughter's only real friend, perhaps, as she gropes her way into English life, he cannot cause another woman of his own choice to replace her."

"Good point, Your Grace. Very wise indeed. It is understood that the husband must name and control the members of his wife's Household, but this is a most reasonable exception."

The Duke sits down to terminate the audience. He is bored. He feels like a gossip. Almost anything would be more engrossing than this discussion of a distinguished royal marriage in his own family, which is habituated to such honors. He had said what was expected of him. Duty has been served.

The Prince goes into a mighty rage when told that the Duke of Brunswick insists that his daughter be allowed to name one of her ladies-in-waiting as being her own choice and an Englishwoman of impeccable background. The Prince says such things are in his province alone, that only he will determine who is to be established in his wife's Household. Malmesbury reports that the Duke is so convinced of the rightness of his attitude on this matter that he has demanded that it become a condition in the marriage contract. To overcome the problem Malmesbury sees to it that the essence of the matter is conveyed to the King through the Government. The King terms the request utterly reasonable; overrides his son. The Prince is so affected by frustration and fury over this setback that he needs to be bled to keep him from violence. He is a bloody-minded man who will not suffer any woman to defy his will.

When he is calmer, the Prince demands to be told the Duke's choice for an English lady-in-waiting. The King tells him the lady's name, as it has been provided to him, smirking his pleasure as he does so. "Lady Joyce Anglesong," he says. "That is the woman they want by the Princess's side."

"Oh, my God! Oh, my God!" the Prince cries out,

striking his forehead heavily with a fist. Anglesong is the most singularly difficult woman in England.

On Thursday, the 4th December 1794, at 11:00 A.M., Monsieur de Feronce, the Duke's legal adviser, with his secretary, Nongre, arrive at the small Brunswick palace assigned to Lord Malmesbury to conclude the signing of the marriage treaty. The treaty is drawn in English and in Latin—Malmesbury objects to French in official documents. It is done word-for-word according to his instructions. After the signing, Feronce presents the Earl with a snuff box from the Duke and a diamond watch from Princess Caroline. He gives Mr. Ross, Malmesbury's secretary, 150 ducats. The signing of the treaty is the most legal and effective form of marriage. There will be a confrontation marriage, a wedding, after the royal couple meet, to make the English people happy, but this marriage, executed by Lord Malmesbury and Feronce, is the real one.

After the presentation of the gifts Malmesbury walks, behind what is most certainly not a codpiece, with the Duchess in the palace gardens. Even though she is a bagpipe of a woman, he knows what an important moment this must be in a mother's life. The Duchess does not even cast as much as a wondering eye at his court trousers.

"I hate being on my feet," she says in German, "but I am so nervous. Weddings are torments."

"Ah, well, Madam," Malmesbury says, "all's well." He speaks English to remind her that she is *royally* English, sister of the King of England, whose ambassador he is; not a German.

"I feel so *agi*tated," the Duchess continues in German, or near German. She actually uses the Yiddish word *Ungepatchket* causing Malmesbury to cringe with dismay. "I feel I must *plead* with you to become Caroline's adviser in England. She is such a *silly* girl! You can have no idea! If she were not my daughter I would tell you that she must have something wrong up here." The Duchess taps her forehead, appalling Malmesbury. Tact is certainly thin on the ground in this lady's garden, he thinks.

The Duchess goes on. "She has this hidden capacity, which she does not keep hidden for long unfortunately, to get herself into *enormous* trouble. She needs your steadying hand so badly."

"Insofar as my government sees fit to assign me, I shall offer all support to the Princess," he says.

Her eyes fall. She starts, lightly. He must be wearing two codpieces! she thinks.

That afternoon Lord Malmesbury makes a formal call upon the Princess to inform her that the treaty is concluded, that she is now the Princess of Wales. This realization makes no more of an impression on her than it had upon her father. She and her husband share the same ancestors; are of precisely equal royal station.

She speaks to Malmesbury in her own sort of English, which cannot be called anything but charming because it is such mixed-up pronunciation, grammar, syntax, that no one could feel she is attempting anything more than a brave experiment. "What do you think would make the besser Princess of Wales, Malmesbury," she asks. "Meinself oder the Hereditary Princess?" The Hereditary Princess is the colossally dignified Princess Louise of Mecklenburg-Strelitz, the niece of the Queen of England and her choice for the post of her son's bride.

"There is no need to conjecture, Your Highness," he answers in French to stabilize her. "The treaty is signed.

You and only you are the Princess of Wales."

"You must not avoid. You must state so."

"Well! I can tell you who *I* think would be the Prince's choice," he replies in English because they are speaking of the British royal family.

"Which?"

"You."

"Why?"

"Because you possess by nature what the Hereditary Princess does not have and can never acquire—beauty, grace and an ever-growing feeling for tact. Further, the qualities which the Hereditary Princess has—each one of them—are qualities which you most certainly will attain."

"What are those?"

He ticked them off on his pale, thimble-shaped fingers. "Prudence, discretion, attention and—tact."

"I need those?"

"You cannot have too much of them."

"How comes the Hereditary Princess who is younger as me, to have them more than?"

"Because, at a very early period in her life, her family was in danger. She was brought up in need of the exertion of the mind. Now she derives the benefit."

"Ach! I shall never learn that. I am too open, too idle, too *légère.*"

"Fear not."

"I fear."

"When you are in a different situation, you will see. You do not need these forebearing virtues here the way you must have them in England. Only commune with yourself, Princess. Question yourself, and you will also act up to the situation."

Caroline likes the way his skin is stretched over his

head; not too tightly, not too loosely. She thinks it is a great joke that he has the wit to stuff his court trousers with that codpiece. She adores the humor of it. And his lips. They are fat little things, quite juicy leeches, she thinks. She hopes the Prince is going to look this good to her because she doesn't believe that miniature portrait of him for one moment. Everyone has run to tell her how much he eats and drinks, so he cannot look like he looks in that portrait. She flutters her eyelids at Malmesbury as she has often practiced in her mirror. She says, "My aunt, the Abbess, says you are a dangerous man."

His face goes ferocious with irritation. "Your aunt has forgotten that twenty years have elapsed since she has seen or heard from me," he snaps. "Further, such an insinuation is a tacit accusation of my being very foolishly principled."

"Ach! I have offended you! Perhaps I think too partially of you myself." She finds herself most partial to him at the moment because Papa has forbidden her to see any other man alone. She feels herself growing moist. Suddenly she wants to peel off his court trousers and find out for all time what he really has beneath that giant codpiece. He, sensing the nature of her thoughts, holds her off with a glare.

Between Malmesbury and Caroline there exists about the same age difference as that between Tristram and Iseult, but Malmesbury is more experienced and realistic than Tristram. Secretly, Malmesbury likes taking sexual chances (the vaster, the better), but he keeps a tight grip upon this aberration. His small adventure with the Marchioness of Horne is a chancy thing in terms of the handicaps it could place in the way of his career should her elderly, powerful husband object. In her case he has given in to his need to take sexual risks because she is so impressively imaginative about the techniques of the sex act and because they are a long way from Whitehall.

But the Princess of Wales is so *available* and, in his view, so adorable. He knows how helpless he can become about kind, amiable women whose dispositions exercise the most basic form of good manners: consideration. He knows, from her dossier at the Foreign Office, that the Princess is wholly kind, unaffectedly kind; as generous and as open as a pretty woman should be.

To summon revulsion, which will prevent him from going one step further, he forces himself to think of the inheritance she and her first cousin, the Prince of Wales, have received from Sophia of Hanover, that fountain of taint whose legacy in the blood has sent much of the family mad for short or long periods of time. Who knew what such a legacy might enable this woman to be capable of telling of such an experience? If he dared to do what he would not do?

However, in a real sense his fears for her are stronger than his desires for her. He fears for her because of the enduring strength of the whims of the Prince of Wales. Thinking of the contrast between this young woman's life now and what it will need to become in England makes Malmesbury wistful about what the shocks of change will do to her. She excites his sympathy. Someday perhaps the sympathy will grow to a point where he will need to comfort her. But she is a political woman. She was born within a fixed scale of things.

"Damme!" Lord Malmesbury suddenly cries out in bed with the Marchioness of Horne who (to cope with what could most definitely be called Malmesbury's lifestyle) has just brought off for both of them an incredibly involved sexual positioning system.

"It's the newest thing from the Orient," she tells him, panting.

"I object, on behalf of the Princess of Wales, with all of my vigor," the now totally unbelted Earl snarls, "that people such as Lord Coomber and the Vicomte Bertie Caen and that pouncing-fiend, Bocca, and Lord St. Helens and that immense Major von und zu Tytell of the King's German Legion all imply, so very snidely, that there is some sort of *stain* upon her reputation."

"It is a great number of men all implying the same things," the Marchioness murmurs. "And I would venture few of them know each other."

"Pluralties do not convey right or wrong, Marie-Louise," he answers severely.

"Just the same, Jimmy—"

"What?"

"Lord Holland did say that any young English traveler—provided he be of good family—who has been through Germany on the Grand Tour would, if asked, tell the Prince that the character of his intended bride is considered extremely loose, even for Brunswick, where they are not exactly *nice* about female delicacy."

"Damn Lord Holland! The swine! Why doesn't he go and say that to the Prince instead of spraying it all around, one leg high in the wind, like some talking dog! This kind of talk can stir up the Queen beyond all the furies. It is what she already believes."

"Lady Jersey is very well with the Queen, you know," the Marchioness says, her breathing gradually returning to normal. "She often goes to Windsor and appears as a sort of favorite."

"Poisonous!"

"Should not the King be prepared for the different possible irregularities which may be noticed in the conduct of the Princess? If the King knew, the Queen might be at least partially disarmed."

"I have bald orders. The King wishes me to have no discretionary powers. I may not comment, give advice or information either to His Majesty or the Government on anything pertaining to the subject of this mission."

"How very odd."

"How very wise. If I may not pass advice or information to the King himself, it becomes quite clear that I most certainly may not be required by the Prince to give information to the Prince."

"Oh, dear. The Prince. At some time in the future there will surely be something he will think you ought to have told him."

He grinned at her. "Hence the bald orders. And let us never forget that it is still possible that she will greatly amuse him."

The Marchioness sighs. "If only she understood merely *basic* cleanliness. She has a smell, doesn't she?"

At noon the next day, insofar as he is able to approach the matter as a gentleman, Malmesbury has an earnest conversation with the Princess about her cleanliness of person and of speech.

"Customs differ in each country," he says. "And it must be accepted that people of other countries take their habits and customs very seriously, thinking them to be the only proper customs in the world."

"Which customs? Which habits?"

"Well! For example, Princess. You wear coarse petticoats, coarse shifts, and thread stockings."

"I know about me, Malmesbury. Tell me about English customs, please."

"You see, Madam, in England the Princess of Wales is thought of as wearing silken undergarments which are ever being laundered with extreme care for freshness and daintiness. That is *it*, you see. The Princess of Wales *must* be personally dainty. Why—the Prince himself takes as many as four to six baths a day! His bills for perfumes for his own person are enormously high. One could say that the Prince is almost wholly absorbed with the importance of personal cleanliness."

"Self, self, self—always thinking of self. I do not have time for that."

"I would give you no credit for boasting of a short *toilette*, Madam," Malmesbury replies sharply. He is appalled at how much this point in her education has been neglected; at how her mother, a *royal* Englishwoman, was insensitive to it. "As *well*, Princess," he continues sternly, "allow me to say there is a further point of personal comportment which will seriously affect the Prince. You must not—you *may* not—continue to speak slightingly of your mother, a royal duchess, sister of the King, aunt of the Prince. To speak so meanly of her as you do, to become peevish, to laugh at her or about her, is not only extremely improper but radically wrong."

Caroline does not understand what Malmesbury can be saying about the way she smells. Everyone smells! she insists to herself. No one has ever said to her before that she smells somehow different from the way other people smell. Malmesbury is a man of great probity; that is self-evident. He is in no way a cruel man; she knows he is trying to do everything in his power to have her shown in

the best light when he brings her to the Prince. But can
there be something wrong with his nose? People wear
eyeglasses, people use crutches, why shouldn't there be
people who have defective noses?

She decides to humor him because he deserves that
attention. He cannot help it if he is the only man in the
world who thinks she smells peculiar. She is twenty-six
years old; no one has ever mentioned it before, so the poor
man has a problem which must be respected. She must
make a proper response so that he will know that she has
listened to him carefully and appreciated what he has said.

"You are trying to make me bad, Malmesbury!" the
Princess shouts at him. "A man and a woman, for that is
what the Prince and I are, want to marry, then get into the
bed and make babies, but first everyone must yell on her
about how her underwear is dorty and how she is not kind
from her to the mother." She bursts into tears.

"Weeping is an evasion," Lord Malmesbury says with
exasperation.

Malmesbury devotes the next week to politics, attempting to persuade the Duke to accept command of the
Prussian army and the combined Austro-British forces. He
does not mention money; therefore, the Duke's glory being
so intact, he does not wish to disturb it by military losses
to Napoleon. Having been set back in this quarter,
Malmesbury returns to instruct the Princess.

"I im*plore* you, dear Princess," he says with such compelling earnestness that it gives her a scratchy feeling along
the base of her belly, "to avoid *any* familiarity with the
English at *all* costs. You must have no confidants other
than myself until you know who your friends are. Further,
at all times, avoid giving your opinion. You may approve

of the weather but do not admire it excessively. You must be perfectly silent on the subjects of politics and party. You must endeavor at *all* times to be well with the Queen."

"My father, who hates the Queen, has explained to me all my life how to handle the Queen. Better, please, tell me how to handle Lady Jersey."

"Who? What? *Han*dle?" Where did these people learn to speak? He makes it sound as if the Princess were implying a brutal sort of fondling. "Lady Jersey is merely your lady-in-waiting. She will defer to you."

"Oh, yes. Ho, ho, ho. But I must certainly see her as an *intriguante*, would you not say?"

"I would not!"

"You will not deny a *connection* between her and the Prince? That she does things with him which are un*speak*able."

From far, far off, as from a distant star, he answers. "In regard to Lady Jersey, she and your other ladies-in-waiting will frame their conduct toward you by yours toward them. And, I protest to you, this conduct should not be too familiar nor too easy."

"I want to be popular!"

"Bah!"

"You ask too much, Malmesbury! You think me prone to comport myself too freely."

"Yes. I do think that. It is an amiable quality in a young German maiden lady but—in your new, high situation—such cannot be given away without great risk. As to popularity—that has never been entertained by familiarity. Popularity can only belong to respect which is to be acquired by a just mixture of dignity and affability."

"But they write to me such dorty letters about that woman, Jersey! Yet the Prince makes her to be my Lady of the Bedchamber!"

"What letters, Princess? From whom?"

"I want to be his good wife, but before I ever even see him he puts the dorty mistress in my room to spy on me and make me cheap!"

"What letters, Princess?"

"They are letters! Papa says the friends of Fräulein Rosensweig send them because the Prince won't let me bring her to England for only six hundred pounds a year. She would read to me in English! She would spell in English for me when I write the letters to the Queen. I am not good to spell but the Prince won't let me bring her."

"Do you *know* these letters are from Fräulein Rosensweig's people?"

"How do I know? They are not signed."

"Unsigned letters do not exist," he says with contempt. "Unsigned letters come from the lowest cowardice and conceal, not reveal, the truth. Therefore they do not exist."

"I will soon know the truth."

He sighs because he is not allowed to be as direct with her as she deserves. He extemporizes. "*Dear* Princess, do you think that the Prince, a supreme man of the world, an incomparable leader where the *ton* is concerned, would have preserved himself in a virginal state until he decided, this very year, that you were to be his bride?"

"That is a crooked answer."

"It concerns the truth."

"How do I say? What will *they* do when the Princess of Wales, driven mad by the faithlessness of her husband, has her own lovers? What of that?"

Malmesbury stands staring at her with the full, heavy dignity of an erect otter. "It is *death* for any man to assume an approach to the Princess of Wales."

"I think you are mistaken."

"It is our *law!*"

"Impossible."

"Guilty of treason and punished with death. If she were weak enough to listen to him—so also would she be."

"Gott im Himmel!" Caroline cries out, holding the sides of her face with both hands. "What have they got me into?"

Ah, babies—babies! When her first-born, little George Augustus, is brought into her view, so smitten with him is his mother, Queen Charlotte, that she causes him to be modeled full-length in wax and keeps the doll on her boudoir table on a cushion under a glass bell. Frequently even then as in later life, she is not sure whether she is more drawn to the offspring or the effigy.

The Queen loves making babies. The King is no slouch at it. Between them they have thirty in all; fifteen live, fifteen wax. What a nursery it remained!

The Prince was born in 1762, nineteen years before his father, and his father's Prime Minister, Lord North, lost the American colonies. The arbitrary and oppressive financial policy which the King adopted toward those colonies caused the outbreak of American revolution in '75; a war which ended in '81, at which time the King removed them from his mind.

The King takes an alarming interest in the education of his sons. For sound, kingly reasons (for millennia kings have hated their eldest sons, who wait for the kings' deaths to take power) he seems determined to keep his eldest son, heir to the throne, a child as long as possible. Little George, keenly intelligent, suffers deepest psychological pain striding about the palace corridors in long baby clothes until he is twelve years old. This humiliation is at the core of his being at every age he reaches. The more he resists the

King's need to keep him insignificant, the more the King forces him, ordering the tutors to flog him again and again in a single day. Raw from the cane, the Prince often rushes to the door of his father's sleeping room at early mornings to pound at the panel and shout out such slogans as, "Wilkes forever! Number Forty-five forever!" Wilkes had criticized a speech of the King's in the forty-fifth number of *The North Briton*.

All authority oppresses the Prince, filling him with the consuming terror of being made ridiculous. Conversely, it gives him a hunger to impress, to make a great and always ostentatious display to prove his worth beyond any possibility of doubt. As this hunger grows he satisfies his need for overwhelming display with money from the bank of his father's prestige. The terror of ridicule is a cage that separates his sympathies from his constancies, especially in his relationships with women. As soon as a woman he loves operatically proves that she does not find him ridiculous, he rushes out to the next gigantic love affair, proving that keen intelligence and cool good taste have little relation to the foundations of emotions. Scalded from the time he reached the first consciousness of pain, he spends the rest of his life seeking endless skin grafts for the torn patch on his soul: a rent which cannot be mended.

More than a dozen court ladies are ever welling up to comfort him as he grows older. At seventeen, he is a stunningly attractive boy. "His countenance is of a sweetness and intelligence quite irresistible," writes Lady Hilary Brown, the Canadian beauty.

It is from a distance that this beauty and charm seem to change, distort. The public, who do not know him, seem to see him through the distant, stony eyes of his father.

When the Prince is eighteen, while the American revolution rages far across the sea, and still further away across his mind, while watching Garrick's version of *A Winter's Tale*, he sees Mary Robinson onstage. As it happens, Mrs. Robinson's husband is deceiving her as to his morals (and other things). But her upbringing insists that a woman's highest duty is to continue to be a faithful wife. She has a child. She works in the theater only to support her child, her husband, her husband's mistresses, and herself.

For many months she refuses to meet the Prince. He writes to her twice a day. He sends her flowers, which she feeds to hack horses; jewels, which she returns. At last, a meeting is arranged by Sir Thomas Buckley, press lord and patron of tennis. The outcome is inevitable once the simple-hearted woman actually encounters the gale force of the Prince's power to please. The Prince overcomes, beckoning her into a tender country. At one day's end a boat glides to a river gate, and Mrs. Robinson is walked across a nightsward into the Prince's rooms.

There are two years of great victories upon the bedsheets. There are over four hundred pitiably loving letters from the Prince before the day when he meets her in Hyde Park and turns his head away as if he does not know her. By then she has given up the stage and, needing to entertain her Prince, is over £7000 in debt, enraging her husband. But her temporary visit to the Prince's life serves. It demonstrates what will be his lifetime pattern of confrontations with women and other objects.

Georgiana, Duchess of Devonshire, describes the Prince well when he is twenty. "He is rather tall and has a figure which, though striking, is not perfect. He is inclined to be too fat and looks too much like a woman in men's clothes. He has a great knack of quickness and, like the King, knows all that is going forward. He has his father's passion for knowing who and what everyone is."

There is talk of his conquest of the easily conquered Grace Dalrymple Elliot, whose illegitimate daughter may be his. Nearly all the women are older than himself: Lady Augusta Campbell, the beautiful, wayward daughter of the fifth Duke of Argyll; Lady Melbourne, whose fourth child, George Lamb, is said to be the Prince's. The extravagant Georgiana, who describes him so well, and her beautiful sister, Harriet, both bed him. All of this huffing and puffing takes place while Mrs. Robinson soars on the wings of love.

When the Prince comes of age, the government votes him an income of £50,000 a year. All previous heirs to the throne have been given £100,000 a year, but the obstinate, cheese-paring King insists that his eldest son receive only £50,000 at a time when money is worth less than when royal heirs got double that amount. Wars have made currency inflation a very real thing. A simple example of this is the rising price of admissions to coronations. A ticket to the coronation of Henry I cost one crokard, but Henry II's went up to a pollard. At any of King John's frequent coronations the price soared to a suskin and, by Henry III's time, it cost a whole dodkin.

In addition to the £50,000, revenues from the Duchy of Cornwall bring the Prince approximately £13,000 more each year. He is installed in Carlton House, Pall Mall. No sooner is he in possession than he begins work on the alteration and improvements of his exterior life just as mightily as he has always worked on improvements for his self-esteem. He collects a racing stud. He patronizes prize fighters. He gambles. He gives breakfasts for the great patron of the Whig Party, Sir Martin Gabel, which do not end until six in the evening. At one such interminable breakfast the table is set for two hundred beneath rococo lanterns fastened prettily to the vaulted ceiling. On the wall above the Prince's head is an illuminated crown— different each time—sometimes in rhinestones, more often in flowers, but once painted in multi-dimensional *trompe l'oeil* holding down soaring portraits of the Prince by James Richard Blake and projecting the letters GP. Directly behind him are stands draped with heavy crimson satin, piled high with silver-gilt plate. There are sixty attendants. One of these stands within a complete suit of armor because Gabel likes to fancy that he lives in the times of the Wars of the Roses. The Prince describes Gabel as "a Spanish grandee grafted to a New World potato."

On the table in front of the Prince is a miniature fountain whose waters flow into a silver-bedded stream to the right and left of him. The stream runs the length of the long table top, is bounded by mossy banks, and contains water plants, flowers, and tiny metallic fish which either swim gaily under the arches of the miniature bridges or float belly up past the diners.

The women are ablaze with breakfast jewels. The Prince is wonderfully easy and courteous. It is a fun breakfast that costs £43,000.

The Prince's Household is composed of: Sir Herbert Mitgang, treasurer; Colonel Franz Heller, confidential counsel; Colonel John MacMahon, private secretary; a vice-treasurer, a vice-chamberlain, a keeper of the wardrobe and a gentleman porter; four clerks, five pages of the presence, a housekeeper, an inspector of the household, a maître d'hôtel named Smadja, famed throughout Europe, a *tapissier* and assistant, a butler, a table decker and assistant, two surgeons of the household led by a formidable healer, Lord Weiler, and forty-three servants. It is a staff for one man's carefully studied bachelor life.

The Prince's perfumers, Bourgeois Amick & Son, have yet to bill him for less than £90 each week for his cold creams, almond pastes, lavender water, scented bags, jasmine pomatum, arquebusade, huile antique, essense of begamot, eau de miel Angleterre, vanilla, eau de Cologne, rose water and perfumed almond powder. He spends nearly ten times that amount each month on his tailors, drapers, hatters, hosiers, mercers, lace merchants, kilt makers and furriers. He sends for toothbrushes by the three dozen. One afternoon he buys thirty-two walking sticks for at last, he feels, he is in a position to avenge himself for his father's ten thousand cruelties. The sweetest revenge is to waste money on manly clothes to pay back for that long, dirty swaddling dress his father had nailed upon him in the cold corridors of his childhood. The more he spends, the more his father suffers. There is a war to the death in Europe. The people are being squeezed for every penny for cannon and the fleet. The more the Prince spends of his country's money, the greater his father's pain; therefore the more he spends.

All at once the Prince has the damaging meeting with the hardship of true love in the bounteous form of the twice-widowed Mrs. Fitzherbert. The Prince is twenty-two. She is a motherly, matronly, calorically fulsome twenty-eight. Her response to the surgings of his uncontrollable love are shocking. She *refuses* to enter into any irregular union with him. Moreover, she is a Roman Catholic and, according to the Act of Settlement, if the Prince marries a Catholic, he will be disqualified for succession to the throne.

The Prince weeps by the hour. He has himself bled by Lord Weiler, hoping this will diminish his ardor much in the manner of slamming a window sash down upon an erection to discourage it. He rushes to Mrs. Armistead's little house in Chertsey (where she is living with Charles Fox, the Prince's closest confidant; a Whig leader) and rolls upon the floor, striking his forehead, tearing his hair, and having hysterics because Mrs. Fitzherbert will not cuddle him to her pink-and-white bosom. It is no laughing matter. Mind and body are being torn apart, Mrs. Armistead tells Fox.

Mrs. Fitzherbert leaves for France, alarmed. The Prince's debts are now tremendous. His IOUs are being grabbed at discounts. He becomes so accustomed to living under pressure that he increases it by telling friends he will quit England and the Crown for love.

His adviser, Sir James Harris, later Lord Malmesbury, stops this. He speaks to the Prince with stern logic.

"But my heart is *breaking*, Harris. My mind has left me."

"May I suggest, Sir, the idea of your marrying?"

"I will never marry!"

Harris presses. "You must marry, Sir. You owe it to the country. And to hold the affection of the nation after you become King you must marry and father upright Protestant heirs to the throne."

Mrs. Fitzherbert returns to England. The rumor persists that the Prince is prepared to offer her genuine marriage. In an urgent letter Charles Fox advises the Prince with all alarm. In answer, to resolve matters, the Prince stabs himself—but safely, in a prudent area. A few days later he writes to Fox saying that he has given up all intention of ever marrying Mrs. Fitzherbert. At once, he marries her secretly in her drawing room. She promises the Prince that, during his lifetime, she will never acknowledge the marriage.

They are married on the evening of the 15th December 1785. Fortunately, someone remembers that the Reverend John Burt is available in Fleet Prison where he is locked up for debt, but, although in technical theological performance he is impeccable, he is not a clergyman who can keep a secret.

By mid-1786 the Prince's debts have mounted beyond all self-indulgence. Members of the Household have not been paid for months. He and his brothers, the Dukes of York and of Clarence, borrow 350,000 guilders at 5 percent from bankers in Holland and ruin the firm by failing to repay the loan or even pay any interest. The Prince's messengers are dispatched to Germany, Holland, and Belgium. Attempts are made to raise loans from men who are to be rewarded with titles as soon as the Prince has the power to confer them. Desperately, he shuts Carlton House again. His racing stable is (almost) dismantled. Tradesmen not only refuse to send him food but stop his carriage in the street to demand payment.

In June 1794 the Prince finds the slinky Lady Jersey, then shares bitterness with his beloved wife when he sees that there is no longer any room in his life for her. His beloved wife learns of this in an odd manner. The Prince is to meet her at a dinner, in Bushey, at the Duke of Clarence's house. On her arrival, as she overbrims with endearing pink blandness, she is given a letter from the Prince. The letter states he will never enter her house again. There is neither quarrel nor coolness between them. The letter of the day before had burst its trousers with love for her.

When she is brought round after crashing to the floor, Mrs. Fitzherbert goes abroad.

The elderly, compulsively overdressed Lord Jersey is appointed the Prince's Master of Horse.

Lady Jersey plays the harp for the Queen, who is greatly pleased that her father is a Church of Ireland bishop. Lady Jersey is forty when she gathers in the Prince; nine years older than he is. She has two sons, seven daughters, several of these by her husband; several less legitimately by William Falkner, Clerk of the Privy Council, and a few by Lord Carlisle. She is a sensual, unprincipled, heartless woman who regularly assures the Prince that the nexus with Mrs. Fitzherbert was never wise and that her Catholicism is the real cause of his fervent unpopularity across the country.

In August 1794, his financial condition worse than it has ever been, the interest upon the interest of all loans threatening to strangle him, the Prince goes to his father, on holiday at Weymouth, and announces abruptly that he has severed any possible ties with Mrs. Fitzherbert and is ready to enter "a more creditable life" by getting married.

His father considers the Prince gloomily. After some silence he says, "I will send some confidential person, with your consent, to report on various *Protestant* princesses."

"My choice is made, Sir."

"Is it?"

"I have long admired the political, military, and private character of the Duke of Brunswick, Sir. My choice is his daughter, Caroline." The Prince doesn't give a fig who the woman is to be. He is marrying to get money. He chooses Caroline because she is the daughter of his father's once-favorite sister. He hopes the choice will make things easier to get the most money.

While Lord Malmesbury is sent to Brunswick by the King to go forward with the arrangements for the marriage treaty, negotiations with Parliament are opened concerning the Prince's debts and income. At last the fullness of the Prince's true, current debts are revealed to the British government. They amount to the immense sum of £630,000, all of it incurred since the Prince's financial settlement of 1787. Pitt proposes that the income from the Duchy of Cornwall, £13,000 a year, be appropriated as a sinking fund which, at compound interest, would discharge the debt in twenty-seven years, and that £25,000 should be deducted from the Prince's income for the payment of the interest on the debt.

"To think," the Prince rants to his peculiar brother, Ernest, "that the Prince of Wales, heir to the mightiest and most meaningful throne in Christendom, should be reduced to marrying for money."

3

As soon as the Marriage Treaty has been signed in December 1794, the Prince acts. He has the highest regard for Malmesbury, but Malmesbury is the King's man in this, and he is unable to trust the King's arrangements. He meets with Colonel Heller and with Major Hislop, who is an aide-de-camp on his brother Frederick's staff.

Colonel Franz Heller, the Prince's confidential counsel on loan from the King's German Legion, is a wide, debauched-looking man who wears a white beard to cover overextensive duelling scars. George III, King of England, is also King of Hanover. The German Legion is a blood-sworn German bodyguard who would forfeit their lives to protect the King's. Heller is as German as Malmesbury is British. His appearance of debauchery comes from a rupture of the peroorbital fat around his eyes due to a weakness of the orbicular muscles, producing deep-brown bags under his eyes which are as large as mice drowned in strong coffee. He is a professionally sinister figure. He is the King's informer on the Prince, as a matter of duty and of his own nature, but he feels enormous loyalty to the Prince. Once each month the German Legion holds its regimental mess at whichever palace the King is residing. Colonel Heller attends these reunions. At the finish, while the officers of the Legion lie strewn around the company room, Heller slips off to report to the King on all of the Prince's deeds, thoughts and plans.

More deplorably, Colonel Heller is also a paid Napoleonic double agent and has been throughout the war. Not that he doesn't love the King, Germany, and the Prince in that order. He loves them. But the more money he can earn the more he can lend the Prince at 40 percent interest, so, on his meager salary, it becomes necessary that he undertake outside employment.

Heller is portly, speaks music-hall German dialect English, broader even than Caroline's—for that matter even broader than the Queen's. He has the ability to terrorize anyone the Prince wishes brought to heel. This power is invaluable to the Prince, who can get no one but Heller to do what he asks.

Major Hislop is straw-colored and doctrinaire. He has been overseas in regular army service for so long that he is impressed by the Prince, overwhelmed by the grandeur of Carlton. Moreover, he is there at the direct order of Prince Frederick, commander of British forces in Europe.

They sit at a glossy, long table. "You will proceed to Brunswick and make yourself known to Lord Malmesbury by delivering to him a letter which I shall give you. You will tell him that I have expedited everything on this side of the water and that I hope he will make every exertion possible to deliver the Princess here as near the twentieth of this month as possible. Bring her through Holland."

"Holland? *Holl*and?" Hislop shrills. "I should think not. The French are all over Holland."

"The Prince says Holland," Heller barks, revealing a corner of his menace. "You will hack your way through."

"Hack?" Major Hislop cries. *"Hack?"*

"I shall expect to hear from Malmesbury not later

than the sixteenth stating that the date of departure has been fixed," the Prince says flatly, closing the meeting.

In Brunswick, Malmesbury, a student of the Prince for a decade and a half, trusts whatever he senses about what the Prince may be plotting. He writes at once to the Duke of Portland, a confidential friend and cabinet minister, telling of Major Hislop's visit to Brunswick delivering an urgent letter from the Prince ordering immediate departure with the Princess of Wales from Brunswick, through Holland. Malmesbury outlines his difficulty by stating that he is under the King's immediate command, cannot act but by the King's special order, and that no orders have been forthcoming from the King. "If the Prince should be displeased with me," Malmesbury writes, "for non-compliance with *his* wishes, I entreat Your Grace to justify me when any justification may be necessary." He dispatches the letter, sighs deeply, then takes up the pen again to write to the Prince.

> Sir:
>
> Although I am in daily expectation of orders none are yet arrived and the sharp frost and easterly wind now set in may prevent my receiving them for some time. I can only repeat, Sir, that on this side of the water no delay has arisen or will arise, and that not an hour shall be lost whenever it shall please His Majesty's ministers to inform me to what place I am to conduct the Princess, a point which was certainly not determined on the date of my last letters from England.
>
> My apprehensions for Holland are very great and the same easterly wind which produces the frost also keeps the fleet from arriving at Texel; and were I to undertake to recommend to Her Royal Highness to go as far as Utrecht, I should expose her to all the uneasiness and

disquietude attendant upon an invaded country, probably to insult, and possibly to danger in the extreme, since it would be almost as difficult to retrograde as to attempt to cross the sea.

Therefore, until I can be satisfied that the fleet is at Texel, and that the attempts of the enemy to penetrate into Holland on the side of the Goree or by the Moerdyk (should it be frozen as it probably is) have failed, I shall not feel justified in my own mind, or acting up to the sense of very high duty reposed in me, were I to move forward.

I am myself so very anxious that Your Royal Highness should find every principle of happiness, that my judgment may be a little warped by my wishes; but I am sure I must have lost every power of discernment if there does not exist in the mind of the Princess the most fixed intention to make your happiness the study of her life, and in her heart every affection to promote it.

I am &c,

Malmesbury

Although the Marriage Treaty is signed on the 4th December, the journey to meet the English fleet does not begin until December 30. However, because it is a period of war favorable to enemy victories, it is not only the severe frosts that keep the British navy out of harbors to pick up Caroline. It is not until the 28th March 1795 that Lord Malmesbury is able to get his charge safely aboard HMS *Jupiter* in the River Elbe, off Stade, twenty-two miles west of Hamburg.

Preparations for the journey begin when, at 2:00 A.M. on the 26th December, orders arrive from the King telling Malmesbury to set off with the Princess at once. He is to take Caroline to Texel, on a West Frisian island in the North Sea, where a naval escort will meet them. The Brunswick court goes into a frenzy of preparations and leave-taking.

At last they start out: Caroline, Malmesbury, and the Duchess; three female attendants, including a Mrs. Keifetz who will read to the Princess and work out her spellings for her. The two other attendants are chambermaids. There are cooks, guards, hostlers, farriers and slops people. From the moment they are on the road the Duchess takes fright at the nearness of the French and announces that she intends to return to Brunswick. "If I am taken," she says to Malmesbury, "the King will be very angry."

"He will be very sorry," Malmesbury corrects, "but

Your Royal Highness must not leave her daughter."

At the start of the journey the procession of coaches is long with proud burghers, but it grows short as the delays go on. Lord Malmesbury's coach takes the lead. The Princess follows in the Hanoverian state coach, Hanover being the kingdom of the reigning British family. Third comes the coach of the Duchess and her jangling coterie of ladies-in-waiting. Carriage number four is *celui de la garderobe* carrying the close stool for escapement of digestive pressures. The fifth coach is devoted to *la cuisine.*

Caroline has insisted that Mrs. Keifetz ride with her in the royal coach. Mrs. Keifetz is the wife of a learned doctor who spends his life being summoned back and forth across northern Europe to treat the various lesions which are constantly popping out of court life. Mrs. Keifetz is an old, old friend of Caroline's and, when they are alone, she is a direct woman. They speak German.

"I think you've been boxed in a trap," she says as the carriage moves along.

"Keifetz, for once don't think. I can remember a lot of happy hours in my life which always coincided with when you were not thinking. For one thing you don't know what you are talking about. What are you? A very nice woman who is a doctor's wife. Does that reflect England? Does that reflect the brilliance and depth of the Court of St. James's?"

"But you know all about it."

"Who better? We are all the same family, the Prince and I. If the doctor were your first cousin, wouldn't you know how his uncle taught him how to think and feel?"

"That's not how royals work and you know it," Mrs. Keifetz says. "They don't teach the children, they hire other people to do it. Listen, I hear a lot. There has been plenty of talk for ten years about this Prince. He's woman-crazy and everybody likes him except the British public, his father, and the British government. Soon, he'll have you to not like him."

"You are worried about my future?"

"Yes."

"Please. Don't worry. And please. Don't talk for a little while."

Caroline wants to be cheered up. Malmesbury has told her she smells bad. The Prince is preparing to show her Lady Jersey in a cruel way. She doesn't expect to go into a grown man's life and have it change abruptly. She understands that it will take a little time and a great deal of attention to every detail about the Prince to make him want to have Lady Jersey go away. But it seems to her, just as it does to Mrs. Keifetz, that by making Lady Jersey his own wife's Lady of the Bedchamber, he is seeking to create pain. She wonders if perhaps he is just a weak man who doesn't know how to unburden himself of Lady Jersey. That must be it. He has allowed her to become such an intimate. The entirely mocking title of Lady of the Bedchamber has been shown by her to him to mean so much to her that he can't deny her. It *must* be that. A healthy man, a single man, has a mistress who exploits him. Well, she'd soon settle *that* to his satisfaction. One week after the wedding she is going to free him from every one of Lady Jersey's slimy chains.

Malmesbury sends Major Hislop to precede them as they travel, grateful that the Prince has not sent Colonel Heller. Hislop will give notice in case of danger from the French, who are fighting somewhere ahead of them. The first night the party reaches Peine, near Neustadt. Daily they move from town to town through bitter cold. They are held up at Osnabruck at first because of the French who are, just then, being driven back by General Dundas and Lord Cathcart, then halted again by severe frost. On the fourth day Malmesbury receives letters from the Prince urging them on but at the same time describing the situation in Holland as being fraught with peril. The Prince's eagerness is defined by his desperate need for the money the government will confer after his wedding.

The Dutch dikes have been opened. The entire country is flooded, then sealed under great sheets of ice, frozen hard enough for the French to march across. On the sixth day Malmesbury decides to go on. He has a galling scuffle with the Duchess over the amount of tips she wants to leave for innkeepers and attendants, making her give fifty gold louis much against her inclination. They get as far as Delden when a letter from Lord St. Helens orders that on no account must they come into Holland; the French have crossed the Waal. Malmesbury turns the coaches instantly back to Osnabruck. All through the night they hear the thudding of cannon. The Duchess wets herself in her coach.

Osnabruck has the advantage of being as close to the port of Stade as to Texel. Malmesbury rides in the Princess's coach for the last twenty miles of that leg to lecture her sternly.

"I am displeased with you," he says.

"What have I done?" she wails.

"I grant that you have a ready conception, but you have no judgment. You let yourself be caught by your first impression, you leap at your first impulse—and you are too prone to confide."

"Please don't be cross with me, Malmesbury."

"I want you to understand. Your life is ahead of you, and you love life—good life. But when it turns, if it turns —what then? In the hands of a steady, sensible man you would turn out well, but under the circumstances—where you will find faults perfectly analagous to your own—life will turn on you."

"You are a steady, sensible man, Malmesbury."

"I am indeed."

"I wish Papa would let me marry you."

He snorts. They ride in silence into Osnabruck. His larger worry for her is that she will not wash, and there does not seem to be the remotest possibility of getting her into the habit of washing. Despite the talk they had, she still wears coarse petticoats and rarely changes them.

They leave at once for Hanover. Count Kielmansegge places his chateau at their service. Each night Malmesbury sits with Caroline in the library. He continues valiantly to try to teach her all the things her mother should have taught her. On the fifth night, the evening of the day he has had a dispatch from the Foreign Secretary, Malmesbury explains how her father, and her mother, have asked him earnestly for his protection of their daughter. "I told them that, no matter what happened, I would do whatever I could to protect you."

"Protect me? From the French?"

"From the greatly unexpected nature of your new life."

"The Prince? Protect me from my *husband*?"

"No." He paused, gazing at her. "You will be a very important woman in a strange country—that is, a country wholly strange to you." He spoke slowly.

"But protect me from what, Malmesbury?"

"Yourself, perhaps. You will need English counsel on

hidden English customs, and you must have this from someone whom you trust."

"I have you!"

"Not for long, I fear, Princess. My new orders came to me today. One month after I bring you to the Prince I am to be assigned to Rome."

"No!"

"I will think of you always." The sentence is as far as he is willing to go. "More importantly, I am going to leave you with the true companionship of a strong, courageous woman to whom no English door is closed."

"A *woman*? Who is she? Where is she?"

"She is Lady Joyce Anglesong, daughter of a sixteenth duke. She will be waiting for us aboard the naval vessel that will carry you to England."

The Duchess is, by now, put out about everything, disagreeable, cold, and ill-mannered. She fights like a tigress against holding court every Wednesday, but Malmesbury wins out. She cries out in her strange German that her nephew, the Prince of Wales, is a *Hochstapler*. Malmesbury speaks in an intense, terrifying voice to her. "Madam, you will *not* refer to the Prince of Wales as a *Hochstapler*, and furthermore, as long as you accompany this expedition through Germany, you will speak only in English as befits a member of the British royal family. *Is that clear?*"

At last, on the 19th February, it is settled that they are to embark from Stade. The travelers leave Hanover on March 24. The Duchess does not go with them. On Saturday, March 28, they embark on the Schwinde River in a Hanoverian boat. When they reach a point nearly two miles from the British squadron, they are transferred into an English man-of-war barge. At 7:00 P.M. they board the

Jupiter while the quiet air is **shattered** by a salute from her guns; then, from across the water, comes the returning cannonade from the fleet.

Lady Joyce Anglesong awaits the Princess. She conveys the slightest apprehension at Caroline's certain assurance of happiness.

"But how can it be oder ways?" Caroline asks gaily. "Am I not going to be married to the handsomest prince in the world and live in the most desirable country in Europe?"

5

The family name, Anglesong, commemorates the terrifying battle cry of the Germanic tribe of Angles who, with the Jutes and Saxons, occupied England from the fifth century A.D. England is named for the Angles. Her hills and shores have rung to the blood-chilling war screams called the Anglesong.

The Anglesong tribe is first mentioned by Cornelius Tacitus in the first century B.C. According to the Venerable Bede, their continental homeland was centered in Angulus, now identified as Schleswig. They spoke a language called English. Through a succession of ancestral women, Lady Joyce is closely related to the Colonnas and Orsinis of Rome. Her forefathers had leaned into Italy to find her foremothers. She does not look English. Nor does she look Italian. She looks Asiatic with black hair and vivid cheeks on dark skin. She has a slow smile and a rough tongue. Her conception of herself is as a warrior chieftain.

It was Lady Joyce who financed the research and writing of (then edited) Mary Wollstonecraft's *A Vindication of the Rights of Women* in 1792, the seminal work which challenged the idea that women exist only to please men and proposed that women should receive the same treatment as men in education, work opportunities, politics and be given the right to the same moral standards. It will be Lady Joyce who, when she reaches seventy-six, will influence Karl Marx and with Marx will found Socialist Study

Groups, the intellectual child's Sunday School. She sees it as her sublime duty to hack away with might and main, with her wits and with her strength and courage, to establish women's civil rights and to liberate all women by the outset of the nineteenth century. She stands for the necessity for equal rights for women. She has chosen to be educated as a lawyer of durable political resilience. She does not practice law but her counsel at law is sought out confidentially by the leaders of both Parties. She is twenty-four years old; two years younger than the Princess.

She controls the Princess's amiability with ease. "The Prince has agreed to post me to your Household as your lady-in-waiting. We must agree on one thing clearly. I am not your lady-in-waiting."

"No?"

"Absolutely not. I am your lawyer and counsellor who, because of present-day customs, in order to accept this commission which Malmesbury has asked me to take on, needs to pose as a tittering, niggling lady-in-waiting, a mindlessness who feeds upon gossip concerning backward people."

"Backward people?"

"Who shall be nameless. Next—we are locked into this cabin so I will thank you to remove those unspeakably rank clothes, get into the tub, allow Mrs. Keifetz to scrub you well, be dried and powdered, then sufficiently perfumed, after which you will kindly enrobe in silken garments suitable to a Princess of Wales."

"Yes. Thank you. I will do that."

"Are you prepared for your husband?" Lady Joyce asks while Mrs. Keifetz undresses the Princess.

"Prepared? How?"

"He is an outrageous child. You will need to become

accustomed to living with a willful, tantrum-ruled, infantile and self-indulgent male, one of the most unacceptable I have ever observed."

"I shall keep an open mind."

"When possible speak to him in German so that your English does not enrage him."

"Enrage?"

"He considers himself a master of elocution. He admires precise English speech almost to the point of instability. He would forgive a murderer with beautiful English speech before a saint with a German accent such as yours."

"*Mein Gott!*"

"And the matter of Lady Jersey. She is his mistress."

"I know that."

"You know rumors. I tell you the facts. She is a titled whore with the morals of a sow and an enormous capacity for self-love. She will show you no pity. *However*—this is my urgent advice to you. Ignore her in whatever she does. Give her much rope. Sit back and wait. Then—when the correct moment comes and we will agree when that moment arrives—we will break her back."

"I cannot tell you how interesting this chat has been," the Princess says as she steps into the tub.

6

The weather at sea is enrapturingly beautiful over the weekend but, on Tuesday, a fog creeps in. On Wednesday the ship has to drop anchor for fear of running aground. After dinner on this dolorous day, the Princess asks Lord Malmesbury to attend her in her cabin. They are alone. She says, "My fear of Lady Jersey has come back."

This irritates him. "Why should you, a Princess of Wales, fear Lady Jersey, who is not only beneath your rank but whom you have never met and do not know?"

"I know that she sleeps with the Prince. I know the Prince has to put this woman as the lady of my bedchamber. How can the husband put his slut into the cage with the new wife? If he can do that, how can he care about the *spirit* or the *feelings* of me in a new country which is their country together? To be the King and Queen?"

Malmesbury stands very close to her as if he could shield her from these misfortunes with the strengths of his body. Out of this wish, his body speaks to her; rises to meet her. She misunderstands his compassion and confuses it with her own loneliness and desire. Her arms reach up to him and pull his face down to hers. For the short instant in which he allows his mouth to remain within hers he is aware that there is nothing revolting about her odor, that every living thing has a characteristic odor and that hers is not only sweet and pleasant, but compelling. He remembers that it has always been women who have run to him with tales about her scent. No woman could judge it. And cultivated women cultivated spectrums of artificial perfumes. He fits these broken impressions together in the time of lightning. He feels desire for her but his lifetime of conditioning, a reflexive measure having nothing to do with conscience, makes him draw away from her and step backward. He stares at her silently; almost reproachfully.

She says: "You spring away but you do not want to. Pity me, if that is the only way it can be. I must know somebody wants me. That would make everything which is going to happen to me when I step upon England something which I can bear."

"You are the Princess of Wales," he answers shakily.

"You are such a man who would not stop for that."

"No!" It was a great no. "I am a man who will not start for that. This is not a matter of what you feel now and what you fear. It is a matter that tomorrow may be worse. As it grows worse, the need to know that you are loved and my own need to shield you will become greater." His voice hoarsens with pain. "We will find ourselves deeper and deeper in a forbidden bog. There is only one disgraceful end for that." He bows to her, turns away, and walks to the door of the cabin.

"Malmesbury!"

He stops, his hand on the door, but does not turn.

"Please—love me?"

He opens the door.

"Lord Malmesbury!"

He turns at the door, but keeps his hand on the knob.

"In case one thing might be stopping you, as a gentleman of the old school, I must tell you that I am not a virgin."

He stares at her expressionlessly.

"I am not even remotely, by any measurement or allowance for fewest numbers, a virgin."

He stares at her stolidly and silently.

"All right. Then tell me this. I must know this. Do you refuse to see me as a woman because the smell of my body is offensive to you?"

His eyes grow softer. He sighs lightly. "I adore the smell of your body," he says. "The smell of your body will stay with me for the rest of my life—a perfume, an intoxicant—and a loss. We are who *you* are, Princess. Who you are, to me, is the smell of holy incense."

He leaves her alone upon the planet.

At eight o'clock the next morning the Princess climbs down from the deck of the HMS *Jupiter* into the royal yacht. She arrives at Greenwich at noon. A member of the family of Thomas Great, apothecary, greets her with the traditional gift of candied eringo. The King's coaches are not waiting to take her to London because Lady Jersey has delayed them. The Princess nearly suffocates with impatience during the damping wait of one hour, thirty-six minutes, with the governor of the hospital and his sisters. These are her first moments in England.

At last, Lady Jersey pours into the room, a train of feline bones and hungry eyes, ready with her first blow. After being presented by Malmesbury, Lady Jersey says to the Princess, "That dress simply won't do for London, Your Highness."

"*Zookers!*" Lord Malmesbury exclaims.

Caroline was dressed very carefully by Mrs. Harcourt, her lady-in-waiting, in a muslin gown and a blue satin petticoat. She wears blue and black feathers on a black beaver hat and looks fetchingly young and pretty. But she

feels less than naked. Malmesbury doesn't seem to understand what is happening to her. Lady Anglesong is long on
her way to London in a chaise. Lady Jersey bundles the
Princess out of the room. She is stripped down while Lady
Jersey makes clicks of disapproval as if this small German
body itself is certain to be found unacceptable to the
Prince. She stuffs the Princess into a poorly fitting white
satin dress that makes her look pudgy and wide, then
crowns her with a feathered turban "brought especially
from London."

The Princess gasps with outrage when she sees herself
in the mirror. "This is a *foolish* dress," she yells, "and that
thing you have put on my head is worser."

"To the contrary, Madam," Lady Jersey drawls.

"No, no! This is the dress for you! It suits you exactly!
You are going to wear it to London."

"You honor me, I am shaw, Princess," Lady Jersey
answers languidly. "Howevah, this *beautiful* dress and this
stunning chapeau were chosen for you by the Prince of
Wales. He has commanded me to dress you in these and he
commands you to wear them."

They go out to the coaches where Malmesbury waits.
"Look at this terrible dress!" the Princess shrills at him.
"Look at this awful hat! She says I must wear this by the
Prince's command."

"It seems a suitable dress, Princess."

"Suitable? Suitable for scrubbing the floors! This is
how they will see me for the first time and they will think
it is me. Help me into the coach, please."

"I will sit beside the Princess," Lady Jersey says.

"You will sit facing her," Malmesbury snarls.

"Sitting with my back to the horses makes me sick."

"If you know that riding backward makes you sick

you should never have accepted this post. Ladies-in-waiting only ride backward. Very well. I shall put Lady Montant into this coach. You will ride with me and Lord Claremont."

"I will sit facing the Princess," Lady Jersey says coolly and climbs into the coach. The royal procession sets out for London accompanied by a detachment of hussars.

"I understand you are the Prince's bitch," the Princess says pleasantly to Lady Jersey.

"Whaaaaat?"

"Ach! My English. I meant to say—of course—the Prince's slut. Is that the right word? Or do I say—his whore?"

Lady Jersey attempts to reply, but the Princess leaves her nearly apoplectic by holding up her gloved hand. "Do not chatter, please. I must look at England."

She looks away beyond the coach window, but in her mind she sees the mute and florid miniature which had so counterfeited the Prince; the husband who is so bent on being her enemy. His true ambassador faces her now. This ambassador has been instructed to convey that a state of war exists. He has never seen her. He does not know her. But his intention cannot be mistaken.

In almost every village they go through the people have crowded out of their houses to see her pass, to shout their benedictions. All the way to London she is showered with welcomes and expressions of deep pleasure for her presence. At half past two the coaches arrive in Cleveland Row, a part of St. James's Palace. Caroline is met by Colonel Heller, who genuflects before her, then brings her to the Duke of Cumberland's rooms. The Duke, the Prince's somewhat tilted brother, Ernest (who is later to murder his naughty valet in his bedroom), is at the threshold to receive her. He is a tall young man with a hard and amusing viciousness which is conveyed to the Princess not only by the advanced quality of his leers, winks and body touches, but also by his left eye socket, so horribly wounded at Tournai.

The Duke withdraws, rather surprising her by not exposing himself indecently. Lord Malmesbury opens the windows to the balcony. The Princess goes out to face the multitudes, to curtsey sweetly to the crowd of more than seven hundred which has been waiting hours to see her.

"How thrilled and honored I am," she proclaims in a clear voice, reaching all of them, "to have this, mein first meetink with the brave English people—the best nation on the earth." She bows. They cheer. She curtseys. They cheer more loudly. She throws them kisses. They exult. These mutual ecstasies might have been exchanged indefinitely but for the Prince of Wales roaring into the room to demand that "this vulgar scene" be terminated at once. Malmesbury draws the Princess into the room from the balcony and closes the door.

She faces a tall, burly, purple-faced man in a cruelly corseted hussar uniform, his eyes popping from the tight lacing. "If there is to be any grand waving to the populace," he sneers at her with his treble voice piping, "be assured that I will do it."

The small figure in the grotesque white dress and the comically feathered turban tries to kneel before her Prince, but he raises her and embraces her. They freeze. His nostrils contort, then wrinkle downward while his upper lip makes a reverse arc below. He thrusts her aside, perhaps not meaning to be rough but nonetheless achieving it. He strides away from her. He glares at Malmesbury with hurt dismay. "I am not well," he says. "Pray get me a glass of brandy."

"Sir—had you not better have a glass of water?"

"No!" the Prince shouts. "I will go directly to the Queen." He races out of the room to his Mama.

"*Mein Gott,*" the Princess says. "Is he always like that?"

"He feels poorly. Not at all well, I am sure."

"Whatever he is, he is very fat and he is not nearly as good-looking as his portrait."

"Flurried, I would say. He will certainly be different at dinner."

She sighs. "Everyone deserves himself. Including him and including me. We are what we are so we become what we become. But seeing what he has become, what will become of me? I did not please him."

"A temporary matter, Madam."

"How tired I feel. I must rest before I face this awful dinner which is to be followed by the rest of my life."

The Prince lifts a glass with a shaking hand, staring at his brother, Ernest, and Colonel Heller. "She smells like a dustman," he says as if he had ever smelled one of these, his voice pleading for pity.

"I didn't actually think so," Ernest says. "But then I'm not much for drenching myself in perfumes. What did you think, Franz?" They speak German.

"She has a healthy woman's smell," Colonel Heller replies honestly, for he is evaluating a German princess.

"She smells *different*—even exciting," Ernest says.

"How very good of you not to deny that she smells at all," the Prince says tartly.

"She surely doesn't have an *unpleasant* smell."

"She has skin like a boiled egg."

"Albuminous and smooth, yes."

"There is a gap between her teeth. The Germans are not only supposed to be terribly clever but they are famous for porcelain. Why have they not done something about that gap?"

"You are too concerned with artificialities, George," Ernest answers smoothly. "That gap happens to be a perfectly charming gap."

"And I hate tallow hair."

"That's news."

"Have you spoken with her? That is, have you heard her? And she'll sound just as bad in French, you know."

"Then speak German to her."

"What would the King say to that?"

"Then teach her English. Proper English."

"They never learn. Listen to Heller. He's been here since he was a youth, and he still speaks like a music-hall comedian."

Heller looks extremely hurt. "We would all sound peculiar speaking Chinese, Sir."

"How she pulls me *down!* The world knows how I adore exquisite English speech."

"Why bite yourself, George?" Ernest asks gently. "Nothing will be changed about your life—exactly nothing. Except that you will have more money."

"Easy enough for you to say, but it is I who am going to have to live with that smelly *thing* for the rest of my life."

"My dear George, regard me, your brother. I am in bad shape. Certain people are pressing. I must get three thousand pounds or there is going to be a disgraceful difficulty. The King refuses to see me. You must help me, dear George."

"I will not, for one moment, refuse you, Ernest," the Prince answers reluctantly. "I promise to think about it."

When Ernest leaves them, the Prince asks Heller, "Have you been thinking hard, Heller?"

"Yes, Your Highness."

"Have you solved anything?"

"I see ways."

"Which ways?"

"You must deliver *quid pro quo* or the money will stop. The Princess must produce an heir."

The Prince sinks his head into his hands. He moans. "That is obvious, you fool. What sort of a solution is that?

How can I do it? How can I bring myself to produce an heir upon a body such as that?"

Colonel Heller allows sufficient time for his pause. "Nonetheless, Your Royal Highness, that is where we must begin to seek solutions," he answers slowly.

The state dinner that evening for the Prince and Princess of Wales is sponsored by the Vice-Chamberlain, the Earl of Rockrimmon, on behalf of their Majesties, who are not able to attend but whom they will all join afterward. Everyone who drove from Greenwich with the Princess is invited.

The Prince and Princess face each other at the center of the long table, in accordance with the equality of their royal rank. For, after all, Caroline's family created the English royal house of Hanover through the Stuarts. The second style of George I of England was Duke of Brunswick and Luneberg. By blood or by marriage Caroline is connected with the great European dynasties: Romanoff, Hohenzollern, and Hapsburg. She is the King's (her uncle's) own choice as Princess of Wales. Lord Malmesbury sits on the Princess's left, the Vice-Chamberlain on her right. Lady Banne Shannon Phillips, Countess of Rockrimmon, sits on the Prince's right. The Countess of Jersey sits at his left.

It is a terrible evening for Malmesbury.

It is bad for the Prince, who regards what happens as a conspiracy to ridicule him and make him appear insignificant.

It is bad for the Princess because it hardens the Prince's contempt for her into hatred, sets her before the court as a vulgar buffoon, establishes the Queen as being right about her, reducing the King's protection of her.

It is a wonderful evening for all the other guests, particularly for Lady Jersey.

At the start of the pageant, the Princess stabs them with her most malevolently summoned eyes, as the Prince fawns upon Lady Jersey, as she amuses and delights him to a degree which appears to exceed all previous measure. The Princess becomes certain that Lady Jersey is rudely fondling her husband under the table.

When, at last, the Princess will accept the affronts no longer—on top of everything else her husband pretends she is not in the room—her heavily accented voice occupies a freak silence which happens at that moment.

"I do believe the lady slut is fondling the Prince's parts under the table," Caroline exclaims to Rockrimmon. There is a common gasp but no other response. As the Prince sips punch from Lady Jersey's glass, the Princess snatches the Vice-Chamberlain's glass, drinks from it, then *gargles* the punch. Like a great stage magician she uncoils chains and snakes of heroic stupidities. She says loudly, "The Prince's whore has such a huge behind. But I think perhaps that is where the Prince likes to give it, *hein?*" She grins at the Prince, then passes the grin around among all the guests. She winks at him slowly and drolly. She brings up a forefinger to her closed eye and holds it there. The brilliance of her clowning releases her audience involuntarily from their inhibition. They explode into laughter.

When relative silence is restored she says, "To tell you the God's truth, you know, the Prince—and I see him today for the first time—is not a fellow who looks like he would like the woman. I think perhaps he more likes little boys." The gasp of the room is like the onset of a vacuum. The Prince goes pure white. Lady Jersey smiles her pleasure.

"Tell me, somebody," the Princess continues loudly. "What do you think? Does he keep his whore Jersey to read to him?" Then she leers horrendously at Lady Jersey, closes the same eye in that elaborate wink, then brings up the iron forefinger to reveal to all that, of course, she is merely spoofing the Prince. No one makes the mistake of laughing. Malmesbury is unable to speak, eat, drink, or move. The Prince looks dangerously ill. He is panting shallowly. Malmesbury feels the tragedy keenly. He knows there is no exit for her. She will crash against the same frightening things for the rest of her life. He has known many royal courts. They are rigidly the same: upholstered prisons with glass walls varying in styles but not in intrigues, jealousies, lying, cruelty and dissimulations, the same wherever power rests, the same polluting influence whether at the court of an Emperor or alight with the nimbus of a president of a republic; endless plotting, petty passions, while the human contrivances they spawn can deaden the heart and the mind. But this is impossible to explain to the Princess. When, at last, she knows it, it will be too late.

The Prince rises. He leaves the room, trembling with rage. The Princess actually believes her wit has triumphed.

Everyone eats and drinks with balance. Lady Jersey chats across the table to Malmesbury and Rockrimmon. At last they all cross to St. James's Palace. Caroline is presented to the wary King and the savagely glacial Queen who does not hate Caroline only because her son has recounted what happened at dinner, but from royal necessity. Caroline is the woman who, too soon for the Queen, will sit upon the Queen's throne.

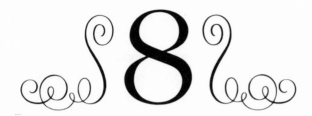

Three days later, on the 8th April 1795, the Prince and Princess of Wales are married in a religious ceremony in the presence of many distinguished witnesses.

Before this public rite, the Prince sits alone with Heller and keens, "What am I going to do, Heller? What am I going to *do*?"

"There is no way to send her back to Brunswick, Sir."

"This is worse than anyone living or dead could imagine."

"Six hundred and thirty thousand pounds is owed, Sir. That is a much more overbearing thing than to have to ignore this girl forever."

"*Ignore* her? I must *sleep* with her! And I must sleep with her and sleep with her again and submit to whatever are her disgusting bedroom fantasies until she produces an heir to the throne. *That* is what this government is buying for their paltry six hundred and thirty thousand pounds. Not my sanity. Not to allow my obligations as the greatest Prince of Europe, but as a stud fee for mounting their sow to give them their heir."

"All they ask is one royal heir, Sir."

"But I cannot bring myself to that! I will vomit all over the bed. I could not sustain any vestige of my manhood in a bed with her."

"There could be other combinations," Heller says simply.

The Prince bridles instantly. "Are you daring to presume that you——"

"No, Sir. No, no. I am a servant. Your wife will be Queen. I would not presume," he says solemnly, thinking of the many, many times he had been to the same well before. "The heir must be in every way—bone for bone and blood for blood—a royal heir."

"How?"

"The Duke of Cumberland is really very badly in need of money, Your Royal Highness. He is your brother, a true Hanoverian. And he does not find the Princess as you find her, Sir."

The Prince's face opens like a lens. "But—would he? —oh, I say, Heller what a bloody *MAR*velous idea! But will he agree?"

Heller allows his face to reveal just a corner more of his sinister power. "He will agree when I speak to him about this urgent matter, Sir."

The Prince begins to drink two hours before the royal dinner party that precedes the wedding at the Chapel Royal, St. James's. He spends the whole afternoon galloping his horse past, then around, then past again, Maria Fitzherbert's house in Richmond. The King's instructions to the Duke of Clarence are that he must stay with the Prince until his wedding. As the brothers ride back from that silent house, the Prince sobs. "William, swear to me that you will tell Mrs. Fitzherbert that she is the only woman I have ever loved."

Caroline sends for the Prince on the morning of their wedding day. She tells him she will delay the wedding indefinitely if Lady Jersey appears there or in her procession.

"Delay it then! Delay it for the rest of our lives, please God!"

"The sort of delay I have in mind," Caroline says pleasantly, "will surely enrage the King. He will send for me but will end up having to come to me. Humiliating for him. I will tell him the true reason for the delay. That you insist that she walk in my procession, that she attend my wedding. Instantly, the King will solve the problem by banishing your slut. Then where will you be, Georgie?"

"You are *not* to call me Chortchie!"

"Do you follow me precisely, Georgie-Porgie?"

"Yes."

"Good. Advise the whore that she is to remain indisposed until notified."

The Chapel Royal glows in soft candlelight. The scene dazzles. Heavy crimson satin drapes the walls. Jewels at throats, wrists, arms, hair, and hands glitter in the right-side gallery where the peeresses sit. Foreign ambassadors are on the left. The Stadtholder of Holland dozes softly in the King's gallery, at the center of his family, opposite the altar. The Archbishop of Canterbury will sit to the right of the altar upon a stool. The Bishop of London will sit at the left. Choirboys and the King's band are in their places. At 9:30 P.M. they begin to play and sing the overture to Handel's *Esther*. Every head turns toward the main door.

An usher raps on a closed door of St. James's Palace. The Household Drums & Trumpets take their places. The door is swung open for the procession of the Princess moving slowly to "God Save the King," led by trumpeters, kettledrummers and a sergeant trumpeter. After these, in solemn order, come the Master of Ceremonies, Sir Norman North; the Bride's Gentleman Usher, Sir Anthony

Jones, who walks between two senior heralds in tabards;
His Majesty's Lord Chamberlain, Admiral Matson; His
Majesty's Vice-Chamberlain, the Earl of Rockrimmon;
then,

THE BRIDE

in her eighty-seven-pound gold filigreed dress, wearing a
crimson coronet studded with large diamonds, led forward
on the arm of His Royal Highness, the Duke of Clarence
in scarlet regimentals, her train borne by four unmarried
daughters of dukes and earls. Bringing up the rear of the
bride's procession are her Ladies of the Household, among
whom Lady Patricia Kavanagh has graciously consented to
take the place of the suddenly ill Lady Jersey.

On entering the Chapel Royal, Her Highness, the
Princess of Wales, is conducted to a seat prepared for her
near Her Majesty's Chair of State.

Admiral Matson, whose lineage can be traced to Vi-
king invaders, and the ermine-bearded Earl of Rockrimmon, return to St. James's Palace to escort the Bridegroom.
The Bridegroom's procession is slightly more crowded
than that of the Bride's; not only because it has become
necessary to accommodate some of his more pressing creditors with the honor, but because a man's station patently
requires more support than a woman's.

The processional order is the same: Music, the Chamberlain, the Vice-Chamberlain; the King's Gentleman
Usher, Lord Sissons; the Prince's Household, including:
Grooms of the Stole, Chamberlains, Gentleman of the Bedchamber, Comptrollers of the Household led by Lord Mitgang, Master of Robes, Grooms of the Bedchamber, Gentlemen Ushers, Colonel Heller looking particularly gala in
a Pomeranian kilt of silver-and-blood plaid, Equerries,

Upholsterers, Librarians, Gentlemen Surgeons led by
Lord Weiler walking beside Sir Morton Stone; Pages of the
Presence, Understrappers, and Creditors.

His Royal Highness, the Prince of Wales, is quite
drunk. He is wearing a richly spangled and embroidered
chocolate-colored suit. The Collar of the Order of the Garter hangs around his neck. He is supported, not alone in
the heraldic sense, by two unmarried dukes; Bedford and
Daithi of Butterfield. As his Royal Highness is conducted
into the Chapel Royal, Daithi of Butterfield mutters, "My
God, Sir, you've got to sober up!"

"No."

"Yes," the Duke of Bedford snarls. "You must, damn
you!"

"I shall never sober up. I never intend to be sober
again."

"We must speak no more," Butterfield says; "he will
weep."

The Lord Chamberlain and the Vice-Chamberlain,
both overeaters, breathe like bellows from all the walking
to and fro as they return to St. James's to attend His Majesty.

The order of His Majesty's procession begins with
Music, then continues with a Knights-Marshal (Lord Sissons has doubled back from the chapel to assume his second style in the second procession), Pursuivants, Heralds,
the Treasurer of the Household; the Master of Horse, Lord
Weldon; two unmarried dukes, Cumberland and Beaufort;
the Lord Steward of the Household; the Provincial King
of Arms, Baron Bocca; the Lord Privy Seal; Lord President
of the Council; the Archbishop of Canterbury, plagued by
a dreadful head cold; all fully flanked by Serjeants-at-Arms

followed by the Garter Principal of Arms carrying his
scepter between two Gentleman Ushers; the Earl Marshal,
Sir William Richert, with his staff; then Princes of the
Blood Royal followed by the sword of state borne by the
Duke of Portland between the Lord Chamberlain and the
Vice-Chamberlain who directly precede

HIS MAJESTY

in the Collar of the Order of the Garter, who is followed
by triple columns: Captain and Yeomen of the Guard;
Colonel of the Life Guards-in-Waiting; Captain of the
Band of Gentlemen Pensioners.

Behind these march the stately orders of the Queen's
party led by the excessively sober Viscount Marek, Lord
of the Bedchamber-in-Waiting; Master of Robes; Groom of
the Bedchamber; the Vice-Chancellor to the Queen; then

HER MAJESTY

advancing as if she is about to bite and rend the chapel
door, between her Chamberlain and her Master of Horse,
followed by their royal highnesses, the Prince's sisters, all
six, then Her Royal Highness the Duchess of York and
Princess Sophia of Gloucester, all supported severally (and
heraldically only) by their Gentlemen Ushers; Ladies of
Her Majesty's Bedchamber, Maids of Honor, and six female Creditors of the Prince's, not all of noble birth.

Within the chapel their Majesties go to their chairs on
the *hautpas* under the blue and gold paneled ceiling by
Holbein.

At the conclusion of the ceremony the entire march-
ing order puzzle is solved again, everyone withdrawing in
correctly splendid tiers after hearing the headcold-ridden
voice of the Archbishop of Canterbury ask the ominous

question: "Does any person know of lawful impediment to this union?"

The Prince, kneeling, stares up at the Archbishop as the high prelate lowers the book, gazes fully upon him, then turns his questioning eyes upon the King. The Prince's maudlin condition shows. He starts up from his knees. The King comes out of his seat like a shot to force the Prince downward again with a heavy hand, whispering to him harshly. No one else speaks out.

The processions file out through the Privy Chamber to the Levee Chamber, where the Prince, in his turn, signs the marriage register with a shaking hand. All at once, the King seizes the Prince's hand and wrings it up and down, again and again. The Prince whimpers through it all either from the sadistic force of his father's grip or at the loss of Mrs. Fitzherbert; his desperation for money; or from his lust for Lady Jersey. He is close to collapse.

Outside, London boils with excitement; particularly among publicans. Hundreds of churchbells ring. The explosion of cannon in the park comes at regular intervals. The streets are lighted with tens of thousands of soft flames from colored candles.

After the wedding there is a Drawing Room, then a supper at the Queen's House, where the Prince gets drunker. Before the supper is over, the Prince goes into a loo guarded by his Pages of the Presence. Within moments, Colonel Heller brings brother Ernest to the place. Behind locked doors they confer in German.

HELLER: Your brother is wholly ready, Sir.
PRINCE (piteously): Can you do it, Ernest?
ERNEST: I shall do it.

PRINCE: Then we leave at your signal. Are you *sure?* Are you convinced you can do it?

ERNEST (amused): Do it? You really are mad, you know, George. She simply is not—indeed she could not be—as bad as you see her. I do believe, to you, she must be some sort of a mirror of the guilt you feel for what you've done to her. She looks very good indeed to me, old cock. Nothing could stop me now.

PRINCE (his voice breaks with emotion): Ernest—about the money. You shall have the money before this time tomorrow night. You must be sure of that.

ERNEST: Be sure, George, that I am now eminently certain of that.

PRINCE: We must produce an heir.

ERNEST: Oh, I agree. At least Caroline and I must.

PRINCE: If she produces an heir, I swear to you solemnly that you shall have payment of so much money again on the evening of the day the heir is born.

ERNEST: Thank you, George. How sordid of us.

PRINCE (clinging to his brother tightly and weeping): You do understand, my dear? I *cannot* do it. I have tried to nerve myself in every way but I simply *cannot do it.*"

ERNEST: No matter is there? We *are* brothers. The heir will be royal. Same bone and blood, won't it, George? Please compose yourself. We must get all of us home to Carlton House.

(He shakes the Prince's hand, pats him on the shoulder, and leaves the loo.) Silently, in three minutes' time, Colonel Heller leads the weeping Prince away.

As Ernest walks to the principal room to join King, Queen, Bride, and merrie throng, he unscrews the top from a small vial and shakes out two yellow pills into his right hand. He stops a footman carrying a tray of filled glasses, removes two glasses, turns away and drops the two pills into one of the glasses of wine. He carries both drinks directly to the Princess, smiling as best he can out of his war-ruined face. "I command my right to drink a toast to my beautiful new sister," he says gallantly, "the most beautiful bride England has ever had." The men within earshot bark "Hear, hear!" The Princess takes the wine, lifts the glass lightly to her brother-in-law. Their glasses clink. They drink the wine down. The assembly applauds.

Sir Ferdinand Fairfax, whose Grace & Favor windows overlook Carlton House grounds, tells Lady Anglesong that during the night he saw the Prince walking up and down in the garden tearing his hair. Subsequently, the Princess tells Anglesong, "Judge, if you will, what it was to have a drunken husband on one's wedding night. He passed the entire night in the fireplace, under the grate where I left him."

The Princess complains to her Lady of the Bedchamber of overwhelming fatigue as she is undressed for bed on the night of the wedding. "I have never been so tired. I can hardly keep mein eyes open."

"You were up with the dawn. It was an exhausting day, and the weight of this dress alone must have borne you down."

"This is no night for rest and sleep," the Princess yawns. "This is one of the great nights of a woman's life." She climbs into bed. "Many men drink too much at their wedding, you know," she says sleepily. "They are nervous. They want to be heroes in the bed with the wife, so they worry. You will see. In an hour or so he will be fine again

—calm and ready." She yawns mightily. "Very ready." She falls asleep.

More than an hour and a half later, the Prince lets himself into the bridal chamber. He holds a glass of brandy. He sways, standing before the fireplace looking down at his sleeping bride drunkenly. His legs give way. He lurches over sideways, falling into the fireplace. As he struggles to regain his feet, his head and shoulders go further under the grate. At last he stops struggling and begins loud, rhythmical snores, tenor to his wife's alto register.

The garden is black with night. There are no sounds of the sleeping city nor any sounds from within the great house itself. At ten minutes before three o'clock in the morning, Ernest, Duke of Cumberland, lets himself into the bedchamber through the garden door. He wears a dressing gown and cavalry boots. He locks the door. Grinning, he strides directly to the large bed and pulls back all the covers. He puts an arm under the Princess's bottom and pulls her nightdress upward over her breasts. He pauses to kiss her left nipple then manages the nightdress over her head. Caroline sleeps, anchored in place by the two yellow pills.

Ernest throws off his robe in the darkness and, opening her legs wide, eases himself upon Caroline and into her. He is almost certain she is not dead because she is so warm; then she mews and whimpers with pleasure several times during the eight minutes which follow, but she sleeps on, her body lax.

The work done, Ernest gets off the Princess and out of bed. He puts on the dressing gown and crosses toward the door to the room. His brother is pressed tightly under his horizontal cage; a zoo for drunks and lost souls. Ernest stares down at him, not smiling. He shakes his head with grim dismay at a vision of the life of this future King. He lifts his cavalry boot high behind himself and drives a hard kick into his brother's haunch. The Prince does not stir. Ernest slips out of the room.

9

The hardly happy-go-lucky young couple spend their honeymoon at Windsor with the King and Queen for a few days; then they go off to a house at Kempshott. Lady Jersey goes with them. She and Caroline are the only women in a house crowded with the Prince's drunken male friends, who sleep with their boots on, under furniture. When they are awake, their language is abominable; their demeanor stained and messy. Caroline's eyes shine with disillusionment, but her manner to everyone in the house, excepting the Prince, is one of besieged endurance. Hopelessly, with the Prince, she falls back upon her arsenal of sarcasm and is greatly rewarded by finding wide breaches in the Prince's emotional armor.

She watches him flinch under her ridicule and remembers. She sees him quail with pain at her contrived vulgarities. Twice, reeling drunk, he throws back his head at the ceiling to scream at her words. These people are primitives, she thinks. Their bodies are formed like Brunswickers', but God has denied them any emotion other than feelings for themselves. My husband is a bold little boy who finds best fun in showing off to his little boy chums as they all soil the furniture with their boots and play at their drinking contests. Jersey is a woman, but they are little boys at vicious play. Jersey knows what she wants. She cannot have the Prince because she is old and she has spawned many bastards by many men, and she is good enough to lie with all of them together with the Prince, but what she wants is what she is determined to get—she wants me not to have the dignity and peace of being his wife because she can never be his wife. I can cope with her, Caroline knows. How does a woman who needs her husband cope with a cruel, small boy who would rather spend his days tearing wings off flies than allowing me to gentle him? If I can find him, it may even be that I can have him. But do I want him? She doesn't have to think long. She is a Brunswicker! She has the heart of a lion! She will find him somehow! She will find him and make him look into her heart and her need.

He flees to Carlton House with Caroline following like the Erinyes.

At Carlton House each levers the other into greater feats of cruelty; it no longer matters who began the war. Then, frantic, the Prince sees no way to halt it. The only armistice terms the Princess will accept are to be based upon the Prince's voluntary decision to take to her bed and dismiss Lady Jersey as the substitute wife. *"Pas de jugement,"* her father had said of her. She has no judgment, no deftness whatever in adapting herself to her new position; no idea whatever of how, possibly, to win the Prince's affections. She is wounded, but she will not permit the wound to heal.

They live under the same roof, but when she demands to be allowed to see the Prince, he will not receive her alone and terminates these icy, official audiences almost as soon as they start. The pace of the Prince's sadism accelerates.

As an automatic rite of the wedding procedure, the Princess was given a pearl necklace. Lady Jersey admires the necklace longingly. One afternoon, while he is drinking with her, the Prince grasps her by the hand, takes her through the corridors of Carlton House to Caroline's apartments, followed by his two Pages of the Presence. He pushes open the door where the Princess sits with Mrs. Keifetz. He is flushed with gin and maraschino.

"Give me that necklace," he says thickly. The Princess removes the necklace from her throat. He snatches the strand of pearls from her and fastens them around Lady Jersey's neck. "Necklace like this belongs on a lady, not a sow," he says.

Caroline hits him for the first time he has ever been hit across the face in his life, sending him to stagger three steps sideways. He is unable to believe what has happened. He is about to weep. His wife has struck him in the presence of his mistress and his Pages but—above all else—she has struck him! She had struck him as a fishwife strikes a street vagrant!

"Strip this room!" he bellows. "Get everything out of this room! Leave two chairs, no more. Strip it, I say!"

The Pages move rapidly—pushing, pulling and lifting heavy furniture. The Prince faces Caroline until only two straight-back spindle chairs and a wooden floor remain— tables, clocks, rugs, paintings, sofas, lamps and bibelots gone. He turns his back on the Princess, takes up Lady Jersey's hand, kisses her palm softly, then swans out of the room with the Lady on his arm.

As the door slams Caroline seats herself in one of the remaining chairs and motions to Mrs. Keifetz to seat herself in the other.

"You see, Mrs. Keifetz? You were right."

Mrs. Keifetz stares at the floor.

"We set out in the royal coach from Brunswick and you warned me that I had been boxed in a trap."

"You mustn't torture yourself, dear Princess," Mrs. Keifetz says.

"No, no. This is not self-torture. This is a confrontation with freedom, that is what it is. I see myself for what they always meant me to be in this Hanoverian family. I am a brood mare. I have been brought from Germany so that he may mount me and fill me with an heir to the throne; then my work will be done. And I will be free!"

She stares defiantly into Mrs. Keifetz's eyes, then her face begins to slip. Her mouth twists. Her eyes retreat into folds. Her expression shatters as if a stone had struck a mountain lake. She utters a terrible cry. "But he will not even mount me, Keifetz. No, I tell you. He will not set me free!"

A compromise in betrayal is reached in Parliament; the worst cheat and humiliation for the Prince on the safe side of his being sent to Marshalsea Prison as a common debtor. His salary, after this heinous marriage, is to be increased only enough to allow him to pay off his debts slowly himself. A Commission of Bankruptcy is to be appointed to decide how to do this. A new Bill is to be passed to make it illegal for him to amass any further debts. The net funds available to him will actually be 21 percent less than before he threw away any chance at happiness by marrying that bitch.

He becomes ill with rage and disappointment. He is forced to accept the terms, but now he has the entire British public as his enemies. He is certain that he has been treated with the vilest treachery. His detestation of the Princess grows bitterer while appearances are kept up. They attend the opera and theaters together. In May, at Frogmore, then at Brighton, they sail together for a cruise just offshore of the towns on the south coast as the people, poor things, stand by the thousands along the shore and wave summer handkerchiefs at them, cheering such utter happiness.

When summer is over, Caroline is left alone again. Malmesbury is long gone to his post in Moscow and Lady Anglesong, while supportive, cannot offer precisely the same sort of solace. The only note of cheer is that the House of Commons, through Anglesong's maneuvering and lobbying, votes her a jointure of fifty thousand pounds a year.

Each Tuesday she assembles all her ladies-in-waiting, excepting Lady Anglesong. She cross-examines Lady Jersey in their presence, believing herself to be witty and thus believing she wins them over to her side.

"Was the Prince very drunk at Lady Hilary Brown's ball?"

"Tolerably," Lady Jersey drawls coolly.

"Does he vomit over you when he comes to your bed?"

"Oh, no, Your Royal Highness. Let us say he comes not only voluntarily but eagerly. But, to answer your question—no, he never vomits near *my* bed, if you catch the distinction."

"It is sad and strange," the Princess says conversationally, "that an elderly woman such as you should, by free choice, come to the end of such an extensively wanton life, with your bastard children all about you—and find yourself in the arms of a drunken, fat, effeminate and probably diseased child-man."

Lady Jersey smiles brilliantly as she closes in with the axe. "In the oldest of homilies, your highness, some of us are lucky and some of us are lonely."

Caroline despairs because she is gaining weight at such an alarming rate. She becomes almost circular; tiny, portly, aqueous. Staring at her body one morning she knows she must seem to everyone else to be pregnant. It is utterly baffling, but there is no other way to account for this, and she fears to ask a doctor. If she is pregnant, she must see a priest, not a doctor, because if she is pregnant then it will be a virgin birth. How could she be pregnant? He has not so much as touched her arm. She knows he is capable of anything, that he would willingly set some stud upon her—but when? Anyway, how could such a thing happen without her knowledge? She did not drink, as he drank. She did not take laudanum, as he did. It would be impossible for anyone to do that to her in her sleep because not only Sidney Smith but also two other Englishmen at Brunswick told her she had the most sensitive sexual repository they had ever performed upon. She knew that to be true. If someone had been ordered to enter her while she slept, she would have known it because she would have felt it so keenly. But—if she is pregnant—whose child could it be? She is certain of one thing, they all looked so much like one another that even a fool such as the Prince would not take the chance of ordering some Captain of the Guard upon her, conceiving some evil way that such a thing could be done without her knowledge. It must be one of the brothers—if she were pregnant which is impossible—one of those abysmally stupid royal dukes. But—if they had found some magical way to do it without her knowing it was happening and if one of the brothers had entered her —which one? She hoped not that grossly fat Frederick. Clarence was hardly capable of getting his trousers off. Edward was a ninny. That left Ernest and Augustus. Adolphus was far too young. She hoped—if such a thing had happened which was utterly impossible—that it had been Augustus. He was so healthy and so marvelous-looking. Then she realized that neither Frederick nor Edward nor Augustus had been in England at the proper time to effect such an impossible pregnancy. If it was a royal duke who had filled her with child, a condition which she did not believe and would not accept, it had to be either William or Ernest. William was out of the question. The Prince simply would not have known how to approach his brother William with such an outrage as this, if it were true, which it most certainly was not. That left Ernest. She shuddered thinking of the evilness, his ruined face, his goatlike sexuality. Even the Prince could not want an heir (whom he must pretend throughout all his life to be his heir) to carry the taint which filled Ernest. She knows she must settle this thing immediately or go mad with circular insanity. She summons Lord Weiler, the Royal Surgeon. He makes an instant diagnosis. "I estimate that you are eight months pregnant, Madam," he says.

She laughs nervously. "I know I *look* pregnant," she says ruefully, "and if I didn't know better, if I didn't know that is impossible, I would certainly agree that I am pregnant."

"I don't believe I follow Your Highness." Lord Weiler, although short, had the dignity of a penguin.

"I mean biology and nature being what they are, it is simply out of the question that I am pregnant."

"If you wish, Madam," Lord Weiler says stiffly, "I shall arrange for another opinion, but the outcome of that opinion will not differ from my own."

When he leaves, Caroline sends for Lady Anglesong who says, on entering, "You are deathly pale, Madam!"

"Lord Weiler just told me I am pregnant."

"Of course you are pregnant. Everyone knows that. But what else did he say which has frightened you?"

"Everybody knows I am pregnant?"

"Of course."

"Anglesong—listen carefully to me. I did not know it."

"What?"

"Anglesong—he never touched me. He hasn't been near me. Not ever."

"We will eliminate misunderstanding. Do you mean the Prince has not cohabited with you?"

"No."

"He has never entered you?"

"Damn this! No!"

"Now—I ask you this as a lawyer who has examined your dossier at Whitehall. Have you been entered by any other male since your arrival in England?"

"No."

"Did you and Lord Malmesbury have intercourse during the four-month period when he was the only male you were allowed to be with?"

"I tell you with all my heart that I wish I could answer yes to that, Anglesong. I tried but his duty kept his fires out."

"The answer is no?"

"The answer is no. With regret."

"Then you are the victim of the oldest flummery that royals have ever perpetuated. They put a man upon you."

"Impossible!"

"Madam—you are *very* pregnant."

"How?"

Lady Anglesong shrugs. "They drugged you on your

wedding night. The Prince stayed drunk. At a properly late hour the substitute arrived and entered you."

"You are sure of that?"

"Your Highness—consult the nearest mirror."

The Princess claps her hands together with a tremendous bang. "Then it is over!" she howls with delight. "The entire miserable marriage to that slobbering, drunken effeminate pig is over and done. I have delivered what he bought me for—he will get his heir and he will take it directly to the royal pawnshop and exchange it for money which he will spend on perfume." She laughs fully, happily, in the highest glee. "*Mein Gott*, Anglesong," she sings, "do you know what this means? I shall never have to look at him from the moment my baby arrives!"

"There is always light at the end of the tunnel, Madam."

"And, by Gott, if I could ever only be sure who it was who placed this babe inside me, I would drag him into bed and give him such enormous pleasure as he deserves and as he certainly never got from me the first time round!"

As the day of the birth draws near, the Prince is in such an ecstasy of greed that he takes to prayer. If the heir comes soon and lives—oh dear God, the heir must live!—he can never again have a financial problem in his life. Why —he will be able to buy Antoine Careme for the kitchens at Brighton straight from the kitchens of the Tsar of all the Russias!

The Princess is in labor. The Prince is on and off his knees like a curate with a weak bladder. The door to the lying-in room must be kept open by law. Lord Weiler enforces this as does the Archbishop of Canterbury, head cold well cured, who wanders in and out of the dim chamber amid Caroline's shrill outcries and wretched groans. The Prince races from room to room: consulting doctors, official witnesses, dictating letters to creditors who are in the offing; promising Sir Herbert Mitgang an Earldom (when he should be in a position to confer it) for Sir Herbert will head the Parliamentary Committee which can double the Prince's allowance when the heir is born.

Lackeys hurry to and fro with trays of refreshments while Caroline suffers. The Prince sometimes has two filled glasses in hands at the same time. The Archbishop and Pitt, the Younger, the Prime Minister, stare at his heroic appetites and movements with saddened disapproval. But it is not only the stimulation of the thought of the money which has brought on the Prince's histrionic agitation. He is overwhelmed with the realization that having given the nation an heir, he will be free to separate forever from this impossible woman.

At 9:20 P.M. an infant's cry is heard. Princess Charlotte is born. More wine is brought. The country's leaders come forward to congratulate the Prince. He weeps with relief. He weeps with gratitude. He cannot stop weeping. He suffers "a total and acute nervous breakdown" before the eyes of England's government, flopping about like a great haddock thrown up from the sea; sobbing; shrieking. Bedded by Lord Weiler, he is convinced that he has only a few hours to live; he dictates his will. In it he acknowledges Mrs. Fitzherbert to be his wife and leaves her all his possessions. He leaves the Princess of Wales one shilling. At last in three weeks, he recovers and destroys the will and leaves at once for Brighton.

The heir is born on the 6th January 1796. On the 10th March the King, at Windsor, sends for Caroline, allowing himself to peer down into the depths of his niece's unhappiness.

"You have my sympathy and support, my dear," he says. "For many, many years I have been filled with dislike and contempt for your husband. Further, you have been wronged."

"Oh, Uncle George! You cannot know what it has been like!"

"We have our feelings, you and I. But we have our duty. Therefore I beg of you to seek reconciliation with your husband."

"My father taught me duty," Caroline sobs. "I never shirk duty."

"How happy you make me."

"But your son must face duty as well."

"Inescapably."

"But he escapes."

"Sadly, yes."

"Then we must have an understanding, Uncle George. Not the Prince and me."

"How?" he asks abruptly.

"If I must stay under the same roof with him, I must have separate apartments, entrances, finances, staff—even dogs and cats. And a guarantee that I do not need to talk to him and must be seen with him only on occasions of state."

"That sounds reasonable," the King answers. "It is like most royal marriages. My own excepted, of course."

"Oh, Uncle George," Caroline says throatily, moving closer to him. "I am so unhappy!" He takes her in his powerful arms and lifts her upon a sofa where he comforts her as he had comforted his wife, the Queen, into fifteen children.

10

The least satisfactory part of horse riding for the Prince is mounting. As he weighs 255 pounds (packaged within a height of five feet eight inches), he can mount only by means of a complicated mechanism: an inclined plane, rising to 2 1/2 feet above the ground, at the upper end of which is a platform. His Royal Highness is placed upon a chair on rollers, pushed up the ramp, and delivered to the platform, which is then raised smoothly by screws high enough for his horse to pass underneath. Then he is let down gently into the saddle.

The Prince has just come in from an exhilarating 9-mile gallop across fields at Brighton. He heads directly for his bath, with entourage.

Boldly, the Princess enters this bath, causing the Prince infernal consternation due to his own shameful knowledge that, before two Pages of the Presence, three Gentlemen of the Bedchamber, and his Master of Robes, his wife is seeing him in the altogether nude for the first time. He realizes how much worse it would be if all these people knew it was for the first time.

He cannot articulate. He roars like a forest beast with a toothache. The six courtiers take this to mean that he wishes them to leave him alone with his wife. They withdraw. The Princess gives him no chance to recover as he stands nude before her.

"I suppose, dear Prince," she says, "that your faithful

courier, Lord Cholmondeley, has not had the opportunity to bring you the message I gave him last Tuesday so, as I never have your gracious permission to see you alone, I am obliged to find you so deliciously naked for the first time in our lives."

"Deliciously," a food word, even a meat word, is *the* word. The Prince's nude body is a huge pink and white and mottled tower of fatty globes, globules, and chunks of sagging fat. Bereft of his corset, his deep, swaying kettle-drum of a super-stomach hangs far downward toward his fat knees with their benign, blind expression, completely concealing his shy genitals. His flaccid, hanging bosoms are like twin hammocks filled with anvils of lard, forcing them downward until they nearly conceal his wee pucker of a navel. His pendulous, trembling chins sway and swing like a pelican's beard filled with excited fish, as his cheeks drop and dewlap into the awful drag of gravity to greet them.

Hastily, he secures masses of Turkish towels and wraps himself mercifully in them. He sits upon a tiny stool, a scarlet face over white wooliness.

"What do you want?" he shrills.

"I want to see you in a tutu." She giggles.

"What—do—you—want?"

"I want your slut Jersey out of my sight. In this the King agrees with me." She turns to leave. He shouts at her to return at once. She pays him no heed. He screams in full tantrum. She turns, grinning, and comes back.

"You must allow me to answer you in German," he says malevolently. "It is essential for me to explain myself without any possible ambiguity on the subject of the un-wise, groundless and most injurious imputation which you have thought fit to cast upon me and now, deplorably, into which you have dragged the King. In the first place, Madam, you insinuate to everyone that I oblige you to dine, *tête à tête*, with Lady Jersey." His voice rises to a grinding squeak. "That is a statement utterly contradictory to the truth."

"There is no one here but us, Georgie. No need to lie. You force her upon me as a lady-in-waiting. A fact is a fact."

"I am more immediately caused to notice the increase in the vulgar expressions you use toward Lady Jersey."

"Georgie, no need to lie. I have always, from the first day I met her, only referred to her as your bitch, your slut, or as your whore. There has been no increase."

"People who poison your mind with vile calumnies concerning Lady Jersey are no less seriously your enemies than mine."

"The wife's enemies should at once become the husband's. That is noble and moral of you, Georgie."

"From the moment of your arrival in this country, Madam, I described to you a woman who is not my mistress as you so indecorously call her, conferring unconquerable disgust upon me for yourself; I described her as a friend to whom I am attached by the strongest ties of habitude, esteem and respect. For months before you ever met this maligned woman you inveighed against her. But let me tell you, Madam, that you make it clear throughout your continuing, vile gossip that the intimacy of my friendship with Lady Jersey, under all the false colors which your slanders have given it, was perfectly known to you before you accepted my hand."

"All that food you eat is turning to fat in your head, Georgie."

"You recited particulars of anonymous letters. You

incite the King against me! When, all the while, the confidence resulting in so long a friendship with this fine woman enabled her to offer advice which contributed not a little to decide me to marry you."

"For that, if for nothing else, Georgie, you should have her cast into the Tower, hanged by the neck, then drawn and quartered."

"Stop this deliberate mockery of your husband! And if you repeat any of these conversations we have had in this impossible place and situation today—I shall turn Franz Heller loose upon you!"

"Tell me, please, Georgie, that you will wholly isolate this woman from my household."

"Yes! And good day to you. You may leave."

"Not yet."

"This is endless!"

"In the future, do not send me messages through Lord or Lady Cholmondeley but, in order to preserve policy, you must give me your orders in writing to abolish all misunderstandings."

He looks at her with loathing. "You may expect a letter from me tomorrow morning. Do nothing until it arrives."

LETTER FROM THE PRINCE OF WALES TO THE PRINCESS OF WALES
30th April 1796

As you so urgently informed me that you wish I would define, in writing, the terms upon which we are to live, I shall endeavor to explain myself upon that with as much cleanness and as much propriety as the nature of the subject will admit. Our inclinations are not in our power, nor should either of us be held answerable to the other, because nature has not made us suitable to each

other. Tranquil and comfortable society is, however, in
our power. Let our intercourse therefore be restricted to
that, and I will distinctly subscribe to the condition
which you require and, even in the event of an accident
happening to my daughter, which I trust Providence in
its mercy will avert, I shall not infringe the terms of
our restrictions by proposing, at any period, a
connection of a more particular nature. I shall now
finally close this disagreeable correspondence, trusting
that we having completely explained ourselves to each
other, the rest of our lives will be spent in
uninterrupted tranquility. I am, Madam, with great
truth, very sincerely yours,

GEORGE P.

✧ book two ✧
emancipation
(1801–1814)

TORY GOVERNMENT UNTIL 1806
PRIME MINISTERS: *Henry Addington, Viscount Sidmouth, to 1804*
Pitt to 1806

WHIGS TO POWER 1806–1807
PRIME MINISTER: *Lord Grenville*

TORY GOVERNMENT UNTIL 1827
PRIME MINISTERS: *William Bentinck, Duke of Portland, to 1809*
Spencer Perceval to 1812
Robert Banks Jenkinson, Earl of Liverpool, to 1827

1

Caroline is moved out of Carlton House. By custom the baby is left behind. The Princess shrugs and explains to Mrs. Keifetz, "Royals are raised as professionals by impersonals." She takes a villa at Charlton, near Greenwich, not only because it is comfortable for her, but because it is uncomfortable for the Prince in that it is a house which was once occupied by Mrs. Fitzherbert. The King appoints Colonel Franz Heller as Controller of the Princess's Household. This is not at all uncomfortable for the Prince. The Princess is beginning to see the clearer outline of her life's work: to provide endless psychological harassment of the Prince. She studies her career gravely. She has to grope toward it at first but, as it shows in sharper and sharper delineation—as clear as her own pain—she works to perfect each vision.

"If you are determined to do this, then you must proceed from policy," Lady Joyce says. "You must not improvise. Let the husband improvise the whims and misfortunes and indulgences of this kind of marriage. If you have negative ambitions for your husband, then you must accept what you are going to do all in one piece, like a rich carpet being rolled out ahead of you on which you may walk toward your goal. What is your goal?"

Caroline beams. "My goal is the mental and physical destruction of my husband and the eventual isolation from him of all public affection."

"You are sure of that?"

"Oh, yes."

She sets out to perform at her "famous" dinner parties, which are eagerly supported by what the Prince has always referred to as the *ton*. She behaves more scandalously at each successive party, determined to have the Prince regard her as a dangerous force to be appeased. She forgets, perhaps, that she is also the future Queen of England. Most gravely, the Prince and his mother learn (through spies placed by Colonel Heller) that the Princess keeps an elaborate notebook about the private characters of the foremost people. The Princess occasionally shows the notebook to acquaintances to be sure the news gets back to the Prince. It is a dangerous book for her. Becoming preoccupied with the joy of all this (for she has succeeded, without much wheedling at all, in persuading Colonel Heller to accept a stipend from her purse to report all of the Prince's reaction to her) she makes the gross mistake that is the second turning point of her life.

Momentarily preferring peaceful relations between them, at the beginning of December 1798 the Prince invites her to dine at Carlton House and also to settle there for the winter. Instead of looking forward to the possibility of her own secure and merry future, instead of seeking the balanced counsel of Lady Anglesong, she harkens back to her father's court and its freedoms for all to come and go and do as they pleased. She ignores the reality of agreeing to live part of the year under her husband's implicit protection. If she could see beyond the hurt he has dumped upon her, she might build her own world apart from his, see as much as she wants to of her own child, be satisfied with her position as future Queen, and have an animated and interesting life.

Most fatally, she refuses.

The unexpected peace offering comes from the Prince not because he has relented or forgiven, but because he is now tired of Lady Jersey and wants to be rid of her. Mrs. Fitzherbert has returned from Europe, and he wants the respectability of a settled, family-man Prince to return himself to her arms.

There is resistance from these two ladies; the one going out, the other coming in again, and from the public who bloody well expect a man to live with his wife and child.

To conduct an effective campaign, he wants everything to appear as if in correct order.

Lady Jersey is summarily removed from the house adjoining Carlton House in June 1799. Her husband is formally dismissed as Master of Horse. Lady Jersey refuses to acknowledge any change in their relationship until Colonel Heller is dispatched to speak to her privately. She withdraws but tells the *ton*, "There is a Popish combination against me." She is finished.

"Well," Caroline says gaily to Mrs. Keifetz. "I have dumped the slut."

"Don't give yourself too much credit. He was sick of her."

"That doesn't matter! She's gone! She was my enemy and she lost the battle! Papa would be very proud of me for standing unvanquished on the field."

"Unvanquished by her, you mean."

"My God, how you love to chew little bones, Keifetz! You certainly don't think the Prince's wife, Mrs. Fitzherbert, is any rival? That is to say, as an enemy who would rather see me humiliated and ruined than see me free? She is a nice, motherly woman. I wish her well and I know, because she is a good woman, she wishes me well. And she is his wife, you know, Keifetz. I have no idea in God's world what I am supposed to be in this country beyond brood mare, but she is his wife."

The public observes Lady Jersey's departure and cheers Caroline wherever she goes. Often she goes to the King and he cheers her. But she will not move into Carlton House, and therefore Mrs. Fitzherbert will not be placated. Mrs. Fitzherbert is upset by the Prince's unfaithfulness to two marriages. She understands the necessities of Law and the State which require his alliance with Caroline just as she knows—as a Catholic— that she and only she is his wife.

Caroline upsets the Prince's dearest plans. She continues her career of attacking him and mocking him. She begins little afternoons with jolly tars. They are not youths but experienced, dangerous womanizers who range from the forceful seventy-year-old Lord Hood, governor of Greenwich Hospital, to Lord Amelius Beauclerk, early thirties, who commands ships, to the old friend and playmate, Admiral Sir Sidney Smith, immortal defender of Acre. Two other principal spread eaglers are spotted among the jolly tars: the rising politician, George Canning, a future prime minister, and a good portrait painter, Thomas Lawrence. Canning, after a "little afternoon" with Caroline, when the Princess somehow gets her little hand inside his trousers, writes to a sage friend, "The thing is too clear to be doubted. What am I to do? I am perfectly bewildered." Rounding out the Princess's congregation of good fellows are the great (even if he has to admit it himself) Sir Walter Scott and Spencer Perceval, who will be the Tory prime minister very soon. As sure as Caroline works to see that the Prince is aware of what must be going on with the jolly tars, et al, so doubly does she work to be sure that he does not know that twice a month the King comes to comfort her.

Unable to bear the flood of dirty laundry that chutes out of the Princess's "famous" parties and her "little afternoons," the Prince summons Colonel Heller. "I want you to find me suitably shady people of an acceptable class," he says. "A man and wife."

"It is done, my Prince."

"Her viciousness will go on, you see, the Prince says in achingly suffering German. "She will continue to debase me." He begins to weep because he has taken too much laudanum that morning. Colonel Heller stiffens, hardly breathing. He hopes desperately that he is not going to be ordered to kill the Princess of Wales, who is, more than anything else, a *German* princess. The Prince looks up through his tears and says harshly, "There is a legal way to stop her."

"Legal, my Prince?"

"Evidence must be delved which will prove to the King, to this government, and to the public, that the way she conducts her life gives me the right to divorce."

At the next regimental mess of His Britannic Majesty's German Legion, held at Windsor, Heller eats with his comrades, as prescribed. They are all large to huge men, as befits bodyguards, and they eat enormously: *Wildschweinschnitzel Kalt; Aalpastete Kalt; Kräuterroulade Rebhuhn; Verputzte Kartoffelwurstchen;* finishing off with great omelets called *Alsterblick,* made with eggs, bananas, chocolate, rum and honey. Before, during, and after the meal they drink from quart tankards of beer. Heller pretends to be drinking with them but only puts down three quarts. When the meal is over and everyone is drunk, the wrestling ritual begins: four officers, stripped to the waist and glistening with sweat, circle slowly around the grinning Major von und zu Tytell, to attempt to bring him down. When the food and the beer has brought them down, Colonel Heller slips up a dark staircase, along passages of the castle, across back corridors to a red door. He knocks. He listens. He enters, locking the door behind him. The King, behind a tall, heavy screen, cannot be seen. Heller hears the grunted signal to begin. He reports all the Prince's fears, tears and conclusions.

"This is as low as he can go. It is tragic and corrupt." The King thinks of his wife and daughters and their voices nipping at him about the Princess of Wales.

The King regrets needing to use his niece in the upcoming operations against his son, but there is no better way. The Whigs grow more impatient. He knows that what seem to be casual meetings are really party councils. He knows that the Whigs seek any means to retire him so that, under a carefully stage-managed and blandly credible complexity of political actions, they can move his son to the throne. He knows they count upon his falling ill again. In history, when all other things seemed ready and equal, politicians had even contrived to cause kings to fall ill to gain their ends. But, although it would require the unfortunate use of his niece, he would nevertheless have to set things in motion to make certain no Whig considered political conditions ready and equal for such a coup. He would need to show his son to be an unstable cuckold and a fool in the eyes of the people. He would have to keep his son and the Whig Party off balance like that for as long as he had the strength. When strength failed, he would leave more than detailed instructions for the leaders of the Tory Party to follow for the proper manipulation of his almost gaudily imperfect son.

"How will you do it, Heller?" he asks from behind the screen.

"I shall study Dr. Gotlieb's files, Sir. They know the contents of many closets."

"Manufacture nothing!"

"Only her natural conduct will be observed and recorded, Sir."

"How long will it all take?" the King asks, to determine how long he will need to deprive his niece of comforting.

"A few months, I estimate."

The King sighs. "But you have never been right. Well —be thorough, Heller. Good night."

Mrs. Fitzherbert sits out of reach at Castle Hill, Ealing. Her position, made clear to the Prince through Ernest, is: "The link once broken can never be rejoined. Even if we were to make it up, he would not remain constant for a fortnight."

The Prince mounts an intense campaign to convey to Mrs. Fitzherbert that "Everything is at an end in *another quarter*. He writes her wild letters. He sends her a locket containing a miniature of one of his eyes by Cosway. He becomes so frenzied that Lord Weiler fears for his sanity.

> IF YOU WISH MY LIFE YOU SHALL HAVE IT. . . . OH! OH, GOD, WHO HAS SEEN THE AGONY OF MY SOUL AND KNOWEST THE PURITY OF MY INTENTIONS, HAVE MERCY ON ME: TURN ONCE MORE, I CONJURE THEE, THE HEART OF MY MARIA TO ME, FOR WHOM I HAVE LIVED AND FOR WHOM I WILL DIE. YOU KNOW YOU ARE MY WIFE, THE WIFE OF MY HEART AND SOUL, MY WIFE IN THE PRESENCE OF GOD. I AM WRAPPED UP IN YOU ENTIRELY, NOTHING CAN ALTER ME, SHAKE ME, OR CHANGE ME. ALIKE YOURS IN LIFE OR DEATH.

Through elaborate arrangements, confederates, and priests, the Prince is alone at last with her against her wishes. "It is no use, my dear," she tells him gently but firmly. "We cannot find peace together in this life."

"I am not able to accept that," he says with an emotion-thickened voice.

"We must accept destiny."

His voice rises an octave. His stuffed face goes crimson. "If you do not take me back instantly, I will stand on rooftops and trumpet out the truth."

"The truth?"

"That I am legally married to a Roman Catholic commoner, thereby losing my royal patrimony forever!"

"George!" Her pinkness fades. She is frightened. She pleads for time. The Prince has two of his sisters waiting in an adjoining room. At a signal they burst in to urge Mrs. Fitzherbert to accept their brother. They take her away from the Prince. Father William Nassau of Mrs. Fitzherbert's church in Warwick Street is waiting for her. He tells her he is willing to go to Rome to lay her case before the Pope. Weeping, she thanks him and returns to the Prince.

He thunders at her. "Think not that prayer or any advice will make me delay my purpose. Thank God, the witnesses to our marriage are still living."

"Oh, George! Darling George!" she cries. "I love you truly. I know that, in this rage of love you feel, you will most certainly ruin yourself if I ignore you."

He springs to embrace her. She repulses him so hard, with a clever use of her large hip, that he rams into a heavy table, caroms into a wall and, losing his balance, falls to the floor. On his hands and knees he gapes up at her. "We may not as much as shake hands!" Mrs. Fitzherbert says sharply, "until I gain permission to reunite with you from the Pope."

In 1801, the King appoints the Princess of Wales Ranger of Greenwich Park. The Queen's indignation at this is immoral.

This is the beginning of a plan which Colonel Heller has developed for the King, entailing the Princess's move from Charlton to Montague House, the beautiful mansion with great lawns and tall trees which is the perquisite of the Ranger. The King puts Heller in charge of the Prince's Household, which he runs as efficiently as his utter Germanness suggests. From Windsor and London, word goes out quietly from the King, the Queen, the six princesses, and the Prince that, at risk of losing royal favor, the Princess's "famous" dinners are to be shunned. The *ton* disappears.

The Princess is a gregarious, hilarious woman. New guests of less impeccable reputations and less high stations are brought in by Colonel Heller to fill the gap. "The King has commanded me," he tells her, his voice breaking, "but the heart in me which was once young, in a strong body which once knew you, commands me far more poignantly to protect you . . . in my own quiet way."

The Princess flings a roguish kiss across the small salon, the door locked, a large admiral's fore-and-aft hat hanging over the keyhole from its handle.

"Your *quiet* way, Marxie?" When she became amorous she always called him by the diminutive of his middle name. "What excites me about you is your noisy way when you take a woman to enormous pleasure."

His tunic collar tightens. His trousers tighten. His face flushes as he breathes shallowly. She puts her hands into her bodice and scoops out both breasts. "Come and get them, Marxie," she says.

3

At Montague House, with its serene seclusion, Caroline reverts to her happiest days at Brunswick. She sculpts a charming bust of Princess Charlotte. She collects nine small children of cottagers, proclaiming that she will educate the small boys to be seamen and the little girls to be housewives. She invents and makes dozens of ingenious toys for them. She chats with them in her hilarious way. Everyone at court, at Windsor and London, considers all this to be too awfully laughable and unroyal. Some say she has taken on the nine small children to carry her love letters and that no less than nine would be adequate for the task.

When he is certain that everything has been established into a settled and smooth routine at Montague House, Colonel Heller visits a Lady Douglas in London who has come recommended to him from the archives of Dr. Gotlieb, information accumulator for the German Legion. Lady Douglas is the adorably pretty young wife of Sir John Douglas, a Colonel of Marines, stern, elderly and impoverished. They are helpless snobs. At their first meeting, Colonel Heller tells Lady Douglas that he knows precisely where she has come from in her long, difficult climb to her present title. He cites how much she had formerly charged men for privileges, and he sympathizes with her ambition for her husband. "Would you like your husband to attend the Duke of Sussex as Master of Horse?"

"Oh, yes!" Lady Douglas breathes.

As they sit in the squalor of two bare rooms in which Sir John and Lady Douglas are forced to live, he tells her that the Duke would insist upon providing the Douglases with a fine country house.

"Then what?" the adorable young woman asks.

He smiles at her evilly. "You will meet the Princess of Wales, you will observe her actions closely, then you will tell me what you have observed. Could you do that for me?"

"I am certain I could. But there would be a need for certain bona fides. We should insist upon being established in the Duke's Household before I could undertake the observations upon the Princess."

"*Ja, ja.* You must be. Or else how will you get the fine house to make you the Princess's neighbor? Remember this and this only. What I arrange, I can aaaalzo take away. *Hein?*"

"Quite."

Lady Douglas is sewing when Sir John returns from his day-long tramping in the streets to keep himself from the squalor of the rooms in which he has installed his touching young wife. He is silent as he sits on the bottom-sprung chair facing her.

She says, "I have good news."

"About what, my dear?"

"About your career, John."

He snorts.

"The Prince of Wales sent his Confidential Secretary here to see you this afternoon."

"The *Prince?*" He is nearly unmanned.

"His name is Colonel Heller. Very military, very

brusque—just your sort of man, John. He wanted so much to see you, but he could wait no longer; then, to my great honor, he entrusted his mission to me to offer to you and will return in a day or two for your response."

"My response?" Sir John was very tired; deeply tired into the folds and creases of his spirit. He was not at all the man he had, perhaps, once been. All he had left was his fine military record, his military dignity, and a faded sort of military beauty.

"The Duke of Sussex has requested you to become his Master of Horse, John. They have offered us a beautiful house in Blackheath."

At the end of October 1801, shortly after the King has left Montague House on a visit to comfort the Princess, Lady Douglas sits at the window of her new house watching the snow fall. Through the snow come two elegantly dressed women on foot. As they come closer, Lady Douglas sees that one of them, dressed in a lilac satin pelisse, a lilac and sable hat and yellow half boots, is the Princess of Wales. Lady Douglas hastens to the door.

"Are you Lady Douglas?" the Princess asks jollily as she comes up the garden path. "I have been told you have a beautiful child. I would like to see her. This is Mrs. Keifetz." The Princess leads the way into the house.

She is delighted with the child. They play together for more than an hour while Lady Douglas entertains Mrs. Keifetz apart.

Caroline wonders, as she plays with the child, if everybody's baby she sees and adores, the babies who are rolled in prams, the babies in paintings, whether they were —well, whether most of them were the children of the two parents whom the world thought were their parents. She is baffled as to who it could have been who had given her Charlotte. She no longer thinks it was Ernest. Ernest is too very peculiar sexually. He came into a room leaving sweat-prints on the floor; then he lost his hand in the butler's trousers. It couldn't have been Ernest. Lord Perman, who knew everyone and everything that happened at court, had told her that there was absolute proof that Ernest had murdered Sellis, his valet, because he had been madly in love with the man and the man refused to have anything to do with him except to wash his socks and press his handkerchiefs. The sergeant of the Cold Stream Guards, on duty at St. James's where Ernest lived, had found Sellis lying on the bed with his hands straight down and the blood all in a froth running from his neck, with the white-handled razor on the floor eight feet from the bed. She has become sure it was not Ernest who won her on her wedding night. He is so nasty he would have told her. He would have suggested that they blackmail the Prince together.

It could not have been Heller. If ever a child did not look like Heller it was Charlotte. Children simply could not look like Heller, and she knew Heller. If he had been the man on her wedding night, he would have come to her later to brag about it. Not to brag about mounting her, but about how of all men, he had been chosen by the royal family to produce the heir they must have. That was his essential character.

Somewhere out there lived a very discreet man who had entered her, pleasured himself, and left her with a baby she had had no idea she was having. But all that made no difference. She had the child, a beautiful, sweet and loving child even if they would not let her see her. Now there was this beautiful, sweet, and loving child—amiable, dear and everything else children were. She would love this little child until they returned her own child to her.

When the Princess leaves, she invites Sir John and Lady Douglas to join her for dinner the next night.

They get along famously from the first dinner party onward. To ingratiate herself with the Douglases, whom she regards as sticks but whose little daughter she can see may be able to lighten her days and not only bring much marvelous fun but enable her to get through such dinner parties as these, she flatters Lady Douglas outrageously. "She is a*dor*able!" the Princess cries. Hardly a week passes that the Princess does not exclaim to all present about Lady Douglas's loveliness. She kisses her cheeks, embraces her and, as always, manages to convince herself that she has not made her point. She goes further and further. "I tell you, you are beautiful—different from almost any Englishwoman." She turns to the dinner guests assembled. "Look at her arms! They are fine beyond imagination. And the bust is so good. And her eyes! Have you ever seen such eyes?"

It gets the dinner party started, she thinks.

During a "little afternoon" when the Princess and the jolly tar Sir Sidney Smith have finished rolling about on the sofa and the floor of the Blue Room where the large admiral's fore-and-aft hat hangs permanently on the door-handle over the keyhole, they sit on the couch and, while the Princess diddles him, she says, "I have found a beauty for you and I have got her all ready for you."

"How very kind," Sir Sidney says. "One can always tell who are one's real friends. Who is she?"

"She is a very silly little piece but extremely pretty. And she has an old husband."

"If you won't tell me who she is, then who is he? Oh, I say! What a gifted touch you have!"

"You taught me."

"But who is he? A man likes to know whom he is cuckolding."

"Sir John Douglas."

"My old messmate! How will you arrange it?"

"I shall appoint her as temporary lady-in-waiting when Lady Montant takes her annual voyage to Naples. I will put her in the Round Tower across the garden. She knows well now what a marvelous bedfellow you are, so I shall leave the rest up to you."

"Jolly good! Oh, I say! This chat has me all stirred up again. Down on your back on the carpet you go!"

On the evening of Lady Douglas's fourth night in the Round Tower, the Princess puts the cherry on top. "He has learned things in the Orient which few European women have ever experienced. I cannot *tell* you what it feels like!"

"But—what does he *do*?"

"There is no use trying to describe it—it is all sensation—vast, enormous sensation—one must *experience* it!"

"But—I mean—oh, I say—I could not even *think* of such a thing," Lady Douglas gasps, her eyes glazing.

Twenty minutes after the Princess leaves the Round Tower, Sir Sidney taps lightly upon Lady Douglas's door. It is five minutes to eleven. She appears startled. She assembles her features into fright. "I am Sir Sidney Smith," he says. "I had to know you."

As she totters backward, eyes covered with an opaque film, he lets himself into the room. He locks the door. He hangs his fore-and-aft hat over the keyhole. Slowly, he undresses himself to reveal to her his true fame which is not as the hero of Acre. She stares, greatly moved. He reaches out to her. She comes to him. He peels the night-dress from her shoulders, over her hips, and lets it fall. She pulls him downward. He enters her in what surely does not seem to be an arcane oriental manner, but she cries out with delight just the same as if he were the brother-in-law of Genghis Khan who has descended upon her.

Two nights later, remembering something she forgot to tell Lady Douglas, the Princess slips into a peignoir and flits across the garden to go up the stairs to Lady Douglas's room. From within it, she hears Heller's harsh voice. She listens, titillated, but the feeling does not last because Heller is saying, "The Princess is a silly woman? We know that. We do not need that kind of information. We want evidence of adultery. What men does she take in the day and in the nights? I want lists from you."

"I can give you such a list," Lady Douglas says calmly.

"Names, places, dates, what they do to each other, what they say to each other. Every day?"

"No. Not every day. But almost every day. She really is insatiable."

"After you give me this list, you will break into the room where she lies with a man with two of my servants and a magistrate."

Outraged, but still not really shocked or surprised, the Princess backs down the stairway and runs across the lawn giggling. Sidney's little piece was selling her to a German who had been her lover since she was sixteen, and they were both going to try to make a terrible thing out of bedding. Well! She must teach some lessons!

She writes a short note to summon Anglesong. Serenely she allows herself to be clothed for dinner in a dress which seems to be alternating satin panels of brass and mustard. Lady Joyce is to arrive from London after the dinner.

At dinner Caroline chats amiably while eating an amazing meal of boiled chicken and potted lamprey which she insists upon having served on the same plate. When a servant whispers that Lady Joyce Anglesong is waiting for her in the Blue Room, the Princess rises and leaves the table.

She enters the Blue Room, waves amiably to Anglesong, and locks the door. "Well!" she says with glee, "I have personally discovered that the enemy is mounting a major attack. How this will appeal to your devious little heart, Anglesong!"

"What have you discovered, Your Highness?"

"You see, I forgot to tell Lady Douglas that I had arranged for her husband to be awarded some inconsequential decoration—those things are so important to the Douglases—so I slipped across the garden and climbed to her rooms. Before I could open the door, I heard Heller's vulgar voice."

"Heller!"

"Wait. This is delicious. He was instructing her as one instructs a hireling. He was telling her that the time had come for Lady Douglas to get solid evidence of my adultery. In the plural, I expect. And Lady Douglas replied she could do that easily."

"I am shocked. I am made ill with disgust," Lady Joyce says, "but I am not surprised."

"Great generals should never be capable of being surprised," the Princess says. "Next, after Lady Douglas has provided such a list, she is to choose the time to break in upon me while I am in the arms of a man or men, to be accompanied by two servants and a magistrate."

"A magistrate? I see. The Prince wants to collect legal evidence for presentation to a formal court."

"I know what I am going to do," the Princess says. "I was curious to know what you thought I should do."

"What is your plan?" Lady Joyce asks, always the lawyer who gives nothing until perhaps a few others might come up with some sound ideas.

"I shall continue to be jolly with her, of course. Although I shall not give her the opportunity she is convinced awaits them—the chance to come crashing into some orgy which would have me at the bottom of it—I have decided to do for her a much, much greater service: give her a little tableau to report back to her masters which will throw the Prince into a series of somersaults."

"What? What will you do?" Lady Joyce exclaims with alarm.

"I shall convince all of them that I am going to have a baby by one of the jolly tars—or whoever; then I shall convince them that I have had that baby."

"A baby? My dear Princess, you could be put to death as Princess of Wales if they could prove you had a child by anyone other than the Prince."

"Yes. You see? They must *prove* it. But I am going to see to it that I spend at least two nights, very soon, at Carlton House—if only on the pretext of a family reunion with Charlotte and the Prince. If they confront me with having a child by a jolly tar—which they will not dare to do because of my friends, the British public—I will tell them that the baby is the Prince's and tell them when and how the infant was conceived."

"I must say, I can see that this is indeed an inspiration you have had—it presents so many possibilities."

"Tell me the possibilities, Anglesong."

"The Prince's reaction to knowing such an infant is NOT his child—and I am basing my list of possibilities on the assurance that you are going to make them think you *may* have had a child, not that you actually intend to have one—"

"That is correct, Anglesong."

"Then there is the possibility that you *can* drive him mad, Your Highness," Lady Joyce says considerately. "He will know it is not his child. But he will know no way to challenge that it is not his child in face of the evidence of your having been at Carlton House with him, and at the risk of making a cuckold, not to say an idiot, of himself. At the same time he will know that the child—if male—will supersede his daughter's claim to the throne, and that this child, whom he sees as an unknown bastard, may become king after him."

"That is exactly correct, Anglesong. But you overlook the most delicious part of his character."

"What part?"

"When Heller and Lady Douglas bring back word that I am pregnant, he will merely remember that he has never slept with me, so he will convince himself that I have given him grounds for divorce. He will move the Whigs into a massive investigation of me. They will do it because that will greatly affect the King, lessening him in the eyes of the public for having chosen me for his son, while raising the Prince up as a righteous claimant to the throne, by showing him to have been wronged and ruined by his wife."

"But how can that be good?" Lady Joyce cries out in

sudden, unmasked consternation. "You would be walking directly into the trap which the Prince has Heller and Lady Douglas setting for you."

"Because it will be the easiest thing in the world to prove that the baby is not my son—because I will not have a baby and he cannot be my son. We will reveal this *after* my husband has gone through the hue and cry of his hunt for my head leading a pack of politicians of the Whig government. When it is proved that the infant is not mine, he will be triply condemned by the public! The King will be raised up and will be even more my strong protector."

"Very good, Your Highness. Oh yes, very, very good."

"Yet, because he has made his mind think in that dirty way, he will always believe that the infant is my child and that I am holding this son in abeyance to wrest the crown away from his daughter when I am ready to overthrow the line of succession! How he will suffer because of all this! Oh, dear Anglesong—how he will suffer!"

"There is the one other thing, Your Highness," Lady Joyce says in a numbed voice. "You see, I am a Whig. My family has been Whig since Whig politics began."

"I don't hold that against you, Anglesong."

"You see, one should understand, Your Majesty, I am an imbedded Whig. I sit in Whig Councils. I have the confidence of the leaders of the Party."

"So?" The Princess is mystified. "A political party is an institution. We are people. We are friends. If this puts you at odds with the Whigs, well—it was inevitable from the day Lord Malmesbury, a Tory, chose you out of everyone else in England to become my confidential counselor. You have guided me. You have protected me against the Prince by teaching me to use the only weapon I have against him, my imagination. If I bring him down—and thereby lose his potential power for the Whigs—then it is because you willed that for me from the first day you brought me your counsel."

"I concede all that, Your Highness."

"Then what are you trying to tell me?"

"I wish to say that I hope minds more experienced in statecraft than ours are somehow plotting how to turn the Prince away from the Whigs and into the Tory Party. It is just that I would feel ever so much more comfortable if only that could happen."

The Princess retires, choosing Mrs. Keifetz to attend her. While being undressed she says, "There will be much to do tomorrow," she says. "I want you to take a letter to the King and to do some special shopping for me."

> Dear Uncle George:
>
>   I ask your permission to replace my Controller of Household. He is so German that I find myself compelled to speak to him always in German and I find that this has seriously rusted what poor English I have. Otherwise he has been most satisfactorily efficient.
>
>   Devotedly,
>
>   Caroline P.

Mrs. Keifetz questions the shopping list. "Lengths of woolen fabric. Woolen pads? Such large, loose clothing!" Caroline shrieks at the extent of Mrs. Keifetz's dismay.

When Mrs. Keifetz returns the following day bearing a note saying that Colonel Heller will be replaced by the Duke of Kent as Controller of Household, the Princess tells Mrs. Keifetz, "Now—the shopping you've done. We must go about this very carefully. I will watch in the glass while you wrap me around the middle with the pads and the woolens."

Wrapped in the increasing bulk of her ever-expanding costumes the Princess sees Lady Douglas once a week but entertains no male visitors alone. In December, the Douglases are invited to spend a month at Green Horse, Semley, in Dorset, with the Duke's Household. Before leaving, Lady Douglas goes to Montague House to say farewell to the Princess, meeting her as Her Royal Highness returns from church.

The Princess, as Lady Douglas reports to Colonel Heller (who informs the utterly consternated Prince, and as indeed the woman will testify before the Commission later), is carefully dressed to conceal pregnancy. She wears a long Spanish cloak and a great muff. Lady Douglas will testify that she was terribly shaken at the sight. "I had thought, over the past months, that the Princess seemed to be growing larger and larger each week I saw her but it had not entered my mind that she was pregnant. But on this Sunday, I must say, I knew I was facing a woman who was very near her time."

"But! This is terrible! This is not what I wanted at all!" Heller says harshly. "Tell me everything she told you. I must have a very, very believable story here!"

"She told me she certainly understood how I could be so surprised because she knew how to manage her dress. She said it was a special German way she had dressed to conceal the pregnancy."

"German?"

"Yes. Then she said it didn't really matter whether she were discovered or not because if the pregnancy became general knowledge she would blame it all on the Prince because she had purposely spent two nights at Carlton House."

"She did! That is right!" Heller says excitedly. "She came to see her child, and the Prince, out of the kindness of his heart, said she could stay for a few nights if she wished. This is terrible! If this is the Prince's child it absolutely has wasted an entire year for me out in this *verdammt* place."

It is the last time Lady Douglas is to see the Princess before the appearance of the infant. When she returns from Semley in January, she calls at Montague House at once. She is shown into the drawing room. An infant is lying on a sofa covered with a piece of red cloth. The Princess draws Lady Douglas across the room saying, "There he is, the little darling. I had him only two days after you left for Semley. *But perhaps it would be much better if you did not mention his arrival to anyone.*"

The drawing room is transformed into a common nursery. Discarded diapers are strewn about everywhere; the Princess insists upon changing them herself. She confides, "I was able to give it a little milk from myself, at first, but it was too much for me. Now we feed it by hand and it does very well."

Dazed, Lady Douglas asks, "Is—is it the *royal* prince?"

"Let us call him William," the Princess says. "Let us say I *adopted* him from an out-of-work dockhand at Deptford, shall we? Let us say that his wife brought the baby to Mrs. Keifetz who brought it to me." She contrives an elaborate wink. Slowly she brings up her forefinger to point at her closed eye to prove that the wink is there.

"Oh! Oh, yes! I see what you mean."

"Still," the Princess states flatly, "looking at the little thing in another way, I suppose I must say now that I shall never be Queen of England."

"Oh!"

"Perhaps, dear Lady Douglas, you are looking upon your future King."

Lady Douglas rushes to London to report to Colonel Heller who is nearly collapsed by the news. He is so frightened of bringing it to the Prince that he holds back from telling either the Prince or the King until he can have Lady Douglas report more extensive confirmation. But, from the first moment of Lady Douglas's return to Montague House, the Princess eludes her. Mrs. Keifetz stares at Lady Douglas as if she were some species of unclean hyena and offers neither conversation nor information. Lady Douglas takes this hostility and the absence of the Princess to be the result of guilt and fright that too much has been revealed.

Several days later, the Douglases find a card at their house written by Mrs. Keifetz on behalf of the Princess. The message states flatly that Her Royal Highness no longer wishes to be acquainted with them. Lady Douglas's letter asking for an explanation is returned unopened. Sir John Douglas is a man so fierce about his honor that friends say he talks about little else. He is outraged by the Princess's slight. Were such a thing allowed, he tells his wife, he damned well would challenge the Princess to a duel.

"Oh, Jack! Don't be an ass!" his wife replies. "We are now an important part of a royal Duke's Household. There is nowhere in Europe where we will not be accepted socially. And I daresay by keeping our ears open we won't do too badly financially either. She is playing directly into our hands."

Colonel Heller works feverishly with Dr. Gotlieb in the locked rooms at the German Legion's archives. The doctor is an accomplished draftsman and forger. A large magnifying glass is strapped to his forehead. Through it he studies individual strokes and penmanship flourishes which link into the personal handwriting idiosyncrasies of the Princess of Wales. Gradually, with much art, he puts together two obscene pieces of correspondence in the correct style of her handwriting, never hurrying but never faltering, achieving truest effects. Colonel Heller breathes over his shoulder.

The first letter is addressed to Sir John Douglas. It states, in the coarsest language, that Lady Douglas is the avidly willing mistress of Sir Sidney Smith. Across the top of the page are ridiculously filthy drawings of a man and a woman who are labeled, in the Princess's hand: SIR SIDNEY, YR. WIFE. The letter is unsigned.

The second missive is curt: from the Princess to Lady Douglas in the same hand. With disgust, this letter, this curt letter, encloses an anonymous letter in an "unknown" handwriting received, the Princess's note says, that morning. The anonymous letter abuses Lady Douglas in the lowest street language saying that she is unfit to consort with the Princess of Wales and details her physical acts with Sir Sidney. The curt note states that the Princess does not wish to see or hear from Lady Douglas in the future.

"Your best work, Dr. Gotlieb!" Heller cries out happily in their own Thuringian dialect. "There is so much subtlety here! It will take real study by them to tell that the anonymous and the true were written by the same hand."

"But why are you weeping, Franz?"

"Do you think I like to do this to a *German* princess? Whose father is our greatest soldier?"

"You are only following direct orders. Franz, tell me something. Why are we doing this? I am only curious. As you said yourself, she is a *German* princess."

"There is nothing murky here, Dr. Gotlieb. Our

Prince, to whom we have taken a blood oath because he is the son of the King of Hanover, who also happens to be the King of England, wants badly to get a divorce. That is all we need to know. She could be an Irish princess for all we care, once we know what is in our Prince's heart."

"A divorce. Well that's not so easy for a man in his position."

"It is easy because we are going to make it easy. We are going to provide the Prince with all the tools he could possibly need to get himself a divorce."

The letters are posted from central London.

The Princess informs the Controller of her Household, the Duke of Kent, the Prince's brother, that Sir John and Lady Douglas have been annoying her when she explicitly told them she did not wish to see them. She tells him that they, in band with Sir Sidney Smith, were utterly beyond the pale and have been banished from her sight.

She asks him to see them and to settle the matter, if necessary asking his brother, the Duke of Sussex, to dismiss the despicable Sir John as his Master of Horse.

The Duke of Kent and Strahearn, and Earl of Dublin, thirty-seven years old, fourth son of the King, destined to become the father of the shining jewel, Victoria, is an anomaly. He has come home to England after having been exiled into military commands by his father. He has the extremely well-earned reputation of being an inhumane commander who is bestially, nearly insanely, cruel to his troops (and is responsible for at least two known mutinies), yet he is the meekest of men, shrinking from anything which is socially untoward. A fussy man, lacking both sense and empathy, he at no time intended to inflict *pain* upon his men, but was merely experimenting along with the other upcoming trends of the day: could men match the new machines? He tries to make machines out of his men and they resist him. Nothing he does is understood, so he shuns contact with people and their problems and now—*this!*

He flutters out of Montague House, socially disarranged. He does not know these people. It is all most unpleasant. But he has met Sir Sidney Smith, hero and defender of Acre, naval person, good rep, jolly tar and so forth. When he returns to Knightsbridge, the Duke writes to Smith asking him to come round. Smith arrives the next day. Getting things started is extremely painful for the Duke so he does the only thing he can do. He sails right in and tells Smith exactly what the Princess had told him. Sir Sidney listens calmly until the Duke has finished.

"Sir," he says at last. "I shall now state the real cause why I and Sir John and Lady Douglas made application to the Princess for an audience. The *real* cause is that Sir John received a most scandalous anonymous letter, of a kind to cause Sir John and me to set upon each other and cut each other's throats—until we both became convinced that this letter was in the disguised handwriting of the Princess of Wales."

"But—see here—my good fellow!"

"Not only were we unanimous about the handwriting, but the letter was sealed with a seal in frequent use at Montague House."

"But—see here—my good fellow!"

"I said to Sir John—straight out—'You should shoot me like a dog, out of hand, if there is any truth in this,' I said to him! Why—the man is my old messmate, Sir!"

To the Duke this is calamity. He has no way to avoid a scandalous secret. What is he to do? His mind darts and buckles, but when he answers Smith it is with the self-possession which his father has beaten into him with a stick since boyhood.

"My dear Sir Sidney," he says earnestly, "the publication of such a shameful *éclat* would have a crushing effect upon the King's health and must be avoided at all costs if only for that reason. From the delicate state of his nerves and all the additional misunderstanding between himself and the Prince, I feel it my bounden duty, as an honest man, considering the *many* complications which do not entirely meet the eye in these matters"—here the Duke flutters his hands meaningfully at either side of his head and rolls his eyes to communicate utter dismay—"to ask you to urge these arguments upon Sir John in the most forcible manner." The Duke strikes his left palm smartly with his right fist. "To press upon him, to urge him to peer deeply into his conscience as an Englishman, notwithstanding all the provocation which has been given him, to let the matter drop; and pursue it no further."

To the Duke's enormous relief it seems that his wisdom has closed the event for good and for all. He remains in this happy frame of mind for four days until he is summoned to a meeting with the Prince of Wales.

As he enters the large room, he is alone with the Prince, who gets up slowly, stiff with rage, walks to a large Sevres vase on a stand against a wall, lifts it high and back over his head with both hands, and flings it with all his strength into another wall a few feet from his brother. "Why did you not inform me of this business between the Princess of Wales and the Douglases?" he screams. The Duke is greatly shaken.

"It is done! I settled everything!"

"Oh, God! You settled everything. Oh, God—*God!*"

"What is wrong, George?"

"Edward—look you straight. The appearance of this infant whom Lady Douglas can prove is the child of the Princess is an *extremely* grave matter. Anyone with his *wits* about him can see that it may be necessary to institute an inquiry."

"Inquiry? Do you mean—an official inquiry?"

The Prince pounds on a desk to give emphasis to each word. "Why-are-you-such-a-booby, Edward?" he shouts.

The Duke binds himself tightly in his dignity. "I have seen this infant, William Austin, as she calls him. There is nothing grave about him. Just a little baby."

"Just a little baby? Is that all, dear Edward? Well! If this story of Lady Douglas's is believed, then this William Austin, as you call him, may one day lay claim to succeed me on the throne of England! This William Austin, as you call him, may have a claim that can override the claim of my own daughter!"

"Oh, my precious oath!" A light goes on in his memory. "A bastard born in wedlock may inherit."

"By law!"

"How can there be such a law?"

"Because as often as not kings are sterile—for one reason or another. When that is the case, the heir to the crown requires a surrogate parent; that is how."

"But, if the Princess chooses to put forward a claim or if he himself forms a party and lays claim—"

"Yes, you dunce! And what is a female heir against a bastard male? Nothing! Hanover, our German kingdom, is under Salic law whereby no woman can rule. My own daughter, therefore, if she ascends the throne, will either have to create a vassal king in Hanover or lose it for us.

How do you think this maniacally clever German mother of William Austin, as you call him, sees that? She will throw the bastard into the claim to make him King of Hanover, then she will use that as a stepping stone—the wicked, heartless bitch—by which he could demand the British crown as legal heir of our accursed marriage!"

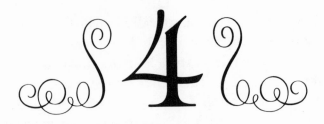

Caroline's mother has never written to her. Caroline cannot remember ever seeing her mother's handwriting. She thinks her mother once knew how to write, perhaps. She is such a lazy woman that she must have been a lazy child, and Caroline has long ago shrugged off the need for any attention from her mother because her attention, when given, always resulted in something disastrous.

Her father writes to her at each equinox, faithfully, if (Caroline wonders) mechanically. She wonders if he writes because he thinks about her and worries about her well-being or if, as the sun moves into a new position between the northern and the southern hemispheres, it nudges him sharply to remind him that he has a daughter exiled in England who would, perhaps, like some news from home.

His letters are filled with news. She can see the people and even think she is smelling the old smells; listening to the old bedroom intrigues. She reads them all five and six times over with much poignant longing.

Signorina Gustoso has hidden her shoes so that she will not have to get out of her bed until late spring, but I would not think of finding them for her for the bed is her *milieu* [he writes about his young Italian mistress]. She is so lazy (your mother says and who should know better?) that she does no credit to her homeland. Now, that, my dear, is a comment. But she is a happy girl, and very comfortable as well as comforting to me, as youth should be for old warriors—as happy and as comfortable as I am sure you are in your new home.

Fräulein Rosensweig is very sad to have taken up the post with the Swedish ambassador at the court in Berlin. She writes to me plaintively, but resistibly, "But what will the Princess do if she returns for a visit?" I assure her that it will be many, many years before this can happen, that your place is now in England where you will prosper mightily.

Mademoiselle von Hertzberg sprained her ankle the night before last while waltzing, which will give some idea of how fast they are writing waltzes nowadays. Your mother (who has stood up twice in the last six years) says this is a fitting thing for people who waltz as much as Mademoiselle von Hertzberg does. You may be sure that, as soon as she is able to stand, she will be up and waltzing just as furiously fast once again. I enjoy waltzing. As I am certain you must do night after night in the arms of your handsome young prince.

Do not fret if you do not have time to write. I understand the pace of life at such a court as yours. But, if you do find the time, please be sure to write in German to save us both the strain. Whether it is language or distance or time, I see you too obliquely through your letters as if the lens were turned round or as if the sun were glittering upon uniforms far across a field of battle decades and decades ago. I must be older. It is not only logical, but my eyes are not what they were. Nonetheless my heart has in it no doubt of the fullness of your daily happiness in your new home.

> With love and pride in my fine daughter,
>
> Papa

Caroline understands his letters. They make her happy because they make her homesick. His words of understanding of her happiness she knows are orders to perform her duty in the face of anything. They remind her forcibly that she is a Brunswicker! And that Brunswickers

have the hearts of lions! Now that she has left her father's
house, she knows, in the light of how very unhandsome her
elderly young prince has turned out, the only true duty
about which her father cares: she must not complain. She
must do all that she has to do but never complain to him
about it.

Early in 1802 the King relapses into the symptoms of the serious illness he suffered in 1788, becoming so mentally deranged that four "keepers" need to be assigned to protect his person from himself. It is the family disease which affects the mind, but it is not a mental disease. It obtains a unique place in the annals of medicine. The disease necessitates the establishment of a regency. Physicians find themselves arbiters of government.

The King acts quite mad, but Lord Weiler insists that his ministers consider more gravely his physical symptoms, which, at times, become so severe his life is in danger! These are severe abdominal pains followed by muscular weakness and stiffness, which is variously diagnosed as "rheumatism" and "gout." The legs are badly affected. There is constipation, racing pulse, sweating attacks, insomnia, logorrhea, delirium. There is a traumatization and fragility of the skin and a total intolerance of sunlight; all of it packed into the legacy handed down from Sophia of Hanover.

Just as Lord Weiler is about to give in to the politicians and to public opinion and agree that the King cannot govern, there must be a regent, the King makes a complete recovery, returning, in moments, to his normal constitution and personality, in charge of himself and his country.

This frustration for the Prince, coupled with the

worry about William Austin and the distaste for using the Douglases to rid himself of Caroline, is unbearable. Once before he has seen the purse of England in his grasp and once before his father has snatched it out of his hands by recovering. The disappointment is so great that the Prince almost goes through the same terrible cyclone of body and mind as his father has. When he stabilizes, he is confronted with the intolerability of the King's public sponsorship of the Princess to protect her from the Queen, her daughters and the Prince. In the Prince's view, the King is doing this despite the Princess's known misconduct.

Once a week after his recovery, the King calls on Caroline at Montague House. The public cheers him along the roads of his way from Kew to her. Caroline is their darling and wronged heroine; brave but defenseless. They love their King even more because he demonstrates the need for loyalty.

He arrives at Montague House, avuncular with all, offering messages of kindness and good humor. He receives the homage of the Household. He compliments the Princess before all on the amiability of the surroundings and the maintained serenity of her Household. He explains to all how hungry he is. The Princess leads him to the Blue Room, which is set out for dining, including the large admiral's fore-and-aft hat hanging on the doorhandle over the locked keyhole.

The King ignores the food. They sit on the sofa. He holds her hand in a desperate grip. "Do you know what Lord Bute said to me very late in 1759?" he asks her. She knows well what Lord Bute said. This is the sixth time she has heard it in the six visits he has made since his recovery.

"No, Uncle George."

"He accused me of growing grave and thoughtful and

said to me it was entirely owing to my daily increasing admiration of the fair sex."

"You were a young man. That was natural."

"I was young. I was a boiling youth of one-and-twenty. My mother pleaded piteously with me for so long to resist the charms of those divine creatures that I would have, then, been ashamed to have become their prey. They wanted me. Oh, yes, they wanted me! I could think of myself then, only of myself. Youth is the time of thinking only of oneself."

"What is more logical when we are young, Uncle George?"

"Just before Christmas in 1759—how poignantly I remember!—there came across the Irish Sea a child of fourteen who was as beautiful as a girl can be. She brought to me a pounding passion. Despite my mother I was—and I am—a passionate man, passionate beyond most men."

"There is so much beauty in memory, Uncle George."

"She was Lady Sarah Lennox, fourth daughter of the second Duke of Richmond and great-granddaughter of King Charles II," the blank-eyed, slack-jawed King says. The pace of his voice increases. His cheekbones glow but he is far far back in the long ago. "She appeared as an angel of excitement at St. James's Palace with her sister, Amelia, the Countess of Kildare." His grip on Caroline's hand tightens painfully. His eyes protrude.

"Henry Fox described her best. He said: 'Her beauty is not easily described otherwise than by saying she had the finest complexion, most beautiful hair, and prettiest person that was ever seen, with a sprightly and fine air, a pretty mouth with remarkably fine teeth, and excess of bloom in her cheeks.' But that is not really describing her, for her great beauty was a peculiarity of countenance that makes her at the same time different and prettier than any other girl I ever saw.

"I had no thought of amusing myself with her," the old man says in a distant voice, "but she possessed my mind. Sleep forsook me. When I could not stand the pain of not having her, the sharpness of my passion drove me to seek counsel. I went to Lord Bute, the only man I have ever known who found deep happiness in marriage. He said to me from his experienced compassion, 'Think, Sir, who you are. Think of what is your birthright and what you wish to be.' I agreed that although I must possess a woman's body I would habituate myself to denying my duty were I to lie upon any woman than she who was to be my lawful wife. He told me we must get some account of the princesses of Germany."

He has opened his trousers. His erect penis is in view which he holds with one hand while he clings to Caroline with the other. "Although my chastity had hitherto remained inviolate, notwithstanding my age and its passions, it was not to be expected that such a fast could much longer be observed," he murmurs dreamily as he stares upon his clutched member. "So they found me my wife and I lay upon her ceaselessly through fifteen children and I am a better man for it." The movement of his right hand increases. "But I never possessed that beautiful child. I never spent myself upon her helping her to spend herself. I lost all that beauty. I turned my back on that body so fair. I have her in my mind every day of my life. I subdued my passion by the strength of my reason, my principles, and my sense of public duty."

A weak trajectory is turned upon Caroline's forearm. The King leans back on the sofa, his eyes closed. Caroline reaches a napkin from the lunch table. His grip loosens.

She adjusts his clothing, then moves to the table to eat her lunch. The King sleeps for thirty-five minutes as she eats alone and fears becoming old.

He leaves Montague House congratulating everyone and enters his carriage to return to Kew.

6

The Tories stand for the rural squirearchy; the Whigs for the great landowners, the aristocrats, the city business interests.

Inevitably, the Princess has evolved into a political object. The Prince is a frenzied Whig because this embarrasses his father, who exemplifies the committed Tory. His father's entire domestic policy has been characterized by a prolonged effort to break the power of the Whig Party, which had maintained control of the government under his two predecessors, and to restore the royal prerogative to the position that it had occupied under the Stuarts. The Prince intends to sweep the Tories out when he becomes King; to maintain the Whigs in power for, collectively, they have been his major source of financing. Unknown to him, his father has anticipated this and has delivered a sealed letter of instructions to Lord Liverpool as to how the Tories are to confront the Prince when the day comes that he must take power because of the King's inability to govern.

The Prince wants an inquiry made into his wife's catalogue of shames in order to be rid of her forever. The Whigs, well informed by Lady Joyce, want this inquiry because it will embarrass the King and the Tories politically. On the 1st June 1806, with the Whigs in power, a Commission of Enquiry, constituted entirely of Whigs, is appointed to consider the strange case of the Princess of

Wales; an inquiry which will come to be known as The Delicate Investigation.

In fact, the investigation is so delicate that it is contrary to the laws of the land. It takes evidence on oath. It does not summon the Princess to be on hand to defend herself nor appoint counsel to represent her interests. Without the aid of a jury it will decide whether she is guilty or not guilty of flagrant adultery, motherhood outside acceptability for a Princess of Wales . . . and other heinous acts.

Lady Douglas's testimony is considered first: that the Princess is a strange woman who had embraced her and had told her what nice arms and sweet, black eyes she had; that the Princess ate immense quantities of fried onions and potatoes and drank ale in bed. She testifies that the Princess had confessed that she was going to have a baby of her own; that her practice of taking unwanted babies into her protection is not as innocent as it seems; that the Princess told her no one would know she was pregnant because she knew how to manage her dress but that if she were discovered she would blame it on the Prince. She had purposely slept two nights at Carlton House to establish this.

LADY DOUGLAS: She said to me, I have a bedfellow whenever I like; nothing is more wholesome, and she urged me to amuse myself with Prince William of Gloucester. She told me, straight out, that she had lain with Sir Sidney Smith, the hero of Acre, and said he liked a bedfellow better than anyone she had ever known.

Sir John Douglas testifies that he has seen the Princess stand up on a sofa, put her hand on her stomach and say,

"Sir John, I shall never be Queen of England." He testifies that he "greatly suspects" Sir Sidney Smith to be the father of the child.

Household servants are called to testify. Some say Sir Sidney Smith had "often" been seen in the Princess's house early in the morning at least two hours before footmen would allow anyone in. A woman servant retails hearsay evidence (which is accepted) that she was once told by a second woman servant that a third, Mary Wilson, had once gone into the Princess's bedroom to make up a fire and had found her and Sir Sidney Smith in such an indecent position that she had immediately fainted at the door. The court asks what the Princess and Sir Sidney had been doing. The witness says wild horses could not drag such words out of her.

Other servants report varying counts of eleven to sixteen different men kissing the Princess on the lips. William Cole, who has twenty-one years in the Prince's service (ten years with the Princess as Page of the Backstairs), deposes that he took some sandwiches to the Princess and found her in such a position with Mr. George Canning "as to alarm me very much." Asked to describe the position, he says, "I am neither willing nor capable to do such a thing." Cole testifies that in November 1801 the Princess "suddenly" grew very large—although she seemed to flatten out and swell up at will.

However, in a score of almost four against one, the other servants of the Princess's Household rigorously deny that there has been anything improper about the behavior of the Princess at any time. Maids testify that never has the Princess's bed shown "evidence" of two people having slept upon it; that such "evidence" would be inescapable. Servant after servant testifies that the Princess was not pregnant at any time, in any year; that she may have been alone with Sir Sidney Smith but that she has been alone with many other men as well because she is a concentrating conversationalist and listener.

Sir Patrick Crowley, the personal physician to the Princess, testifies that if she had been pregnant he most certainly would have noticed it.

Admiral Sir Sidney Smith, the hero of Acre, in his testimony, denies, disapproves and detests any and all suggestions that he and the Princess have not acted with propriety. He makes a simple request: that the Douglases be ostracized from human society for their persecutions of this kind woman. Thomas Lawrence, eminent painter, and George Canning, potent statesman if that is not too incriminating an adjective, admit to having been alone with the Princess.

"It is a condition of her friendship," Lawrence testifies.

"Nothing ever passed between us which I could have had the least objection for all the world to have seen and heard," deposes Canning.

The conflict of evidence disturbs the Whig commission. They decide to reject hearsay evidence out-of-hand. Testimony from former servants of the Prince's has to be regarded as suspect. Documentation of a most final nature is at last produced by Lady Joyce Anglesong, which proves beyond a doubt that the infant in question was born at the Brownlaw Street Hospital on the 16th November 1801 to Samuel and Sophia Austin and was christened William Austin. The mother is accompanied to the court by Lady Joyce Anglesong; both testify.

The mother testifies that she frequently went to be given food at the kitchens of Montague House. After her baby was born, she took it with her there. A lady of the house, Mrs. Keifetz, suggested that the Princess might adopt the child if the mother could bear to part with it. Mother and baby were taken to the Princess who touched the baby under the chin and said, "Oh, what a nice one! How old is it?" The mother answered, "Two months." The Princess turned away, the mother testifies, and spoke to Mrs. Keifetz in a foreign language. Mrs. Keifetz told the mother that the baby would be "brought up and treated as a young prince." The mother agreed to the adoption. She came back to Montague House regularly to see the baby and to collect an allowance for the education of another child from the Princess. Her husband found regular employment on the docks through the Princess's influence.

Caroline waits, with the air of a woman who has been listening to an engrossing story of high adventure, at the Anglesong house in Audley Street, for the outcome of the investigation. She hears the horses gallop through the gate and the carriage groan to a stop two stories below. Someone is running up the marble staircase. Lady Joyce bursts into the room, her olive cheeks glowing with excitement. "The Commission has announced, Your Highness," she says gaily. "It amounts to an apology to you."

"How very nice," Caroline says.

"They are now in the process of explaining to all of England that there is—in their words—'no foundation whatever for declaring that the child now with the Princess of Wales is a child of Her Royal Highness or that she was delivered of any child in the year eighteen hundred two.'"

"Georgie must have word of this by now."

"Their proclamation states that you are a kind-hearted, generous woman."

"You said—tell England?"

"The same thing. Everyone at court, everyone who takes sides in this battle, will know all about it by tomorrow morning. The public is very keen about these things."

"And what did they do to temper the reputation they have given me—or someone has given me—perhaps it is I who gave it to me—that I indulge—in their words for I would have phrased it differently—in inordinately reckless behavior."

"Nothing whatever. But what does that matter? They had to leave the Prince some little scrap upon his plate."

Sir John Douglas is dismissed from the Household of the Duke of Sussex. He and Lady Douglas return to a two-room flat in East London because she decides it will be better if they "disappear" for the time, yet conserve the small amount of money they have been able to get together until Sir John decides to accept another post.

Sir John is very bitter because he does not understand what has happened. He cannot account for the sudden change of affections by the Princess of Wales, but to him this is a peripheral thing; a "social" matter. What he really cannot understand is how the Duke of Sussex, whom he had not yet met, could possibly find a stain upon his honor, Sir John Douglas's honor, which could result in the disgrace of being replaced in such a vital post as His Grace's Master of Horse.

"I will be frank with you," he tells his wife. "This is the end of all roads for me. I am an old man and I have been disgraced without a vestige of guilt. As a man of honor I say it is only fair to tell you that I am going to kill myself."

"You may kill yourself when I leave you, if I leave you," Lady Douglas says. "Until then I wish to hear no more of the matter."

Wherever the Princess goes she is cheered in the streets or applauded as she sits in her theater box.

The Prince has to be restrained in wet sheets and bled to keep him from doing serious damage to the beautiful furniture at Carlton House.

The Queen requires the King to announce that the Princess can no longer be received as an intimate of the family and that "no nearer intercourse than outward marks of civility can be admitted in the future." The King agrees because, as he says, the Princess has become a "female politician," a condition far worse than moral turpitude.

7

Caroline's father, the Duke of Brunswick, takes a frightful wound in the face at the battle of Auerstedt. He is dragged from the field. He dies in exile in Denmark. Caroline is bewildered by his death. She knew that he would die one day, but she had always been certain, from the time she had been a little girl, that she would die before he did. He seemed immortal to everyone. Europe had not had a commander so valiant in the years of his life. He exhaled the pleasures and the gallantries in a way that no emperor or king or man had ever done. That he could die in battle seemed an impossibility to her as if secretly she believed that he had been bathed with Siegfried and was impermeable to the machines of war.

She retires to the Blue Room at Blackheath and fixes the admiral's fore-and-aft hat over the keyhole so that she may weep unobserved. She remains in the room for three days, remembering how it had been when she had not lived in England, when she had been with her father in her father's palace and he, the greatest warrior for all of the monarchs of Europe, had drawn the mighty, and the charming, and the brilliant, and the exciting people of the world to his roof as honey draws flies. Alone in the darkened room she is able to mourn her father as he would have had his death celebrated: with memories of marvelous music from massed violins, as bolt upon bolt of shining, shimmering colored silks, as jewels and mattresses and long, short, fat, and thin legs carved out of rose were opened to him. As she had slipped the key secretly into Lord Dickie Adler's hand, or Bocca's hand, or jolly Smith's hand and then disappeared across the ballroom to lose her mother's eyes, then up the back stairs to her room until they came to her: ardent and very, very happy with life and with her. She thought of Captain Manning's cold belt buckle pressing again into her soft belly with the rhythm of a printing press until she laughed with joy and many orgasms to think that the belt buckle of the Irish Guards would be printed upon her spirit for the rest of her life.

Her father faced life and dealt with politics. In England they faced politics and tried to deal with life; all of them failing at the court. The Prince held orgies of men and women entwined and encircling sweat-and-sperm-filled rooms but it was she who was marked here as the wanton because no one knew how to deal with life, or wives, or love.

They had touched her with their wands, which were like blind men's canes extended to find power and, feeling her not as a woman who hurt, who was bleeding her life away through loneliness, but as a conduit to power, they had transformed her with those wands into a political pile of opportunity; a stink; an excresence which all "good" people deplored.

Now her doltish brother would be the Duke of Brunswick. If they had been able to change sexes he would have made the dull-headed, insensitive, uncaring and perfect wife for the Prince. She would have been a proud and worthy Brunswicker Duke in her father's steps; the one who loved him and understood him and knew what his essence represented to the world—an essence which she would have expanded and made to shine gloriously for all

the days of her life never mind on the field of battle—
people did not need that kind of battle when they had
English princes—but upon the ballroom floor at great
galas, upon great carved and glistening hardwood beds and
floors, in the music and in the poetry and sculpture which
he had made so possible. She would have expanded all of
that if she had not been a woman who had been exiled by
her father to this callous land.

8

The Princess begins her long education in directly involved politics with the tutelage of the Tory Party under
the firm guidance of its leader, Spencer Perceval. The
Commission which investigated so delicately sat from the
first to the fourteenth of July, but at no time did any official
hint of what was taking place reach the Princess. In mid-
August a copy of the Commission's report is presented to
the King. A most incomplete copy is brought to Montague
House by a footman; an insult which is so recognized as an
insult.

The Tories rally round the Princess, sternly advising
that she complain to the King, which she does. There is no
reply from the King. The Princess writes again stating that
she wishes a complete copy of the Investigation so that her
legal advisers may prepare her defense. The Lord Chancellor is ordered, by the King, to send her a complete copy.

Caroline hugs a letter from Lord Malmesbury. Writing from St. Petersburg he says:

> I ask you to pay heed. You are in the greatest danger.
> Princess! Mark these words well because you must see
> yourself as an object in a life-and-death struggle between
> two political parties. The one, Whig, battles to return to
> power. The other, Tory, is determined to use you as a
> lever to dislodge the opposition. The poisonous element
> in this, my dear, is that the Prince is not only an
> avowed Whig supporter but is also so passionately

partisan against your cause and will prod and beat the
Whigs onward even beyond points to which they would
have been willing to go to maintain their power. I pray
that you are with Lady Anglesong consulting at every
available moment to divine what your survival strategy
must be. She is a Whig of ancient Whigs. But first she is
a woman of exalted honor who has pledged to be your
true counsel. So you must lean upon her. I am too far
removed to be of help. My information, though
constant, is mixed and at second-hand. But I can urge
you to the most necessary caution and protection. You
must abjure all impulse in this matter! You must live
within your head, not your heart. You must listen,
listen, and listen to Anglesong's counsels, for she
understands your peril and possesses sources of
information that are without flaw.

The Princess knows she must win back the King's protection while he is still alive and sane. She sits with Lady Joyce for hours, arguing over which is the best procedure.

"The Whigs are about to fall," Lady Joyce says. "Their government is finished, so what you must do is to consolidate your position with the British press and public."

"I must do that as well, yes. But the key to everything right now is the favor and protection of the King."

"That could be a nest of hornets. Best not to disturb the King."

"I don't intend to plead with him, or to put myself at his mercy, Anglesong. That time is past. We require desperate measures or else I might as well understand that I shall be returned to Brunswick."

"What desperate measures?"

"Perhaps it is best that you do not know about it."

"Nonsense! Whatever you do politically they will all think I advised you to do it anyway, so tell me what you consider a desperate measure."

"I shall blackmail the King. It is the shortest cut to salvation—at the moment."

"*Black*mail? The *King?*"

"You see? We won't talk about it anymore."

"We will talk about it! What in heaven's name have you got in your crazy German head?"

"I have written a certain letter to the King. But I have not sent it yet. I want you to read it. You are a realist. You know they can send me back in disgrace. You are brave and you are bold." She opens a desk drawer, takes out a sheet of paper covered with fine, small writing, and gives it to Lady Joyce.

> Sire: It is nine weeks since my counsel presented to the Lord High Chancellor my letter to Your Majesty containing my observations in vindication of my honor and innocence. The world, in total ignorance of the real state of affairs, begins to infer my guilt. From this state I humbly entreat Your Majesty to perceive that I can have no hope of being restored until either Your Majesty's favourable opinion shall be graciously notified to the world by receiving me in the Royal Presence or *until the full disclosure of the facts shall expose the malice of my accusers.* Your Majesty will be graciously pleased to recollect that an occasion of assembling the Royal Family, in dutiful commemoration of His Majesty's birthday, is now at hand.
>
> Caroline P.

Anglesong looks up at her, grinning. "You always seem able to prove to me that you are cleverer than you look," she says. "Send it."

When the King reads the letter, he decides to accommodate Caroline even though he exhibits evident upset at the findings of The Delicate Investigation. He is alone in his willingness to display public forgiveness. The Queen fights him savagely. She demands that Caroline be sent back to Brunswick and forgotten.

"Then you have not read her letter."

"I have read it!"

"Her letter states that she may be forced to give the

whole facts of the case to the public. A copy of the entire
case and all testimony against her was placed in her
hands."

"Yes! And she is totally soiled by it!"

"The Commission looked at the same evidence and
found her innocent. A Whig commission, which acted to
aid the Prince, the Prince's own partisans. What are the
people to believe in but her innocence? You will receive
her."

"I will not, Sir!"

"I put this to you, as well. In her defense, which came
long after her alleged trial, written by damnably clever
lawyers in her name, she points out that the entire investigation was done in an illegal, clumsy and irregular manner
which can be made to appear as an outrageous breach of
justice which I sponsored. You will welcome her!"

The Whig government has been doing its best to lose
Caroline's defense to the charges for more than two
months. It has no intention of expressing any opinion on
it, even when the King sends his second letter demanding
action. The government's policy is to leave all judging to
the King, who is fighting off the Queen on one side and the
Prince on the other while his own body and intellect grow
weaker. When the Ministry responds at last to his second
letter, through the austere Lord Kullers, the position is
that "in view of so broad an acquittal, the Commission
wishes to decline to give an opinion at all."

The King demonstrates royal rage. He thunders that
he will have an opinion at once! The essence of the long,
sullen reply is: "In this situation, His Majesty is advised
that it is no longer necessary for him to decline receiving
the Princess of Wales into his royal presence." But the
government reminds His Majesty that "in those examina-

tions and even in the answer drawn in the name of the Princess by her legal advisers, there have appeared circumstances of conduct on the part of the Princess which His Majesty must regard with serious concern and disapprobation."

The King cuts out the word "disapprobation" and sends the letter to the Princess. She answers with unfeigned happiness and presses for the day of her public meeting with the King and the royal family.

The Prince will have none of it.

He writes to his father saying that he has placed all letters concerning The Delicate Investigation into the hands of his solicitors for "analysis." He states that, inasmuch as he may have serious observations to make on evidence at a later date, he must request His Majesty to defer naming any day for seeing the Princess of Wales.

The King is being cornered: the Queen, her daughters, the Prince and Caroline.

Caroline's adviser, the Tory leader Spencer Perceval, is ready with an axe to crash upon the opposition. He has edited all the evidence of The Delicate Investigation, has had this printed in book form, has stored 5000 copies in secret hiding places all over London ready for distribution to booksellers. Word of the impending sale of such unutterable juiciness passes through the city like strong brandy. Secret agents of the Whig government find the printer, but he can tell them nothing of the whereabouts of the books.

Just as the country is about to explode with the scandal, the Whig government falls. The Tories' first decision as they move into power is that all copies of the book *The Delicate Investigation* must be destroyed. *Instantly!* Perceval collects the 5000 copies and burns them in his garden. A few copies escape into private hands. One gets to New

York, another into the hands of a London Sunday newspaper months later. The government buys back every copy it can find at prices of up to £5000 a copy.

The second decision made by the new government is to request His Majesty to receive the Princess of Wales at court and to grant her apartments at Kensington Palace. On the 7th May 1807 the carriage-and-four of the Princess of Wales draws up once again at the courtyard of St. James's Palace. The dense crowds (organized by Lady Anglesong with £192 of government funds taken from the postal service budget) give her the wildest, most loving, most rambustious welcome of any dignitary attending the King's reception. Daisy Hanly, an Irish actress of small parts in the Haymarket, throws herself on her knees before the Princess, clasps her legs, kisses the hem of her skirt, and cries out loudly for all the attending press to hear, "You are the light of Heaven for us all!" winning a prolonged round of applause from the claque for her reading, eliciting moist eyes all around, as well as a bonus payment of £4.

The King receives Caroline with cordial gruffness. The Queen, center of a glacial tableau composed of cartouches of frozen daughters, stares out at the Princess and beyond her. The Queen nods as if controlled by a machine hidden in a building in Manchester. The Queen is twenty-three years past her gracious prime, when she was thirty-seven and Gainsborough painted her. She stands, magnificent in gold stuff with broad loops of diamonds; her daughters are in immense plumes and pink and silver tissues.

"How very, very rewarding to see you again, Your Majesty," the Princess of Wales says quite loudly. "It seems like such a long time since my wedding." She grins. "I see your *charming* daughters so—surely—somewhere nearby I will find the pleasure of reacquainting myself with your handsome son, Georgie? He is so dear to me. As you all are, of course."

She curtseys and turns away. She leaves casting smiles like bullets through the massed Drawing Room.

10

For the next few years the Princess submerges herself beneath her notoriety in her apartments at Kensington Palace with the little boy, William Austin. She keeps Montague House. Princess Charlotte remains with her own establishment at Shrewsbury.

When the Princess is thirty-nine years old, she has been in England for thirteen years. She tends to overdress except at the bodices, which are cut so low, the gossip goes, that one can see the top of Sir Sidney Smith's head. She uses too much paint on her face to cover the footprints of the wine. She has strong eyebrows, which have grown darker, as has the color of her hair. She is plump; shapeless when she leaves off her stays. Her eyes are more alive than any other eyes at the court, but too bold. Her hair hangs in masses of curls on either side of her head like a lion's mane. Its color, once that of fresh cheese, is now purple. She sets her own fashions in dress and, in consequence, introduces the smirk to British society. She wears gold and silver spangles on her gowns and on her satin boots. She dances with men as if she were standing on the backs of running stallions, guiding them with her hips.

The Prince grows more and more unstable. Reports of his wife are deliberately withheld from him, whenever possible, because they drive him into apoplectic furies. Friends, however, do manage to give him a steady account of Caroline's activities.

As the King, ill once again, sinks beneath the horizon of reality, Lady Joyce Anglesong sits long into nights with the Princess to plot the strategy that will protect her if the Prince comes to power. Anglesong is a vital if invisible power in the Whig Party. Her information, however, is universal; it transcends party lines.

"Your husband is about to forsake the Whigs, with whom he has spent his life, to whom he owes almost everything he owns. Around him the Whigs planned their return to power," she tells the Princess.

"George—a *Tory?*"

"For one thing, Spencer Perceval tells the Prince that he is going to secure the Regency for the Queen."

Caroline shudders. "I would be safer with Georgie."

"Perceval has told the Prince bluntly that they will bypass him because he supports the Whigs—but now the Tories are in power."

"Well, as we know—look at me—he will do anything for money."

"Yes. There you have the reason. He will betray his friends of a lifetime with reasons that he fears Whig reform and their ideas for Catholic emancipation, but the real reason he will turn his coat for the Tories will be to get money."

"What does it mean for me?" the Princess asks, at once fearful.

"It means he will make the Whigs his enemies. They are the most formidable enemies in England. By doing that he has insured your protection. We are going to break his fat, royal back, Madam."

Caroline remembers the King, as does the rest of the nation, as a great, disciplined presence who has now passed to rest on some netherworld isle as a shade. He remains in

England, but as a ghost of Christmas past. She can hear his voice in triple harmony, as if a trio of fine singers had been assembled upon a secret stage, one singing the stern basso, another the avuncular baritone, the third straining its scrotum and herniating its intestinal wall to reach the falsetto high notes of the lover in this brave musical arrangement that has become a threnody.

She had loved him as her uncle for he had taken her father's place. He and only he had sought to see the hostile, bleak world through her eyes. She had been moved by him as a lover; a lover seated beside her or within her, always far, far away from her, thinking, as he made love to her, of that young, fair child from Ireland. He had been a shade then, at the end of his sanity. She prods Anglesong daily to find her news of his mind's way behind those locked doors at Windsor, abandoned by his wife, his sons, his daughters, and his ministers. Anglesong brings reports such as: "Yesterday, the King took four jellies, some cocoa and tea, is totally lost as to mind, conversing with imaginary persons as he constantly addresses himself to Eliza."

Anglesong says that only Ernest goes to see the King. Caroline is baffled.

At noon on the 5th February 1811, the bandsmen of the Grenadier Guards march in their white gaiters into the courtyard of Carlton House, pitch their colors, then strike up "God Save the King" as the first of the Privy Councillors arrive for the ceremony of the swearing-in of the Prince as Regent, in his father's illness.

Perceval has broken the seal on the envelope containing the King's total strategy for the confrontation and manipulation of the Prince when this day came.

The King has slipped the leash of sanity, but from a place beyond the mind he continues to use power through Perceval, who offers the Prince these Tory alternatives: (1) the government will refuse to recognize that the King is incompetent even if they need to replace the physicians daily; (2) the government will recognize the Queen as Regent and will insure that the Queen will recommend that the Prince's income be quartered as a war economy measure; or (3) the government will name the Prince as Regent and increase his income substantially while stabilizing his debts.

It is no contest. It is neither betrayal nor bad judgment when the Prince forsakes the Whigs. The King's pious adoration of the uses of power has blackmailed his son. The Whigs and the Prince are outmaneuvered.

But, at the end of 1811, comes a lovely, light touch of the whip from the now-mad King: when the Prince-Regent presents his bill to the Tories for the payment of his debts amounting to £552,000 and the payment to himself of £150,000 for "Regency services," the Tory cabinet turns him down. They tell him they have no knowledge of any arrangement which the Prince-Regent says he made with them. Spencer Perceval actually laughs at him. The Prince weeps when he tells Colonel Heller about Perceval laughing at him. Heller's eyes go blank. His limbs and his entire body tremble.

Heller withdraws into the officer's mess of the German Legion at Windsor every night and broods with Major Tytell and Dr. Gotlieb over the shame and treasonous contempt which Perceval has poured upon the Prince. Tytell, who has evolved an entire social career out of pulling Heller's leg, supports his comrade with the sturdiest mock indignation.

"You know as well as I do, Franz, that we live good here. They pay well, they feed us all the German food we want, and the beer is direct from Dortmund."

"What has that got to do with this tragedy?" Heller, over the hill to drunkenness, shouts.

"What do we give for the fine honors they pay to us?" Tytell says, winking at Dr. Gotlieb. "We give our oaths, which are our honor, to protect them. Can you imagine this Legion if such a shameful thing had been attempted against the King, Franz? The man who did it would have been strangled with his own scrotum and every German hand in this barracks would pull the knot tighter. But, of course, you are no longer with the King's protection—you have only the Prince."

"I should avenge my Prince's honor?" Heller asks confusedly. "Yes, Martin. You are right. This family whom we serve have lifted me to a place among the most important people of the *world!* I have taken the oath in blood to protect them—" he gets to his feet unsteadily, knocking a tall stein to the floor. "It was never as much as considered by any of us that this protection meant to protect only their lives, their bodies. What is a king, or my prince who will be the king, but his country? What is a country but its honor, Martin? My prince cannot confront his enemies. That is the slime of politics. I must become his sword." Heller reels, then makes straight for the door. "I must fulfill my oath to this family."

"Franz!" Dr. Gotlieb cries out after him.

"Franz! Wait. Come back and sleep! We will talk about it in the morning," Major Tytell shouts after him, laughing. Heller has gone into the night.

Two days later, Spencer Perceval is assassinated in the lobby of the House of Commons by John Bellingham, a

deranged commercial agent who had been easily persuaded by Colonel Heller to punish the Prime Minister for
what he had done to the dignity of a great Prince.

Lord Liverpool becomes Prime Minister.

When the news of the murder comes to the Prince, he
knows in fullest revelation what has happened and who is
responsible. But he cannot act to take Heller to justice
because he sees that it would be like leading himself to the
gallows. He knows he cannot separate himself from Heller
because the murderous German is himself, as he sees himself, a force which willingly, even involuntarily executes
all demands from the underside of the Prince's character.
He beats Heller unmercifully with a heavy stick, injuring
him enough to send him into the German Legion infir-
mary. Then he plunges himself into a bout of drink and
laudanum.

When that autumn the Prince-Regent goes to a
Queen's Drawing Room, there are more than 18,000 people in the Pall Mall outside Carlton House through whom
he must pass to reach Buckingham Palace. His carriage
goes through the crowd in an enormous hush. There is no
sound of applause.

In the north, where the Whigs are strong, walls are
placarded offering 100 guineas' reward for his head. There
is an avalanche of anonymous letters which threaten him
with "the same fate as Mr. Perceval." When the Prince-
Regent attends a performance of *Henry V,* the play's allu-
sion to breach of promise is taken up with thundering
applause because of what he had done, as a husband, to
attempt to disgrace his wife.

To comfort the Prince during these trying days, Colonel Heller arranges with *The Morning Post* to write about

him as "The Glory of the People"; "The Maecenas of the Age"; an "Adonis of Loveliness."

London howls its derision. The *Examiner* publishes Leigh Hunt's article, which states:

> "The Glory of the People" is the subject of millions of shrugs and reproaches. This "Adonis of Loveliness" is a corpulent, purple gentleman of fifty. In short, this delightful, blissful, wise, pleasurable, honorable, virtuous, true and immortal Prince is a violater of his word, a libertine who is head over ear in debt and disgrace, a despiser of domestic ties, the companion of gamblers and demi-reps, a man who has just closed a half-century without one single claim on the gratitude of his country or the respect of posterity.

The Prince immediately orders the arrest of the Hunt brothers.

They are charged with "intention to traduce and vilify His Royal Highness, the Prince of Wales, Regent of the United Kingdom." The brothers are found guilty, fined £500 each, and sentenced to two years' imprisonment. The sentence causes national indignation.

The Prince's health seems to give way altogether. His sight is failing. He gets a numbness in his head which makes him talk constantly about paralysis. His only conception of relief is to be bled, but his body is unable to agree with the theory.

On becoming Regent, he has deserted Mrs. Fitzherbert once again. He takes up with Lady Hertford, who reads the Bible to him. His worse qualities seem to intensify under these attentions. He becomes vainer, crueler, more unstable, harsher. He becomes reckless about being seen drunk in public.

What shatters him most of all is the mounting popularity of Caroline. He is unable to understand how she, for all her sins against him, can have been lifted so high above him. He is the ruler, but she gets the people's love. He detests her far, far into his laudanum-glazed dreams.

11

When Lady Joyce Anglesong brings Henry Brougham to the Princess as her colleague-at-law, it is with the ambitious blessing of the Whig Party. Brougham and the Princess dislike each other from first greeting, yet they are two of the three people who will pave the way for the great Whig reforms of the prison system, of popular education, of criminal law, of Catholic emancipation, and toward a better balance between the value of human life and the value of property.

Brougham is thirty-three years old when he is introduced to the Princess in 1811. When he came to London, at twenty-five, he was already known as a brilliant lawyer, and one of the contributors to the *Edinburgh Review*. His "Colonial Policy," written for that paper, had generated the abolition of the slave trade. Brougham is a genuine reformer, an astute Whig politician able to gain such ends, and a man concerned with injustice. It has become self-evident to Lady Anglesong and to the Whig Party hierarchy that his special talents as a political counter-plotter are now to turn with inhuman objectivity toward the harassment of the Prince-Regent. Brougham has all the Whig newspapers at his disposal. Anglesong will have the generalship of the enormous Whig street armies which make or break public opinion at the level of rumors and panic. Unlimited party funds are placed at the disposal of both.

"Our objective, Madam," he tells the Princess across

the distance of their mutual dislike, "is to make you the most popular figure in England while assuring that your husband is the most despised. The time has come to persuade our Regent to return to the Whig Party."

"How fitting!" she replies.

She feels, rather than knows, that the days of improvised warfare under Lady Joyce's counsel are over. Anglesong belongs to her, she is sure of that, but this Henry Brougham belongs first to himself, then to the Whig Party. Listening to him, watching his eyes, she knows she has become a political commodity to the Whigs. She is the currency they will use to buy the Regent back to the Whig reforms by promising him that they will remove her from his sight and sensitivities forever. Anglesong is powerless against all of them, she keens to herself. I am nothing unless I use them to work for me, use their fortunes and their power, use their newspapers and their great legal minds to reduce Georgie to dust *before* he becomes king. When he does, and I am useless to them again, he will have nothing to do with them for the pain they have brought to him through me. Either I live to dominate the Whigs, she thinks, or I will be exiled to an Indian reservation in America to spend the rest of my days.

She measures Brougham coolly, knowing that he is the total professional Whig partyman. He is a man, she thinks, and all he has at stake is his career and his comfort, so he cannot think about what he must do more than 75 percent of the time. I am a woman who has been mocked and ruined by my husband. I am a Brunswicker and I have the heart of a lion. I have better—I have my father's heart! I will bring Georgie to his knees, then I will grind him to dust before they can bring him around to plead with them to get me safely out of his way. And I am able to think about that—and only that—100 percent of the time. Too bad about the great Whig reforms, whatever they may be.

She looks at Lady Anglesong apologetically for what she has been thinking and smiles sweetly.

Princess Charlotte is sixteen. From both her parents she has inherited a high degree of susceptibility to the opposite sex. Physically she is more mature than any young woman of her age can afford to be. At the wish of the Prince-Regent, who will rarely see her, who has seen her perhaps two dozen times in all her life, she is moved from Shrewsbury House to the Lower Lodge at Windsor to mature under the icy stare of her grandmother. Lady Montant has this impression of Charlotte at the time:

> She is grown excessively and has all the fulness of a person of five-and-twenty. She is neither graceful nor elegant yet she has a peculiar air, *et tous les prestiges de la royauté et du pouvoir.* She is above middle height, extremely spread for her age; her bosom is full but finely-shaped; her shoulders large; her whole person voluptuous. Her features are fine. Their expression, like that of her general demeanor, is noble. She has a hesitation in her speech amounting to a stammer; an additional proof, if any were wanting, that this royal Hanoverian is her father's own child. In everything she is the image of all the royal family males rather than resembling only one of them. She laughs too loud. She seems to wish to be admired more as a lovely woman than as a queen. Yet she has a quickness of fancy and penetration and would feign to rule despotically or I am much mistaken. I fear she is capricious, self-willed and obstinate. Her faults have evidently never been checked.

Charlotte was raised first by Lady Elgin, a tutor named Mr. Trew, and a dresser called Mrs. Gagarin, one of the few among the crowd of surrogate parents bustling around the child who really won her affection. Her aunt, the Duchess of Württemberg, has directed her "principles" in a flood of letters, which have been read aloud twice a day to her, containing such pearls as that if Charlotte were "strongly impressed with the omnipresence of God" it would root out her propensity to tell lies.

Lady Elgin gave up her post as governess in 1804, Charlotte settled at the Lower Lodge at Windsor, an entirely new group of instructors is set in around her. Lady de Clifford became head governess; Mrs. Campbell and Mrs. Udney were sub-governesses. Her educators were two divines: the Reverend George Knott, who was to act as chaplain, and the climbing, boring, pompous Dr. Fisher, Bishop of Exeter, whose touchy self-importance brought contention into the group; life was an endless squabble. Charlotte has loathed the dreary, interfering bishop all the minutes of her hours, all the hours of her days.

Every morning Lady Alexandra Wells takes the Princess for a drive in the Park. Every morning a handsome man on a white charger canters beside the Princess's carriage. He is a gallant; not an official escort. He is Captain Hesse, age thirty, of the 18th Light Dragoons, whose regiment is quartered in town.

Captain Hesse finds it flattering to receive little notes of admiration from the heiress to the throne. He pays court to her for six weeks. Lady Wells, at last, becomes frightened. She is worried that the affair has gone further than mere rides beside the carriage. She tells Captain Hesse that his attentions must cease and Charlotte weeps and rages, but she knows her father already believes Lady Wells to be too lenient, so Captain Hesse disappears.

Within a few weeks, Princess Charlotte is given permission by the Regent to visit her mother more frequently. As she and Lady Wells drive toward Kensington, Captain Hesse rides in casually beside the carriage. He salutes. He does his soldier's best to seem greatly surprised to see the ladies, but Lady Alexandra decides otherwise. She accuses Hesse of making a rendezvous with Charlotte behind her back. Hesse rides off. Charlotte wails as the carriage draws up at the Palace courtyard. The Princess of Wales is waiting at the main entrance.

"What is so dramatic?" she asks amiably.

"There is this *wonderful* officer. He does nothing more than ride beside my carriage, but Lady Wells says it must stop or she will tell Papa I am having some kind of disgusting affair."

"Yes, darling, we see how you feel—but even those most casual equestrian meetings could cause the devil at Windsor. Don't you care. I will make amends for this."

Soon many of those working at Kensington begin to think it is unusual that Captain Hesse's mount is always at the stables while the Princess is visiting her mother. Caroline merely sees it all as a discreet way for her to take on Captain Hesse as a bedfellow. If they think he is there to flirt with her daughter—all the better. What could be more harmless?

Lady Anglesong does not want any large uproars created at the moment. But Caroline's appetite is whetted by all this; it becomes one more game to madden the Prince.

Captain Hesse's regiment is transferred from Windsor to Portsmouth. Caroline gets a stupendous inspiration for the most wonderful way to consternate the Prince. With Caroline's expert assistance, Charlotte is able to meet Captain Hesse in her mother's apartments at Kensington, unknown to Lady Alexandra Wells.

Caroline takes her daughter and the captain into her bedroom. "I will leave you two alone for a moment," she says gaily. "Amuse yourselves." She locks the door from the outside as she leaves.

When Anglesong learns what the Princess has done, she is shocked with outrage. She confronts Caroline. "You cannot deny it! I saw it with my own eyes!"

"What did you see, Anglesong? You saw a door closing."

"I saw the mother of the girl who will inherit the crown of England become a prime procurer in the deliberate seduction of her daughter!"

"That is what you thought you saw, Madam Self-Righteous. Captain Hesse obeys me and his ambition, not his lusts for young girls, if any. As it is, he is fascinated to cooperate with me because he thinks I can win a field rank for him."

"What are you saying?"

"I say that if you don't know what I live for and live to do, Anglesong, then you might just as well go north and open a pub because that is all your mind is good for. Hesse is not in that bedroom to ruin my daughter, as you would put it. As if one could *ruin* a girl so sure of herself and her place—only a little lark on a bed with a healthy man. You should cast about for a little of that kind of ruining yourself, Anglesong! Who would be permitted to believe such a thing as Princess Charlotte being ruined by a man in this kingdom? She will be Queen. She is beyond such silly ruination. But—and this is why I exist—it will ruin my husband. This is my most deeply felt aim, Anglesong. I didn't really need another Captain Hesse for myself, my dear. I have already quite a sufficiency of Captain Hesses and, if you don't think it unseemly for me to say so, he is hardly the stallion he believes himself to be."

"How will it ruin your husband?"

"When the right time comes, he shall know about these adventures of his daughter—*his* daughter!—because, when I am ready, she shall tell him. Charlotte and I have agreed upon all this. She feels contempt for him. And that is an opinion she obtained not from my influence. Do you know he strikes her with his fists!"

"No!" Every feminist drop of blood in Anglesong seems to boil. "The dastard!"

"He is worse."

"Tell me your plot, please."

"Yes, yes. He is now maneuvered to where he continues to believe that little Willikin Austin is my bastard child. Good! The more he believes that, the more he will know that—if he should die—Willikin, not Charlotte, whom he pretends is his own daughter, will inherit the crown. His need to believe Willikin is my bastard will drive him insane because he knows the male Willikin can inherit."

"Is Willikin your son?"

"I will say this much, Anglesong, he is not William Austin. It was well managed. No one can know who he really is nor shall they until after my death; before which I will have driven the Prince-Regent mad. When they ask me if Willikin is my child, I shall answer them—*prove it and he shall be your King!*"

12

The Prince-Regent, the Government, and the Queen wish Princess Charlotte to marry the Hereditary Prince of Orange. Charlotte sees the marriage as the only means of escape from her father and the dinginess of Warwick House, which stands across the private gardens from Carlton House, to which she has been moved from Windsor. The Regent is intent upon marrying her and getting her out of the way in Holland. She is too popular with the public. But Charlotte cannot stand the Prince of Orange. "Sometimes I am obliged to turn my head away in disgust when he is speaking to me."

Prince William of Orange has been two years at Oxford and later with the Duke of Wellington's staff on the Peninsula. He is breezy but bilious. He has a wispy figure, a dissolute face, and the creepy manner of a studied toady. He is not intelligent, not particularly anything. Notwithstanding all his disadvantages as a husband, the greatest bar to Charlotte's accepting him is his insistence that she make her home with him in Holland.

"That is the accepted thing, my dear," he tells her. "A woman's place is at her husband's side, nowhere else."

"I think you are missing something here," Charlotte replies. "You must always—always, William—bear in mind that if I am to be your wife, you will be marrying the next Queen of England."

"The wife must go where the husband goes," he says stubbornly.

"It is out of the question. Even my father, who is so keen on this arrangement, would agree to that."

"No, no, Charlotte! Actually, this is your father's idea."

"What do you say?"

"Oh, yes!"

"He has said nothing to me about any such thing!"

"I should think not, Charlotte. Your father intends to withhold this information from you until after the wedding."

Charlotte leaps to her feet, her face growing red with rage. She sweeps to the door of the room. "That will be all, William," she says at the door. "You are dismissed." She slams the door heavily as she leaves.

In her room she writes a short, imperious note to Lady Anglesong, commanding her presence at once.

"His eagerness for this marriage is to banish you from the country for unassailable political reasons," Lady Anglesong says. "You are too popular among his own subjects, who detest him. Having once got you out, you may be sure he will keep you out."

"How can he keep me out?"

"My dear child, you will be under the control of a person not subject to our laws—a Dutch prince. And you will remain where your husband tells you to remain—he in turn having been instructed by the Prince-Regent—until the Prince is crowned King of this country. Despite how much the people hate him, despite how much they love you—can you imagine anything more absurd than for a possible Queen of this country to be abroad as a subject of a foreign state and incapable, by Dutch law, of leaving its territory without the consent of her husband?"

Lady Joyce suggests that Charlotte write a "careful" letter to her father, which Lady Joyce offers to draft. In the letter, Charlotte requests to see the marriage contract and pleads that an insertion be made in it to prevent her from being taken from England against her inclination. This enrages the Prince-Regent.

After two days he sends word to Charlotte that he will consider forgiving her for having sent the letter if she will withdraw it. If she refuses, he will bring the matter up before the Cabinet. Charlotte refuses to withdraw the letter. There is a day or two of coming and going between the two houses that face each other across the small private park. When Carlton House flings out the example of James II's daughter, Mary, who had gone abroad to marry an earlier Prince of Orange, Warwick House counters with a proviso made by the Peers to prevent Queen Mary from being taken out of the country by her husband, Philip of Spain.

"Dammit! *Dammit!*" the Prince-Regent shouts, throwing a bottle of maraschino across the room at Colonel Heller. "The place across the garden must be filled with lawyers! This is no young woman's answer. It's that damned Anglesong! I knew it, I knew the moment the King allowed her name into that marriage contract with the sow of Brunswick that Anglesong would work to ruin me."

He stalks back to his principal work, which is making out a list of guests to attend Charlotte's wedding. Deliberately he omits the name of the Princess of Wales and sends the list across to Warwick House. Charlotte adds her mother's name, scratches out the name of the Prince of Orange, and sends the list back to the Prince-Regent.

Despite pressure from royal dukes, bishops, generals,

the Prince, and Colonel Heller at his most histrionically frightening, despite slaps from the Queen, and pinches from the Queen's six daughters, Charlotte refuses to give up the stipulation of residence as written in the marriage contract. In the presence of others, Charlotte tells the Prince of Orange that she will not leave England under any circumstances.

"If you are determined in that, then our marriage must be off," he says. When he has gone, Charlotte dashes off a peremptory note to him to confirm what she said; formally breaking off their engagement. She then sits in Warwick House awaiting and expecting terrible events.

On the third day, William sends her a note. He has told his family, but he cannot, as she had asked in her letter, break the news to the Regent.

Charlotte writes to her father.

There is no reply.

The silence grinds on until Lady Anglesong sends three Whig rumor teams into the pubs of London to spread the word that "Young Prinny has thrown over the Frog." Simultaneously, with full authority from Charlotte, Anglesong releases the information to the press that her marriage is broken off for reasons of her attachment to England, which she cannot and will not leave; above all her attachment to her mother who, in her present distressed condition, she likewise cannot leave.

UPROAR AT CARLTON HOUSE!

At the end of three weeks, the odious Bishop of Exeter calls on Charlotte. He weasels around to the barely expressed hint that unless Charlotte writes a submissive letter to her father holding out the hope that within a few months she will be willing to agree to the marriage, the arrangements her father will make—the Bishop purrs—"will by no means be agreeable to Your Highness's inclinations."

Lady Anglesong advises Charlotte to send her father a submissive and affectionate letter but under no misconception to allow it to contain any hope of a renewal of her engagement. At 5:00 P.M. two days later Charlotte is summoned to Carlton House. She refuses to go. Her companion, Miss Knight, goes in her place, pleading that the Princess's knee is so painful she is unable to walk.

"Do you know what kind of a summer this has been, Miss Knight?" the Prince-Regent bursts out. "It is the most detestable I have ever spent—tussling with the Princess of Wales over forbidding her to attend the Queen's Drawing Rooms—suffering the unholy boredom of foreign princes —being insulted by paid political mobs—and now!—now total insubordination from my own daughter! It is too much! All this has worked me into a state of ill-temper for which the only relief is to do something *really* disagreeable."

"Disagreeable, Your Highness?"

"I am sorry to put a lady to inconvenience, but I want your room by this evening. A new, far less friendly group of companions shall take over the Princess. Colonel Heller has found them and trained them."

"In what way have I offended?"

"I make no complaint and will not make any. I may make any changes I please. I blame myself for letting things go on as they have done."

Miss Knight answers stiffly. "My father, having served His Majesty for fifty years, sacrificed his health and fortune in that service as an Admiral. It would be strange, indeed, therefore, if I could not put myself to temporary inconvenience." She curtseys and leaves.

She reports the conversation to Charlotte, who has strung herself up into a state of desperation. In twenty minutes the Regent and the Bishop of Salisbury are announced. "Go to him at once," Charlotte cries, "but delay him as long as you can!" She dashes out of the room through the far door. "I shall go to my mother!" she exclaims over her shoulder.

A white figure that seems to be balancing a white feather on her bonnet hastens through the summer's night down the back stairs and out into London to Charing Cross where she throws herself into a hackney coach and tells the driver he can have a guinea if he drives as rapidly as possible to Connaught Place. She has never been out alone before in her life. The terror of her father loosens. Her girlish exuberance begins to enjoy the novelty. When she gets to the house in Connaught Place, she learns her mother has gone to the Blackheath villa for the day. Charlotte must send a groom off to find her. She sends a messenger to find Lady Anglesong and Henry Brougham. Then she orders dinner.

Within thirty-five minutes many carriages are on their way to Connaught Place separately carrying the Bishop of Exeter, the Duke of Sussex, Lord Mitgang, the Duke of York, Lady Joyce Anglesong and Henry Brougham, Lord Ellenborough, the Princess of Wales.

The Duke of York is made to wait downstairs with the odious bishop. The others are told they can wait, if they must, outside in their hackney coaches. Upstairs, the Duke of Sussex surveys Brougham and Anglesong. "These are, I assume, your legal advisers?" he asks Charlotte.

"Yes."

"Pray, sir," the Duke says, straight to the point with

Brougham, "supposing the Prince-Regent, acting in the name of and in behalf of His Majesty, were to send a sufficient force to break down the doors of this house and carry away the Princess, would any resistance in such case be lawful?"

"It would not," replies Brougham.

"Then, my dear," the Duke says to his niece, "you hear what the law is. I can only advise you to return with as much speed and as little noise as possible."

"That does not fit my plans, Augustus. Thank you."

Charlotte has become obsessed with the idea that her father will force her to marry the Prince of Orange.

"I repeat to you," Lady Anglesong tells her, "that without your consent, freely given, no marriage can take place."

"What am I to do?"

"Return to Warwick House or Carlton House and on no account pass the night anywhere else."

Charlotte weeps.

The meeting continues until well past 4 A.M. when the summer's early dawn begins. It is to be a day of great excitement for the London mob; the day of the election of Mr. Harold Harris, as a Member of Parliament for St. Marylebone. Caroline leads her daughter to a window overlooking Hyde Park. "Look out there, my darling," she says. "In a few hours all the streets and that park will be crowded with thousands upon thousands of people. I will have only to take you to this small balcony, show you to that crowd, tell them your grievances, and they will rise up to do battle on your behalf."

"And why should they not?" Charlotte asks loftily.

"Carlton House will be attacked. Soldiers will be ordered out, blood will be shed, lives will go. If you were to live a hundred years, it would never be forgotten that your running away from your father's house was the cause of so much death. You may depend upon it, my dearest. Such is the English people's horror of bloodshed—your name would never survive it."

"Very well! But there is one thing I shall cling to in my misery," Charlotte says loudly. "Anglesong must write out a declaration that I will not marry the Prince of Orange and that if ever there should be an announcement of such a match, it must be understood to be without my consent and against my will."

"We will do that," Lady Anglesong says.

"I desire that the Duke of Sussex take particular notice of this," Charlotte says. "Finally, I shall not budge unless a royal coach is sent for me."

13

After high-level consultations with the Whig leadership, Brougham and Lady Anglesong move to make the Prince-Regent's conduct against the Princess of Wales a major political issue.

By January 1813, Caroline has not been permitted to see her daughter for more than seven months and the Prince gives no evidence that she will ever be allowed to visit Charlotte again. Lady Anglesong draws up a screed, turgid and weighty with lawyers' marrow, which Caroline signs and which is sent directly to the Regent despite his announcement that he will accept no further communications from his wife. The letter is delivered on the 14th January and is returned unopened the next morning. Immediately it is redelivered with a covering note which points out that the letter contains matters of State importance. It is returned unopened within an hour with a courteous note from the Prime Minister, Lord Liverpool. This time the letter goes back, with a covering letter, to Lord Liverpool, which states that Her Royal Highness cannot believe that the Prime Minister would take upon himself the responsibility of not bringing to the notice of the Regent the contents of H.R.H.'s letter because, if he does so, he will be depriving her of the privilege of petition to the Throne, a right available to the meanest subject in the kingdom.

Liverpool seeks the advice of the Lord Justice. It is a

legal issue, but nonetheless a vital political matter is at stake. They decide that the Whigs would be handed a club with which to beat the Tories if Liverpool refuses to sponsor the Princess's letter. Together, they tell the Regent that, as government servants, they must read the letter to him. He listens throughout the reading, showing no expression.

Liverpool advises the Princess that His Royal Highness, having heard the contents of the letter, was not pleased to signify any commands upon it. Whereupon, to her utmost pleasure, Caroline's rejected position beside that of her daughter, both struck cruelly by her husband, is published in Sir Thomas Buckley's *The Morning Chronicle*, but her chances of seeing her daughter again are ended.

The Regent goes almost feral with rage. "What am I now?" he rants to Colonel Heller. "I am nominated to be the most despised man in my own kingdom because of a corrupting bitch! It is now explained to the nation that, having brutally mistreated my charming wife for years, I now refuse to let her meet my own daughter. Caroline is a national heroine! My God! I have made Caroline a heroine!"

"Temporarily. Merely temporarily, Your Highness," Heller pleads.

"Well! At last! For once you are right! We will see how long that contemptible beast remains a heroine. You will move directly to have the Privy Council re-examine all the documents pertaining to The Delicate Investigation and have them state to me whether or not they concur with my informed decision—forced upon me by the evidence in those documents—that I must protect my daughter from the contaminating influences of her mother."

On the 27th February the Privy Council not only

concurs in the Regent's decision but urges him to continue with the policy. The Council is comprised of Tories. Immediately, the Whigs, Anglesong and Brougham, draft a letter of bitter complaint for Caroline's signature. The Princess declares herself willing to stand for a public examination of her conduct at any time.

This is ignored.

Caroline, feeling great strength and joy in her renewed power to break the Prince, tells Anglesong that she is going to appeal directly to Parliament and demand a public trial. Anglesong is doubtful about this course but agrees to sound out the idea.

Using the paid Whig rumor teams like knitting needles, Anglesong spreads the word of Caroline's intentions through gentlemen's clubs, pubs, at sporting events, in church congregations, at theaters, and in both Houses. Lord Moira floats a counter-rumor telling an acquaintance he knows to be a friend of Brougham's the full details of the case the Crown will bring against the Princess if she presses for a public trial. She and Brougham judge the case the Crown will bring to be so flimsy that Caroline can challenge it with impunity.

At once they draw up a new, longer manifesto. It is sent off to the Speaker of the House of Commons in Caroline's name. It entreats to be allowed to bring the wrongs done to the Princess by the Prince-Regent to the lower House, demanding that she be allowed to clear her name publicly, at the earliest opportunity, and forever. As customary after a reading in the House, the appeal is published throughout the country, if only in the Whig press. As Anglesong had correctly estimated, there is hardly a dry eye in England as people study the injustices done by a callous husband to the woman he married and scorned.

The Tory government rejects any possibility of a public trial. The British nation now sees the Prince-Regent and his government at their worst and lowest—men plotting to bring a fine woman down so that they may all kick her—that the Prince-Regent may utterly desert her.

The Prince-Regent so loses his self-control that any reasoning becomes meaningless to him. He *commands* that the entire case be disclosed as revealed initially in The Delicate Investigation, by publishing it line by line in the Tory press. This creates an exquisite irony. Five years before, Caroline had tried to publish the same papers in the same press on the advice of the Tory Party, to show that a faked case had been engineered against her by her husband. Now, the same maddened husband insists upon publishing the identical material to establish justification of his conduct with his wife.

It is a grave misjudgment. The people answer it with a howl. They see it as a criminal slander against Caroline and a positive admission of nefariousness by the Regent. He has sunk his own ships with his own guns.

Caroline dances with joy. She toasts life.

The hounded Prince-Regent meets with the Prime Minister, Lord Liverpool; Lord Moira, his executor and principal creditor; and Colonel Heller, his implementer and siccarian.

"I am utterly calm," he says the moment they sit down. "You need have no fear of reckless action on my part. I see it all so clearly. She must be induced to go abroad, d'you see? Do you follow my intention here? That will remove her from Whig control and their intensive advices. You may be sure that Lady Anglesong has no interest in living anywhere removed from the wellsprings of British power. When the Princess is abroad, she will no longer have Anglesong's counsels. Next—and this is very important—I cannot score the importance of this surety too much—her despicable animal nature is *certain* to bring her into grievous mischief once she is beyond British controls. When she commits whatever heinous and unnatural acts she is certain to perform and this is imparted to the British nation by appalled *foreigners*—why, it *must* follow that our own public *cannot* place the blame for these horrendous and obscene writhings upon me or my government. Do you see?"

Liverpool and Moira gaze at him thoughtfully.

"To go abroad is *logi*cal," the Prince presses. "The war with France is almost done. She is bored here. I am never going to permit her to see her child again. She will adore to have a merry fling on Continental turf. Therefore —I put it to you—she must be enticed, even bribed into doing just that. Need I say more?"

14

Lord Malmesbury has come to London in advance of the party of Tsar Alexander, to whose court he had been sent as ambassador. On his mind far more absorbingly than the pageantry of welcome and of victory among the Allied sovereigns is his longing to see Caroline and to talk to her. But the past is too great a bar. Several times he takes up his pen to tell her he has returned briefly, but each time he stops himself with a greed for the past, a need to want to see her only as he remembers her; as a young, careless, charming and adorable woman who had trod a primrose path to a bottomless abyss because she would not believe that the real world of all of her life to come had sharpened teeth and relentless jaws.

If he sees her now, his last illusion will be shattered: the illusion of his power over her, the illusion that she loved him, that she wanted him. She is twenty years older —in itself nothing—but his carefully accumulated information has told him that it has been a battering twenty years, filled with poisons and bitternesses. Why should he sit before a brittle, used woman whom he would not recognize physically or otherwise when, by not seeing her, he can protect the memory of a force of true innocence and gaiety, a pretty, kind, and generous woman whose need to give to all others overflowed her own public presence and half-drowned it.

Most of all, what he is determined not to bear is the certainty that they have transformed her into a bore.

One tentacle of the Tory Party reaches out to plan strategy. The projected negotiations with Lady Joyce Anglesong and Henry Brougham relative to the greatly-to-be-desired agreements applying to the Princess's return to Europe, perhaps forever, must be initiated.

A second tentacle, operating through the press knight, Sir Thomas Buckley, plunges into arrangements to secure from the British press whole-hearted endorsements of the Prince-Regent to make certain of a shining public image for the Prince during the forthcoming Victory Visit to be made by the Allied sovereigns. Sir Thomas agrees to temporarily take up the Prince's banner in return for being named Captain of the All-British Tennis Team which will play against Russian, Prussian, and Austro-Hungarian tennis teams during the Victory Visit. Tennis is Buckley's deep, inner life.

The third tentacle is the Regent himself. He concentrates upon the extraordinarily complex plans for his reception of the Allied sovereigns: Alexander I, Tsar of Russia, and his recently widowed sister, Catherine, Grand Duchess of Oldenburg; Frederick William III, King of Prussia, Württemberg and Bavaria; his second son, Prince William; his two princely brothers and a princely cousin; Prince Anthony de Radziwill, husband of Princess Louise of Prussia; as well as nineteen generals including Blücher and Platoff. Prince Metternich will represent the Emperor of Austria. They are all due to arrive on the seventh of June for a great international celebration of their ultimate victory over the French, and they will also serve as pawns in the Tory public relations effort to make the Prince-Regent seem important to the world and therefore to his people. London is giddy with excitement. Everyone is agog to watch multiple royalties pop in and out of state coaches.

The Strategy Planning Commission works behind locked doors.

Sir Thomas Buckley gives to his task of the annunciation of the (temporary) canonization by the press of their beloved ruler his characteristic directness. He visits editors/publishers of key newspapers in turn and explains to them why it is good for the newspaper business to praise the Regent during visits by Allied sovereigns; and then to return to business-as-usual when these people quit London.

"It is the patriotic thing, you see," he tells them. "We can't have all these wogs here and let 'em know what we *really* think of our Prince, can we? It will be a difficult task to lay upon our lads, trying to find pleasant things to say, but it can be done. I tell you it can be done."

Buckley himself puts up prize money for those journalists adjudged to have come up with the most effective idolizing stories. It only costs him £100 (which he charges to the Tennis Association) and it produces prodigies of reporting.

In the *Courier:*

> Among the many instances which have come to our attention, so honorable to the character of the Prince-Regent as a man of feeling, one occurred at the Levee Thursday last when a man who had lost both feet and one leg hobbled before the Prince with the aid of pitiable crutches. This veteran of the wars attempted to stoop to kneel before the Prince.
>
> "No, *no!* You need not kneel!" cried out the Prince, knowing of the man's disability, having met him previously at Brighton when the man had fallen on his face while attempting the same obeisance, badly bruising himself and embarrassing the entire court because the gesture had so offended the Prince. It is time these kindnesses that one discerns in the goodness of the Prince's heart were more publicly proclaimed. For once, he has not asked that they be withheld from publication.

(The writer, Mr. Michael McNay, won a first prize of £35.)
In the *Chronicle,* Mr. John Clohesy won the second
prize of £20.

> Our Prince-Regent is not only a soldier's soldier, a religious
> leader, an example to British youth, and a loving husband and
> father, he possesses uncanny artistic taste, so far beyond con-
> scious measure that its source must be in the fountains of his
> genius, for yesterday he found a painter whom he deemed wor-
> thy of knighthood and, once again, he was right at bulls-eye, for
> that humble painter is now Sir Thomas Lawrence, who is said
> to feel that he is even a better painter for having known the
> Prince-Regent.
> Beyond that, and who could have thought that a man such as
> the Regent, whose life is so demanding of his attentions, could
> ever have found time to read?—and yet—he has instructed his
> librarian to give Miss Jane Austen permission to dedicate her
> next novel to the Prince. Faint with the honor, Miss Austen has
> notified her publishers that she will do so.

The Buckley Awards Contest runs for five weeks. The
Prince-Regent can hardly believe his senses. He has to be
torn away from reading, rereading, scissoring and pasting
the wonderful newspaper features about himself into the
quite slim book kept for that purpose. "They appreciate
me!" he cries out so happily to Colonel Heller. "They see
me as I am, at last! Oh! Then it is worth all the pain!" He
weeps in Heller's arms at the unsullied beauty of justice.

The Grand Duchess of Oldenburg, the Tsar's sister,
comes to England in advance of the main party as if to
measure the ground. She takes over the entire Pulteney's
Hotel in Piccadilly at a cost of 210 guineas a day. She is an
ugly, clever, self-important little woman.

The Prince-Regent and the Duchess take an instant
dislike to each other. He rushes to the hotel to greet her
and she coolly insults him for not giving her time to get out
of her traveling clothes. The dinner at Carlton House in

her honor is a lamentable disaster. She says loudly that the musicians must be sent away as music of such a quality makes her feel ill. The Prince, attempting to smooth over this embarrassment, ventures to hope that a widow of her charm would not continue to wear mourning for long. She answers him with an astonished silence and a Russian look filled with icy haughtiness. She criticizes the Regent's treatment of his daughter. The Regent turns to the Countess Lieven, the Russian ambassador's wife, at his left, and says loudly, "This is intolerable!"

> Handsome, he is [the Duchess writes to her brother, the Tsar], but he is a man visibly used up by dissipation and rather disgusting. His much boasted affability is the most licentious, I may even say obscene, strain I have ever listened to. You know I am far from being puritanical or prudish, but I avow that with him—I do not know what to do with my eyes and ears—a brazen way of looking where eyes should not go.

She maddens him even beyond the elemental chemistries by receiving leaders of the opposition instead of government leaders, by announcing her intention to visit the Princess of Wales, and by spending hours alone with Princess Charlotte in her rooms.

The Prince-Regent summons the Russian ambassador and instructs him to see to it instantly that the Grand Duchess damned well does not visit the Princess of Wales. The ambassador persuades the Grand Duchess away from the visit only by threatening to resign if she goes through with it.

Things get worse when the Tsar arrives. Booted on by his sister's dislike of the Prince, he becomes savagely annoyed at the sight of him. Other fuel for the tsarist rage occurs when Louis XVIII, seated on the restored French throne, decorated by the Prince-Regent with the Order of the Garter, has the effrontery to ignore Russia's sacrifices to bring Napoleon down, and proclaims to the Prince and the press, "It is to the counsels of Your Royal Highness, to glorious England and to the steadfastness of its inhabitants that I attribute the reestablishment of my House upon the throne of my ancestors."

The Tsar is so enraged he refuses to stay in the apartments at St. James's Palace which had been prepared for him. He puts up instead with his sister in Pulteney's Hotel. The Prince-Regent cannot risk exposing himself to the shouted insults from the Piccadilly crowd, so he sends word that he cannot go to the Tsar's hotel.

The Tsar and his sister later claim that they waited to receive him for hours.

The Tsar knows he is a man of divine enlightenment. He not only makes the gross gaffe of going to see all the Whig party leaders, beginning with Lady Joyce Anglesong, as if he were confusing them with the leaders of the Tory government deliberately, but he also insists upon speaking a fascinating sort of English to everyone.

His English speech horrifies the Prince-Regent. It even horrifies Colonel Heller. It amuses the ruling classes and greatly endears the Tsar to the British public. Having learned to speak English at the knee of his Cockney nanny in St. Petersburg, he sounds as if Maurice Micklewhite had been made Tsar of all the Russias. Further, as if intentionally to offend the Prince, he develops a mad crush on the Prince's former property, Lady Jersey, whom he waltzes with continually whether the music is playing or not, dropping aitches all over the carpets.

He gets into a humiliating argument with the Prince-

Regent before massed British crowds when he refuses to enter a Royal coach with the Prince unless his sister is with him. "'Ere! Oi! 'Arf a mo'," he shouts. "Watziss all abaht? Where's me sistuh?"

The Prince-Regent answers with his cultivated speech in which, due to the elegance of every correct nuance delivered, he is universally known to have no phonetical or pronunciational peer. "No woman," he says, measuring the words, honing them as he delivers them, "ever went into the same carriage as the Sovereign when he appears in public as such."

"'Ere, then! Tew bad on yew then, innit?" the Tsar yells. "Yer don't ketch me goin' mivvout me sistuh!"

"Why!" a woman exclaims at the edge of the dense crowd. "'E speaks bee-yew-dee-fool English fer a Roosian."

"Fer a Roosian?" her friend replies. "I wish the Prince would troy speakin' English vat good."

The Prince turns away from the Tsar to stare icily at the women. The two women smile at him pleasantly. As famous as the Prince is for the quality of his diction, there are those who rate him even higher for the measure of frigidity in his steady glance when he has been deeply offended. The two women finally back away and disappear into the crowd.

The blunt King of Prussia does not madden the Prince in precisely the same way as does the Tsar, but he is exceedingly difficult. He will speak only in the Pomeranian dialect calling for an interpreter. He insists upon sleeping on a rough military cot instead of on the great bed of state which is provided for him at Clarence House. His disposition is that of a sulky bear's. As for General Blücher, morning, noon, and night he is raucously drunk. Desperate to get away from them for any length of time whatever, the

Prince arranges for all of them to sit for a painting by Thomas Lawrence. But, however impossible the extended visits are for the Prince, they also bring him happiness because he accomplishes what is, for him, the most important single objective of the Allied victory: both monarchs and Prince Metternich agree to ignore Caroline, Princess of Wales.

The Prince-Regent receives the Russian, the Prussian, and the Austro-Hungarian ambassadors and orders his Prime Minister to meet with them. At each meeting the ambassadors are given the same explicit instructions to convey: under no circumstances of past relationships, family connections, old friendships or feelings of admiration for the late Duke of Brunswick are the sovereigns to agree to receive, to visit, or to acknowledge by letter that the Princess of Wales is in England while they are there. This is impressed upon the ambassadors as being a severe matter of internal domestic policy of utmost importance to the British government which must be observed.

Heller tells that to the Prince. The Prince tells that to Heller. Heller tells that to the Prince again and again. It is a gambit which they know will cause Caroline terrible pain.

Although the Princess sends more than seven letters to each monarch, more than a dozen to the Grand Duchess, four to Blücher and to Platoff, inviting them to Kensington Palace, or for an afternoon in the country at Montague House; offering to visit them; entreating them to give her reasons why they are treating her as if she did not exist; calling upon the services and glories of her late father, the single commander who had fought for all of them so well and so long and who had died in the service of the King of Prussia; pleading for their protection against her husband who, she will grimly prove to them, she says, is studying how to bring about her destruction, they ignore her as if she were invisible because each letter she sends is immediately diverted to the corresponding ambassador, never to be read by Their Majesties.

The effect of the illusion of her own non-being almost breaks Caroline. It is the first time in all the terrible years since she left Brunswick that she gives in to despair. Nothing the Prince-Regent has ever been able to do to her directly has had the crushing effect of this unfeeling avoidance by the people of her family, the people of her childhood; the safety that European monarchy has always represented to her has been denied to her at last.

It is Colonel Heller's plan that this despair will sow the seeds for the successful negotiations for her exile. Her daughter has been ripped out of her life. Her acquaintances are useless ornaments. Her European relations have turned away from her. Her husband is her greatest enemy. Her life is empty. Were she alone she might sign anything. But she is not alone. She has Lady Anglesong, Henry Brougham and the Whigs to protect her and her interests for as long as these coincide with their own. The negotiating teams go to work on the Treaty of Exile in deadly earnest.

15

Anglesong and Brougham face Lord Sissons and Admiral Matson, the two Tory negotiators.

"We will establish this as the basis for these negotiations," Anglesong says. "The Regent is petitioning his wife to leave the country."

"We would deflect that, milady," Sissons answers mildly. "We meet to attempt to find a solution to a bad marriage."

"What you call a solution is the Regent's decision to find a means to cast out his wife."

"No, no."

"The Regent's decision rests upon his wife's departure from this country."

"That is as much to be desired by the Princess as by the Regent," Admiral Matson says.

"Consider please," Anglesong replies sweetly to the two men across the table whom she has known from early childhood, "that you are asking the Princess to become persuaded to give up her only home, her only daughter, the protection of the English people, and a life among dear friends of more than twenty years in exchange for the loss of her principal reason for being, which is instant adjacency to her husband for attacks upon his *amour propre.*"

"Not in exchange for that alone," Sissons drawls. "We offer her fifty thousand pounds a year for the rest of her life—if she remains outside England. Should she return—

and she is always free to return—she would get nothing."

"What else?" Brougham asks.

"What *else?*"

"Of course—what else?" Anglesong says testily. "What else for acknowledging her most urgent motive, that of restoring tranquility to the Regent as well as securing for herself the peace of mind of which she has been deprived?"

"We speak of the upkeep of her Household," Brougham says. "Is one to expect this royal person to travel about Europe alone?"

"She will be able to lay on quite a Household with fifty thousand a year," Admiral Matson snaps.

"Oh, no!" Lady Anglesong objects.

"My dear Joyce," Sissons says, "if we give in on Household you are going to demand funds for her jewels, clothing, entertainment and all else."

"Be certain of it. She is not only a defenseless woman, but she will be the next Queen of England when the Regent is crowned."

"Who would have thought we would come to the crux of all this so soon," Lord Sissons murmurs.

"Crux?" Brougham asks.

Sissons clears his throat portentously. "The Regent must have the signature of the Princess of Wales, witnessed by the Prime Minister and the Archbishop of Canterbury, renouncing any right she might have to become Queen."

"O, Michael, Michael!" Lady Anglesong exclaims. "She is his wife. When he becomes King, she is Queen. No document, no renunciation, can change the custom of centuries. One cannot resign from a marriage nor from becoming Queen when one's husband becomes King."

"The Regent will resign from the marriage for her—

through a divorce. Does that answer the question?"

Anglesong and Brougham look at each other blankly and begin to laugh. They rise from their seats laughing and go to the door where they turn to look back at Matson and Sissons. "Nothing left to talk about, gentlemen," Brougham says, wiping his eyes. "Good afternoon."

The Regent has committed himself to himself. That evening he and Colonel Heller go over the negotiations with Matson and Sissons. The negotiators try to convince him that the Whigs' exit had been merely a negotiating trick; that if they are permitted to stand by the original conditions the discussions will be resumed.

The Prince will have none of it. He is transfixed by the ideal of an England without Caroline. "Our objective is to rid me of her," he says flatly. "Divorce will follow. When a true mess of a woman is allowed to rut through the undergrowths of Europe she will exceed her most shameful previous excesses in this country and—when she does —*we,*" he points at Colonel Heller, "will know all about it with the testimony of unimpeachable witnesses. I shall divorce her. The first step is to get her out of England. The second is to keep her out. Forever."

The nineteen days of negotiating begin at ten each morning and end each evening at four forty-five when the tea wagon enters. Resultant documents are signed by the Regent and by the Princess of Wales, then countersigned by each.

PRÉCIS OF THE PRINCESS'S DOCUMENT

1: The Princess is extremely anxious that the Regent shall be informed of the motive for this letter, and clearly comprehend her past conduct, as politically exhibited. In exacting a justification from this noble nation, her sole protection since the unfortunate disposition of the King, she is to be understood as solicitous only to maintain her rights and her honor, which are dearer to her than life itself.

2: Unwilling to prove any obstacle to future arrangements favorable to the happiness of her daughter; a happiness placed in jeopardy by the public avoidance of the Princess of Wales by the Tsar of Russia, the King of Prussia, and the Envoy of the Emperor of Austria, all her blood relatives who were ordered to deny the presence of the Princess of Wales at the explicit urging of the Regent, the Princess of Wales has, at length, resolved to return to Brunswick, her native country. She may afterward travel into Italy and to Greece, where she may probably be able to select an agreeable abode and to live in it for some years. The Princess flatters herself that the Regent will have no objection to this.

3: The Princess of Wales requests the Prime Minister, Lord Liverpool, to represent to the Prince-Regent that she resigns Montague House and the title of Ranger of Greenwich Park in favor of her daughter as also the house bequeathed to her by her mother. The Princess of Wales hopes the Regent will grant this favor, the last she will solicit.

4: The Princess embraces the opportunity to explain the motives which have induced her to decline the grant of £50,000 a year for life voted to her by the nation in Parliament. She expresses her most lively acknowledgement to this liberal and generous nation for its willingness to grant her such a pension, but she has only accepted £35,000 per year because, as the gift was intended to support her proper rank and enable her to hold a court as became the wife of the Prince-Regent.

5: Such is the decision of the Princess of Wales which she would have made before but for the fear of producing new debates in Parliament. She has therefore waited the rising of Parliament and is now about to depart for Worthing to embark, not intending to return to London.

The Princess of Wales is happy to assure that she will ever be ardently solicitous for the prosperity and glory of this generous nation.

The voluntary reduction of the yearly pension due to the Princess from £50,000 to £35,000 is a ploy of Lady Anglesong's. The gesture underscores the grotesque public profligacy and greed of the Prince-Regent. It shows the Princess to be far more self-sacrificing and noble than he by refusing to take all of it. However, the available £15,000 difference is re-labeled as Household Expenses Fund (Annual) in the (secret) agreement. This (secret) agreement, about whose terms Anglesong and Brougham are adamant, states that it is the right of the Princess to issue her own personal statement about her own views of events which led her to voluntary exile. This personal statement is made in the form of a letter to Anglesong and Brougham which, it is also understood, will be released to the press.

The Prince-Regent's own document, signed by himself and countersigned by the Princess (and initialed by the Archbishop of Canterbury) states:

1: The Prince-Regent can have no objections to the intentions of Her Royal Highness to return to her native country to visit her brother, the Duke of Brunswick, assuring her that the Prince-Regent will never throw any obstacle in the way of her present or future intentions as to the place where she may wish to reside.

2: The Prince-Regent also commands that no obstacle be put in the way of Her Royal Highness, whatever they may be, respecting the house in Blackheath which belonged to the late Duchess of Brunswick, or the rest of the private property of Her Royal Highness. But, for reasons too long to explain, the Prince-Regent will not permit Princess Charlotte to be Ranger of Greenwich Park nor to occupy any of the houses at Blackheath which her Royal Highness hitherto occupied.

3: The Prince-Regent signifies to Her Royal Highness that the Prince-Regent never opposed himself to the Allied sovereigns making a visit to Her Royal Highness during their stay in London.

4: The Prince-Regent will not oppose Her Royal Highness's retaining the apartments in the Palace at Kensington in the same manner as she possessed them while in London, for the convenience of herself and her suite.

The last paragraph was inserted at the Prince-Regent's insistence, to convey the impression that, insofar as he knew or was concerned, the Princess of Wales was merely going to Brunswick for a family visit and would, of course, be returning to London as she willed it. The (secret) agreement withdraws any rights the Princess of Wales might have had to an apartment in Kensington Palace.

LETTER FROM THE PRINCESS OF WALES TO LADY JOYCE ANGLESONG AND TO MR. HENRY BROUGHAM DATED 25th JULY 1815 AND RELEASED IN FULL TO THE NEWSPAPER PRESS OF THE UNITED KINGDOM ON THAT DAY AND DATE

My dear friends:

The Princess of Wales has the pleasure to inform and, frankly, to avow to you, that she is about to take the most important step of her life. She has embraced the resolution of quitting this country for a time and has written to Lord Liverpool immediately to inform the Prince-Regent of her intentions.

My conscience tells me that my conduct is worthy of my character and sentiments and will always remain so. No person possessed of pride and feeling could endure to be so degraded below her rank as Princess of Wales, or even as a simple individual bear to be so hated by the Sovereign as to be debased from his presence both in public and in private. I cannot allow myself to be treated as a culprit by the Prince and his family when my innocence has been acknowledged by Ministers and by Parliament after an investigation which has done away with the accusations of traitors and enemies.

The Princess Charlotte will the less feel the privation of her mother's society as she has been deprived of it entirely for the last two years. During that time nine and ten months in succession have passed away without the mother being allowed to see the daughter. I have even been refused the consolation of receiving any of her letters, and thus my regret at leaving her is lessened for, although living in the same capital, we were not allowed to speak even when we met on our airings. I cannot rest in a situation so unfortunate for myself and so uneasy for others. How much it has cost me to make public this declaration, to say openly that the Prince-Regent has been my most inveterate enemy, imposing upon me false accusers and enemies to my honour.

That which renders my situation still more embarrassing is that this generous nation has shown more devotion to myself than to its ruler, who ought to be the blessing and the glory of his people. I hope, with all my heart, when I have quitted England, the Prince-Regent will make public his conviction that my conduct and my character have not merited reproach and thereby regain the popularity which is due to him on the part of this noble and generous nation.

Caroline

Princess of Wales

book three
revenge
(1814–1821)

TORY PARTY IN POWER
PRIME MINISTER: *Robert Banks Jenkinson, Earl of Liverpool*

1

On the 9th August 1815, the Princess of Wales embarks from South Lancing on the warship, the *Grace of Wherry*, to be returned to Brunswick through Hamburg as if she were a piece of defective merchandise. She is forty-six years old. Her Household consists of three English ladies-in-waiting and Mrs. Keifetz; three chamberlains; a dashing equerry—the same, but now Major, Hesse, he of such breadth and length; and a young physician who is Lord Weiler's younger son. The Major-Domo, two chambermaids and one messenger are German. Little Willikin Austin, now fourteen years old and not as bright as he might be, boards at the side of the Princess.

The beach at South Lancing is crowded with people who have come to see her. It is a bright day. The Princess is very gay as she answers their continuing cheers with boisterous waves of her hand. She wears a dark green pelisse and a hussar cap with a feather. As the *Grace of Wherry* draws away from the shore those who stand nearest to the ship's rail see that the Princess is weeping. Without seeming effort, suddenly she becomes gay and unmoved. "I wonder whatever happened to Lady Jersey?" she asks no one at all.

The visit to Brunswick is as brief as possible. As she and her brother shake hands at meeting, they are looking at others. As soon as possible the Royal party moves south to Geneva, then on through Napoleon's own Simplon Pass into Italy.

The Italian Alps behind her, the Princess models her journey on her own conception of how to burlesque her husband's institutions of which, she decides, his marriage must be considered one. She travels in a phaeton which resembles a seashell, or in an old London & Dover mail coach when it is raining. The phaeton is covered with mother-of-pearl and gilding, lined with blue velvet with silver fringes, drawn by piebald horses with Willikin, whom she allows it to be known may be the heir to the English throne, dressed like an operatic cherub in flesh tights and spangles, sitting up beside the driver. Caroline's high-colored face is comically rouged, surrounded by a pink hat with eleven pink feathers. Her bodice is cut extremely low. A short, white skirt barely covers her knees over two stout, pudgy pink legs in pink top boots. Beside her on the seat is a large, long case on which is printed in large, white letters in English and Italian: HRH THE PRINCESS OF WALES, TO BE ALWAYS WITH HER. It contains an indescribably unflattering portrait of her husband, which she shows to all who will look. In advance of the royal procession of six coaches, on another piebald horse, rides a courier dressed lavishly in imitation of Joachim Murat, King of Naples, whose portraits Caroline has long admired.

"The Regent of England has sent me to you!" she cries out in Italian whenever the procession comes to a gathering of more than three people in the road.

Lady Joyce Anglesong, whom the Prince was certain would never leave the power-nest of England, remains one city in advance of Caroline's tour, much like Puss in Boots. To orchestrate the events which become the scandalous stories of the Princess's astonishing behavior, Lady Joyce sets up hosts and guests for balls, dinners, gambling parties and masquerades night after night. Caroline wears out these assemblies. She refuses to retire, has musicians dragged out of their beds to play on through dawns. She provides her Gentlemen with outrageously embroidered liveries.

At Geneva, pulpit of Calvin, the Princess appears at a ball undressed as Venus: she wears no clothing at all above the waist. At Baden she leads a raucous procession into the opera box of the newly widowed Margravine, shrieking with laughter, wearing a peasant headdress ornamented with the most vulgar sort of infula. She arrives at the hunting party of the Grand Duchess of Zendt wearing a half-pumpkin on her head explaining that her husband wears these throughout the summer months—the coolest sort of millinery. In Genoa she sings with her unnaturally strident voice, itself a major accomplishment of burlesque, from the back of her carriage while showing a prodigious expanse of bosom and two pudgy pink legs in pink top-boots.

Lady Joyce sees that the letters go speeding to London by the dozens. The Hon. Anthony Gornall writes: "That 'Injured Innocence' which made such a run when investigations were delicate would now be booed off the stage." From Milan, Lord Byfleet of Bolt writes to the Duke of Cumberland that the Princess is reported to be insane. "I saw her riding a piebald horse as courier for her own entourage of coaches." Admiral Gelbart posts stories of indecent paintings on her walls and about the "orgiastic" balls she gives. Count Axelrod, the Swedish envoy, writes to the Swedish ambassador to St. James's that she will give directions only with her feet, lifting them high and wide and pointing them in the direction she wishes to indicate.

"I cannot tell you how sorry and ashamed I felt as an Englishwoman," the Duchess Van Itallie writes to eight intimates in London. "Dancing in that room behind hips like onrushing boulders was a short, fat, elderly woman with an extremely red face in a girl's white frock which had no top to it whatsoever, back or front. She wore a black wig, false eyebrows which gave her an intensely fierce look, and a wreath of pink roses on her head. I was staring at her with revulsion when she smiled and called out to me. Do you know what she said to me? She said, 'Kiss my husband's foot for me if you have the chance. I should be very grateful.' I thought she was some new kind of vulgar, paid entertainer sent among the guests to shock them! Bentinck, our ambassador, nudged me and said, 'Do you not see the Princess of Wales nodding to you?' My *God!* I tell you I was sorry and ashamed to be an Englishwoman."

By the time the Princess reaches Milan all the English have dropped out of her Household. Lady Anglesong, entirely at home in Italy for centuries, replaces them with an Italian team (supported by French cooks, Arab footboys, and an Austrian postillion). "These are people we will control when the Prince begins to conspire against you," Lady Joyce explains. "Be assured. You are safe from him with these."

The Italian team includes the Countess of Oldi from Cremona, respectable for both her qualities and her misfortunes. She is plump and placid. Her husband has expelled her for loose conduct. To persons of highest culture she might have seemed distastefully bourgeois but she is amiable, a good listener, and a diligent lady-in-waiting. Her notable trait is revealed at once. She has the keen ability of not seeing what is happening around her. She never notices being deserted by her royal mistress in the middle of the night; always fails to notice when the Princess, in the little white cisvestitic nightdress, carrying her pillow under her arm, returns at ten o'clock the next morning.

The Princess's physician is Dottore Max Jungstein of Como, who is also a distinguished former professor of botany, agriculture, and natural history. He understands vegetable aphrodisiacs which the Princess never needs to use herself but which she insinuates into the food of others from time to time. Her equerry is Chevalier Hanl di Rathfarnami. The Doctor of Laws, Francisco O. Connelle, is her lawyer. "All of these, and the servants, are under instructions to allow themselves to be bribed," Anglesong tells the Princess. "Bribe an Englishman and he feels he must return value received in solid information. But these people are so sophisticated, so inordinately cultivated after two millennia of corruption that they will be able to accept the Prince's bribes regularly and give absolutely nothing in return because they know I can make them far more uncomfortable than the Prince-Regent can from far-off England," Lady Joyce explains. "They will take the money and the detailed briefings from the Regent's agents to fill in their testimony when the time comes. Then, when they do depose, they will confound their suborners by the blandest testimony entirely in your support." She laughs merrily. "It is as though you had been issued a hunting license."

Caroline invents a way to get to sleep. It isn't easy. It takes wine and it takes time. She finds a comfortable position in the bed and tries to enjoy its comfort, inch by inch all along her body, hoping to relax it. If it seems as though her body is willing to cooperate, she thinks of all the young men she could have married; men she has thrown away, or whom her father considered to be politically impossible.

There were German princes, a few Grafs, one very, very rich son of a Frankfurt banker. She remembers a French duke whom Mademoiselle von Hertzberg brought to her father's court. That really might have been a love match— if she could have loved him. He was a visitor, nothing official. She slept with him. If five were the average figure for a lover, he could be rated at almost seven. He fell wildly in love with her or with her father's extraordinary connections with the rulers of the world. He wanted to marry her. He went to her father, who was sympathetic but discouraging. France was in too disturbed a state politically, he told Caroline frankly. Then the man turned out not to have been a duke at all, at least not then. He would be a duke someday when his father died, but for the present he was a viscount. How well she remembers the way he could use his hands to pick a lock when her father locked her in her room after he knew how deeply the young man felt about her. She sighed as she felt sleep nearby. Viscomte Bertie Caen. And now the past and everything but revenge is ashes.

What the members of the Princess's Household also have in common is that they are aristocratically well connected in England. They are intimate with the people of the royal court, the government, and the press in London and find it easy to accept guidance from Lady Anglesong on what they should report to friends in London on a continuous basis. Tireless correspondents, they begin by spreading the word, which goes like a wildfire across Carlton House and Windsor, that the Princess of Wales is taking secret instructions from the Pope with the intention of converting to Catholicism. Next they build an edifice of rumor concerning Willikin and the Princess's proud ambitions to claim the throne of England for him. The Whigs' plan is simplicity itself. The cooperation of their controlled press insists, and induces the British public to believe, that everything they read about Caroline is base lies perpetrated by the Regent's Italian spies. They intend to make the Regent plead with them for some compromise. Hitting London all at once, the campaign has a shocking effect upon the health of the Prince-Regent. It makes him drink and take laudanum at the same time. It causes such severe nervous tensions that the Prince demands to be bled almost continuously. He spends four weeks, two days in bed, very ill, unable to face the world.

Through her own family's connections with the Italian secret police establishment, Lady Anglesong is informed when Colonel Heller and his entourage install themselves silently in Milan at Palazzo Debbitina. The blizzard of rumors from Italy about the Princess has convinced the Prince-Regent that he must begin to cause the evidence to be gathered against her. He also issues instructions to British ambassadors throughout Europe to be transmitted to all governments to whom they have been sent that any favors granted the Princess of Wales will cause the gravest displeasure of the British government. His diplomats are instructed to watch upon and report her movements. Their reports quickly confirm what the scandals have only rumored. So much evidence piles up before the Prince by reason of Lady Anglesong's deftness and the explorations through bribery by his own people that the Prince-Regent feels he has no alternative but to ask his government to undertake an official inquiry into the Princess's conduct.

When Whig headquarters, London, reports this gratifying news to Lady Joyce, she and the Princess celebrate joyously. If the Prince can be moved as their pawn to expend huge amounts of government funds on yet another persecution of his wife, then, when as a result of totally uncooperative witnesses it is shown conclusively to have been the Prince-Regent's total delusion, his own competence will be so placed in question, the press and public of England will so howl with demand for change, that he will have to sue for a peaceful settlement, one which will return a Whig government to power and Caroline to her rightful place in a royal marriage bed beside her husband.

They celebrate all alone at a private dinner party. They bring in musicians. They wear gaudy party hats and occasionally employ noisemakers to express their delight at the Prince-Regent, who is helping them so kindly with their plans. They are two middle-aged ladies. Lady Joyce is forty-five; Caroline forty-seven. But Lady Joyce has not debauched herself as the Princess has. She looks younger than she is, using her eyes to devour the Princess.

"When do you have men, Anglesong?" the Princess asks when they move seriously into the wine.

"I have taken a few when I had the time," Lady Anglesong replies. "But men are very demanding. They want all of one's time. They demand flattery."

"So does everyone. But with a man you get to bed him and that is sublime even when he isn't so good as another."

"To me, balancing against all else, I think the bedding is overrated," Lady Joyce says.

"That's too bad. I could have given you quite a few very good ones. Look at it this way, Anglesong. I am demanding. I take all of your time. But you don't even get the pleasure of bedding me."

Lady Joyce averts her eyes quickly. Her cheeks color.

She takes up a glass of wine to cover her expression and drinks with her eyes closed. "You are different," she says in a slightly trembling voice. "You—you are my career."

The Prince-Regent tells Heller that he can almost feel the pleasures of the certitude of his divorce coursing through him. "I tell you it is now or never," he says passionately. "She is removed from England. Foreigners as well as English report daily on the scandals of her conduct and at least—quite independent of me—these can be proved." The Tory government, raw under Whig attacks, agrees to appropriate money for an inquiry into the Princess's turpitude on the condition that "whatever might be the nature of the evidence obtained, however decisive as to criminality, the question of the expediency of any proceedings must always be considered as an open question."

Colonel Franz Heller, formerly of His Majesty's German Legion, is chosen to head the inquiry, which will be known as The Milan Commission. Administering for him as permanent party in Milan are Sir Charles Chapman, "one of His Majesty's Counsels learned in the law," and Captain John Reese, R.N., assigned to this shore duty because of his cunning as a naval intelligence expert.

The Princess of Wales and her lady-in-waiting, the Countess Oldi, take tea at the Royal Hotel in Milan. It is a rare sunny day in that gloomiest of cities. The lobby and porch where the two ladies sit is bathed in golden light. The Contessa Oldi has asked the Princess to grant an audience to her brother, Bartolomeo Pergami, recently retired from the Italian army, in the hope that the Princess might decide to employ him as a courier.

A tall, brown and heavily bewhiskered young officer of hussars who has a nicely adjusted hang to his furred dolman swaggers out upon the porch and greets his sister with an outcry of joy. He is a man of the world of thirty years; eminently self-contained. His eyes have boredom, boldness, and expectancy all at once. The Princess of Wales is merely as susceptible as she ever was. Pergami falls to one knee and kisses her hand, lingeringly and tenderly. She bids him sit with them.

At the chat he provides a letter from General Bellegarde-Pino, Austrian Governor of Lombardy, which recommends the high character of Bartolomeo Pergami. He seems very beautiful to the Princess.

When the headquarters of The Milan Commission are settled at the Palazzo Debbitina, Colonel Heller's first thought is to search out an irresistibly handsome and healthy young male whom he can plant in the Princess's

Household and who, gaining his way with her, can induce her to do as the Prince-Regent, through Colonel Heller to him, will instruct.

Through Baron Ompteda, the Hanoverian minister to the Vatican, Heller succeeds in gaining a favored introduction to Generale Melvini-Sestero, chief of the Italian Secret Police. After introductions, the Generale feels it will be better if they speak German.

"I am sure you understand," Colonel Heller says, "that the deep anxiety of my government, and of the Prince-Regent personally, concerns the scandalous actions of the Princess of Wales. And you will understand our need to establish an *agent-provocateur* within the Household of the Princess."

Melvini-Sestero nods.

"Therefore, most respectfully, I ask for your collaboration in procuring a handsome, strong young man who will be capable of approaching the Princess of Wales while at the same time understanding that he is under my orders."

"We have two or three thousand young officers in the Italian army alone who could do the job. Each would feel it a privilege to screw a genuine British princess. I will sort them out and advise you."

When Colonel Heller leaves, the Generale dictates a message to Lady Joyce Anglesong in exquisite Italian, the language of happiest conspiracy.

Charming Cousin:
   Your competitor visited me today. Make a good
dinner of him. Invite me to tea so that we may chat—
and laugh. With inestimable admiration,
                                                        ALEAMALIA

The Princess has urged that Lady Joyce hire Contessa Oldi's brother. The sooner, the better, please. At tea with Melvini-Sestero, Lady Joyce arranges with him to send this young male to Colonel Heller in response to Heller's urgent request. This amuses the Generale greatly.

When Pergami meets Colonel Heller, he listens intently to the requirements of the proposed assignment in the Household of the Princess. He asks how much it pays.

"One hundred English pounds a month."

"Cash?"

"Cash."

"That seems all right."

"What does your Italian army rank—*maresciallo d'alloggio*—signify?"

"I was a quartermaster of billeting," Pergami answers stiffly. As a cavalry man he was not allowed near horses because, unaccountably, they all bit him.

"Are you an aristocrat?"

"My sister is the Contessa Oldi." He shrugs with great delicacy.

Heller leers at him. "Do you think you are strong enough for this job?"

Pergami stares at him insolently. "Possibly," he says.

"Good. These are your orders. We will meet in this room on the first Monday of every month. If the Princess moves, we will move behind her and our monthly meetings will be held wherever she is. I want detailed and explicit information concerning all her activities, particularly her sexual activities."

Heller writes to the Prince-Regent. The letter says, in part:

He is an agent who has been sent to me from the highest officer of the Italian Secret Police who vouches for him "in every way." Impeccable references are being forged for him. His male beauty will achieve the rest. I will propound nothing to you on which I have not absolute certainty. I am convinced that the "entry" of our agent, Pergami, will produce the most marked scandal and the most damaging legal deposition when we are ready to take everything forward.

When he leaves the Palazzo Debbitina, Pergami strolls across the piazza to Casa Jemma, headquarters of Lady Anglesong. He ogles Lady Anglesong's secretary who looks at him icily, without interest. Lady Joyce serves him tea. "What will he pay you?" she asks.

"One hundred English pounds a month. How much will you pay me?"

"Fifty."

"Fifty?"

"You have your beauty and your health. What can more money do to improve on that?"

"Superficially it can help me when I am old, ugly, and unhealthy."

"I have better than money for you."

"Please—let us not now count the charms of the Princess as gold."

"Are you not a little tired of being just a little *maresciallo d'allogio?* You—who are about to bed an English queen?"

"Suppose I answer yes, I am tired of being insignificant." He sneers at her pleasantly.

"In Sicily, *mia maresciallo,* I know of a certain property called Franchina. This property confers upon whoever owns it the title of Baron. The new owner has only to apply to the King of Sicily, pay a fee, and become the Barone della Franchina. That is how I think of you. That is how I want you to make the Princess of Wales think of you so that I may petition her to reward you by buying you this distinction which you deserve."

"At your orders, Serenissima! Money need not obtrude into our relationship. Fifty pounds sterling, in cash each month, is more than I deserve."

"You make me happy," Lady Anglesong says. "I propose that we meet on the Sunday evening before the first Monday of each month so that I may convey to you what will be best to report to Colonel Heller."

3

On the 19th October the Princess of Wales leaves Milan along the road through Tuscany and Umbria to Rome. Pergami rides at the head of the procession of six carriages. He wears an astoundingly colorful new livery designed for him by the Princess to resemble a "suit of lights" worn by Spanish bullfighters. She rides, thoughtful, as she considers whether she should ask him to have his left ear pierced so that he might wear a jewel-encrusted gold ring in it. For fifteen minutes of each hour Pergami turns back and rides at the window of his patroness's coach. She looks lewd when she speaks to him. She thinks lewd when she thinks of him. Aieee! She tosses the jolly tars out of her mind; she snorts when she thinks of Heller in bed with her. She quacks with hilarity when she thinks of such bedmates as Sir Walter Scott, Lord Eldon and even the Viscomte Bertie Caen. Only Captain Manning, but not even Sir Sidney Smith, may be included in the pantheon of tireless, heart-filling lovers—an army of only two great men—led by Bartolomeo Pergami. She rests her head back upon the cushions in a way that allows her to watch him as he rides with such *Pfiff* as master of the entire procession. What will she do when he wears out? she thinks. She must return to basic principles: select long, lean men, for their endurance bests any others; choose men who are not less than ten years younger, fifteen years is better; be drawn to non-drinkers or careful drinkers; urge them to dress for the mirror in extravagant plumage and always insist that they ride a horse not less than two hours a day because riding agitates the man's important parts. But she knows it is all just a fantasy. She will wear out long before Pergami becomes exhausted. He is the Latin man of ardor and he loves her because she is always amusing and never complaining; always amorous and never denying. She can sustain his ardor because her experience tells her so. Because she is alone in the coach she luxuriates in a rare wave of self-pity, a luxury which, when in the realistic world, she sternly disapproves. She probably does not have but a half dozen beautiful young men left to her after she wears out Pergami. The self-defeat is in the very nature of the enjoyment of the act itself: one has to remove one's stays and, although the sight of her that way did not put Pergami off balance, it very well could do for those future young male beauties up ahead.

Thank heaven, she thinks, for Dottore Jungstein and his persevering experiments to find the universal aphrodisiac. She falls asleep.

The women of Roman society take pride in their reputations for being fast: a special eminence throughout Italy. They are grossly offended therefore by the bare bosoms of the Princess of Wales at dinner parties and galas because she has exceeded their imaginations. A fad for showing single and double bosoms sweeps Rome. One matron attempts riding a horse while barechested in the Villa Borghese and the flappings blacken her right eye. The city is so amused that all black eyes are called "carolines."

Lady Joyce arranges an elaborate audience for the Princess with her cousin, Pope Pius VII, and sees to it that every available correspondent of the British and

Hanoverian press is at hand for the event. The story is printed that the Princess of Wales will take instructions in Catholicism. The Whig Party from the floor of both Houses of Parliament demands to know why the Regent cannot prevent his wife from committing such illegality.

Caroline tells Lady Joyce that she and the Pope had discussed, in German, how happy the Prince-Regent is with Mrs. Fitzherbert and what a fine woman and good Catholic Mrs. Fitzherbert is. Because Pius VII is of the Chiaromonti family, a third cousin to Anglesong, the Princess wears a fully covering bodice.

For the first time in many years, Caroline sets out to liaise with a bedfellow without caring whether it upsets her husband or not. Her sexual ambitions work into fantasies as the royal party rolls along the roads to the Kingdom of Naples where King Joachim Murat, "the handsomest man on earth," rules with his Queen, Caroline Bonaparte. It is the most abandoned of all Italian courts.

Everything about Naples dazzles the Princess because she is so ready to be dazzled. The precocious vulgarity of the colors of the architecture against the bluest of skies and the matchless blue bay with Vesuvius smoking dangerously in the background, the white and pink city tumbling down hillsides upon such noisy, sensual, excitable people all seems to make her drunk. She abandons even her own weak notions of what prudence might be. For as long as she remains in Naples she abandons sanity as well.

To draw herself to King Joachim, Caroline gives a masked ball in a casino overlooking the sea. Three times during the evening the Princess leaves the ballroom to change her costume. On her third appearance she bursts into the fête as the Goddess of Glory with one pudgy leg bare to the bottom of her waist. She is certainly gloriously ready. She takes Joachim, dressed as a jolly Mediterranean tar, by the hand and leads him away from his wife into a small, richly decorated antechamber. At the end of this room, bathed in light from eleven silver torches, he sees a great bust of himself.

Pergami, the producer of the pageant, hands the Goddess of Glory a laurel wreath. She advances (in a rough imitation of a forest dryad) and crowns the bust with the wreath. Young ladies dressed as muses advance on the bust. They carry silver chisels with which they carve into the wooden pedestal of the bust the word JOACHIM. The Goddess of Glory pays homage to the crowned bust. Deeply affected, and a little drunk, the King of Naples brushes tears from his eyes and hurriedly adjusts his clothing.

The Princess cannot stay out of Murat's bed. As time passes there is the greatest difficulty in getting her out of Murat's bed at all. She conceals herself behind arrases and doors. Naked and large she seizes him from behind when he enters a room, tearing open his trousers and spilling their contents into her until the man shrieks at the slightest unexpected sound near him if he is alone.

His wife tells the court of Naples, which relays it immediately to London, that the Princess of Wales is a sexual monstrosity. "She is insatiable," the Queen says. "I have seen women go mad over him before, but this is the truest and most wholly degenerate insanity."

Murat, deeply pale, hardly seems to be able to speak at all. This suave, experienced satyr solves everything by fleeing Naples to the north. The scandal acquires such solid weight and density, the Neapoliticans are so outrageous in their amusement at their King's flight from the strangling scissor-lock of the English princess's fat legs, that the Queen of Naples orders the Princess to leave the kingdom.

Lady Anglesong is almost feverish with the excitement of buying Italian newspapers and shipping them off to the Whig Party in London by the bale. She urges Henry Brougham to promise Sir Thomas Buckley anything if he will give the story the widest circulation. Buckley promises to keep the Naples Affair prominently displayed "for not less than two weeks" if the Whigs will guarantee, when they come back to power, that they will create a Royal Lawn Tennis Association of which he will be named Chairman for Life.

Numb, sated to her hairline, the Princess totters out of Naples and goes to Rome where Lady Joyce conceives an idea which has them working at a fever pitch of excitement. They commission an unmistakably recognizable portrait, painted by James Richard Blake, Royal academician, showing the Princess of Wales in one plus three-quarters scale, as the Magdalene. Lady Joyce persuades him to re-do the facial expression three times until she is satisfied with its degree of lewdness and hardness. The plump body is scarcely clothed at all. It merely leans against something at its back, slumping, its hips reaching out eagerly for something. When the portrait is completed, they have it framed as hideously as possible, crate it, mark it, FROM THE COLLECTION OF KING JOACHIM OF NAPLES, and ship the painting to the Prince as a birthday gift.

There is terror at Carlton House when the crate is opened and the painting suitably hung so that the gratified Prince may view it. He cannot believe what he sees. He races at it, attempts to pull it down from the wall, uttering piteous cries of rage, but he does not have the strength for the task. He throws ink, food, wine, chairs and vases at it. He screams at his people to take it down, but they will not move within range of the flying objects. At last he is restrained. The painting comes down. He tears loose from his captors and flies at it with a table knife and renders it into tatters. The emotions and the efforts so exhaust him that Lord Weiler insists that he be put to bed. He is bled carefully for three days until he will lie quietly; then he remains there, just staring at the ceiling, for three days more.

Pergami delivers full, detailed sets of notes, drawn up by Lady Joyce, to The Milan Commission. The reports indicate which servants will be most open to bribes, which have been eyewitnesses to the choicest pieces of scandal; how the Princess has urged him to go to England to kill the Prince-Regent so that they may marry. Colonel Heller is helpless with gratitude over his good fortune. The Milan Commission begins to contact members of the Princess's Household secretly. They are amazed to learn that even such people as the Contessa Oldi, Dottore Jungstein, Chevalier Hanli and Excellanza Francisco O. Connelle readily state that they will "tell all" before any official inquiry due to their mountainous disgust with the Princess.

"This thing will be tried in the House of Lords!" the Regent gloats as he reads report after report from Heller. "She is as good as convicted. I am free! *Free!* Isn't this *wonderful!*"

Other informers on Colonel Heller's paysheet—at enormous expense, on which he only pockets 20 percent— include members of the indigent British aristocracy resident in Italy; hotel chambermaids; hackney drivers; journalists, laundresses, and waiters. All but the rankest outsiders have been re-bribed with far more thrift by Lady Anglesong with Whig Party funds. By putting all of them in the way of receiving the bribes from Heller without having any of them arrested by the Italian Secret Police, Lady Joyce is able to bring off her suborning at a cost of less than 15 percent of what the identical corruption is costing the British government.

In January 1816, one after the other, her royal uncles, members of the cabinet, and even the elderly Queen, seventy-two years old, visit Princess Charlotte or summon her to visit to chat with her about her disposition as might concern Prince Leopold of Saxe-Coburg and about what her reactions might be if her father can be persuaded to allow her to marry this young man.

Leopold had spent the winter at the Congress of Vienna seeing to the interests of his brother, the Duke of Saxe-Coburg, and amusing himself. He met Princess Charlotte during the visits by the Allied sovereigns. He worked to make their letter correspondence attractive to her. No matter what his diversion, his steadfast intention to marry Charlotte never leaves his mind. He was too deft to press this while the Regent was still outraged by the broken engagement, but he cultivates the Duke of Kent carefully and, through him, manages to get his letters through to Charlotte herself, assuring her of his steadfast devotion and determination somehow to bring his suit to her. By January 1816, Charlotte is eager to marry him. She is marooned. Leopold's devotion is the only chance at life offered to her. Her mind is so definitely made up that she is impatient for him to come to England to put the matter on a solid footing.

Late in January, Charlotte is invited to the Pavilion at Brighton. The Queen and her daughters are all melting sympathy; much kinder to her than they had ever been before. The Regent is dazed that Charlotte actually seems to *like* to stay with him. Charlotte blossoms. Her father tells her that Leopold, now in Berlin, has received a royal invitation to come to England.

Leopold lands on the night of February 21. He wears a long-skirted coat, a fur hat, a muff, and a sable boa which indicate that in some quarters there is strong enough belief in his chances to advance him working capital. He is penniless. He drives directly to Brighton with Lord Castlereagh.

Lady Jane Montant loses no time in writing to the Princess of Wales:

> Princess Charlotte is radiant with happiness. She sees escape very near. She is so happy and looks so pretty. Prince Leopold is enchanting. His appearance and manner could win any young girl's heart.

They are married on the 2nd May at Carlton House amid crimson hangings, nine-foot candles, velvet cushions, prayer books from the Middle Ages, spectacularly uniformed men, and women who had come afire by standing under showers of precious jewels. Charlotte wears white satin with a wide border of ermine. The Prince wears sombre blue from material used to make the uniforms of Guards officers.

As they leave for their honeymoon at Oatlands, country house of the Duke of York, the Queen makes one last, brave effort to dim Charlotte's vibrant happiness by urging the Duchess Van Itallie to go into the carriage with the newlyweds, to sit between them. "It iss zo imbrober dat dey drive off, t'igh to t'igh, alone," she says. The Duchess refuses.

They settle in to live at solid and peaceful Claremont Park in Surrey with its wide gardens and rustling fountains. Not only is she drenched with happiness because of Leopold—he will allow no interference from the Regent or the Queen. He and his "astonishingly impressionable and nervously sensitive darling" are ecstatic just to be with each other. She loves him as she has not been allowed to feel about anyone before this. She can confide in him. "My mother is bad," she tells him, "but she would not have been as bad as she is if my father had not been infinitely worse."

In May they know they are going to have a child.

Lord Weiler is in regular attendance on Charlotte. She is to have a special *accoucheur* as well; a long, thin man, Sir Richard Croft, who demands blind obedience from his patients. After three months Lord Weiler becomes convinced of the folly of Croft's treatment. But Charlotte depends on Croft and Croft is very obstinate about his method. When Charlotte's spirits are too high Croft counteracts this with further bleedings.

On November 3, Charlotte is taken ill. Croft is constantly with her. He tells her it is absolutely vital that she eat nothing. He will not allow Lord Weiler into the room but passes medical bulletins to him through the half-open door.

At nine o'clock at night, November 5, Charlotte's baby is born dead. At midnight, Charlotte's body begins to turn unaccountably cold. At two o'clock on the morning of November 6, she is dead.

Croft kills himself.

In the sixteenth century, the ruins remaining of the Convent of Sant'Andrea are bought from the Bishop of Como by Tolomeo, Cardinal Gallio. The Cardinal becomes very rich, as holy men can, is made the Marquis de Scaldasole, feels he should entertain more and more and, by the time of his death in 1615, has expanded, improved and adorned the lovely buildings on the shore of the loveliest lake in Europe. He calls it the Villa Salvadore after the most important woman in north Italy. It is inherited by his nephew, the Duke of Alvito. The Sultan of Morocco asks to be allowed to visit it with his slaves, monkeys, multiturbans and protective scimitars. On the death of the Duke, the Villa Salvadore goes to his nephew, the Marquis Calderara, one of the wealthiest and most dissolute patricians of his time.

After a century of decline the property is restored and embellished. The Princess of Wales finds it in the summer of 1816. She has to have its aristocratic isolation, its magnificent gardens and its soul-mending prospect. The house is now owned by Contessa Gina Salvadore over two hundred years after her progenitors had built it. She makes it a condition of sale that the deed must state that she deprives herself of the villa only in order to satisfy a royal wish.

The Princess wants many alterations and changes to be made. She settles in to go to work on these when the news of Charlotte's death reaches her.

"I've known life was going to be bad ever since I was a little girl and they left me alone with strangers," Caroline tells Lady Anglesong. She has been drinking brandy for seven hours. "But I never knew it would get as bad as this. It was always a heavy but comical thing to me. I could joke with it. I could poke sticks into it and make it dance for me. What do I do now? Do I change because of my dead baby? I cannot. My little girl is gone, but no one but you and me knows her death means anything to me. They never gave me anything else but Charlotte and I don't want their pity. It is bad enough that we must all learn that the very beginning is the end of the end. I am losing myself inside myself. I never thought I could do that. Now she is gone. My daughter is gone before I saw her again. Life was my father once. I went out to meet life but he stood there and, blocking the way, became life. After that what was the choice? The Prince—the kind, witty, hopelessly unselfish and considerate Prince. The choice was small, my dear. So Charlotte is gone and I am life. I have become the threat to be jeered at and poked with a stick to make it dance. I am life, but no one will know I ever lived. Charlotte is dead and now I know duty is important, that loyalty counts as gold. One is the mother so one must love the child. While she is alive. One must not use her as a hook of revenge against a man who has no meaning even to himself. Now that she is dead I want to be loyal.

"But why? Hey? Why? Only the thought of him keeps me alive. Charlotte is dead so I can see that I can live in a perfect way by adoring her and forgiving him. I would find peace. Charlotte is telling me that, but I cannot. It is too late to settle for peace. I want revenge. I want to see him broken and insane. I want to live five minutes longer than he lives to see him dead—ruined. Charlotte is dead, but life must become a comic turn again. I will make them all laugh until their malice glows—if they will promise me revenge."

It takes four days before Pergami and Lady Anglesong can get the Princess sober. When she has been stabilized in cold, wet bed sheets to lift her body temperature and reduce movement, Lady Joyce sits beside her as the Princess's china-blue blank eyes stare at the top of the window frame. Lady Joyce persuades her to take part of her Household to embark on a cruise of the Mediterranean.

The Regent thinks of Charlotte when he drinks alone. When he is allowed to talk and move and to think off the top of his head, no thought of her ever comes to him, but he is unable to persuade even the closest friends to stay on and on through night after night to keep him talking and moving. When she comes back into his mind, he wants to scream. She is not unkind as she stands there gazing at him. But he knows about unkindness and who has been unkind. If he drinks more she is more sharply seen, so he must reach for the laudanum bottle to fade her down and down into a wash drawing, then, as his mind collapses from the fatigue of his self-hatred, into an evanescence.

If only he had been able to think of her as his daughter he might never have struck her, he might never have humiliated her. If only his mother had been strong and had prevailed over his father to force a marriage with Princess Louise of Mecklenburg-Strelitz. She was unfeeling. She would have lain upon the wedding bed like a Prussian soldier at attention and received his royal seed so that he might have had a daughter who was his daughter, not a mockery.

Ah, Charlotte, Charlotte—you were a delightful child.

You were strong. You were a woman with your mind determined to have ascendence over anyone who denied you. If you had been my mother, by God, you would not have been my daughter, he thought drunkenly. Years and years and years of worry about such a wonderful child becoming a woman and somehow being taken upon the shoulders of the mob to sweep him out of palaces and place her on the throne and he need never have done that. He could have loved her. He could have used her innocence to bring serenity to jagged times. He could have behaved so much differently that she could have loved him.

The gin and the laudanum lock together like robotic lovers. He sees all of their connected lives in a brilliant light. If he grieved because he had never loved his daughter, or shown her in any way that he had wanted to love her, did his father, mired in madness, think day and night of how he could have changed his life if he had only loved his eldest son?

When Ernest is told the news of Charlotte's death by his wife, Princess Frederica of Mecklenburg-Strelitz, who is also his niece and unopposedly chosen by his mother, he drawls, "Sad, I suppose, but could be for the best. She had the makings of a little radical, that one, and the first thing you know we would have had Catholic Emancipation."

6

The Princess of Wales, Pergami, Willikin and members of the Household are conveyed to Palermo by HMS *Sea Brigand,* a warship having a full crew complement, a facility arranged for by Lady Anglesong through the Whigs in the House of Commons so that the Princess might find a change to affect her bereavement over the loss of the Princess Charlotte. The Regent does not dare to nullify this.

There is not much room aboard for the royal party. Captain Briggs, R.N., puts them in the three sleeping rooms at the far end of the wardroom that fills the entire afterpart of the ship. The largest, on the port side, is fitted up for the Princess. This cabin has a door opening into the wardroom. The cabin next to this goes to the Countess Oldi. This cabin has no door into the wardroom but opens into a third cabin which is to be occupied by the Princess's maids. Pergami is to doss down elsewhere in the ship. All arrangements are made at considerable inconvenience to the officers of the *Sea Brigand,* so Captain Briggs is considerably annoyed when Her Royal Highness insists upon certain remarkable alterations. Countess Oldi's cabin is to be given to Pergami, and the blond, golden Oldi is to sleep elsewhere. Her Royal Highness has no objection to her maids remaining in the third cabin, but the door leading from the middle cabin to the maids' cabin must be nailed shut. A new door is to be cut into the bulkhead so it will open into the wardroom a few feet from the adjoining door to Caroline's cabin.

Captain Briggs, who sleeps in a cabin at the opposite end of the wardroom, testifies later that he never saw or heard anything that could make him speculate. Naturally, he is frequently called on deck at all hours. The wardroom is unlighted at night.

The Princess is enchanted to see Palermo from the sea, on an island which was colonized by the Phoenicians, the Greeks, the Carthaginians, the Romans, the Barbarians, the Arabs, the Normans, the Swabians, the Spanish, the English, and the French. As Caroline approaches the city, Sicily is ruled by King Ferdinand IV, a Bourbon, the family which established the great baroque architecture of Sicily.

A glittering deputation comes aboard to fetch the Princess, bringing a brass band, three banners and two flower strewers. But when Caroline goes ashore, the reception is chilling under the eyes of the British ambassador. Ferdinand IV is entirely watchful of the wishes of the British government. He knows, as few Italians seem to know, that the Princess of Wales is royalty in disgrace; the wife of a ruler who regards her as his enemy.

Caroline refuses a carriage after this reception. She walks through the streets of the city to Palazzo Butera, which has been assigned to her. She descends the Corse Maria Pia di Giorgio from the Porta Nuova leaving the royal palace behind her and walks through a file of great baroque palaces on either side of the street. She passes across the Piazza Bellini, a substantial crowd collecting behind her, attracted by her entourage and her gaiety. Just beyond the church of Santa Maria dell'Ammiraglio she is guided into the small palace. Her first act is to appear on its balcony to curtsey and wave and cry out joyous greetings in Italian to the now very large crowd that has followed her. They cheer. They sing. She sings back to them with that awful voice. They collect one band, then many bands to play for her.

The next evening, moving under veils and in secrecy, the Princess slips alone through the darkness in a closed carriage to enter the royal palazzo by a covert entrance. A Sicilian army officer conducts her to the King. His iciness is gone. He throws his arms around her, as there is no British ambassador present to inhibit him. "You are so kind to understand that I must do as I did at your reception on the pier because, you know—and I am sorry to say it— if it weren't for the British, I wouldn't be here."

"Of course, of course," the Princess cries like a gull. "And what is the difference? You have placated my husband, who is a fool, and when I leave you must think of a way to make it even more insulting."

"Cold, yes," the King says. "Unfriendly, yes. But never insulting. The people love you. I know what happened outside the Palazzo Butera yesterday. No, no, please. Have you ever had a Sicilian sweetie?"

"You are the first Sicilian I have ever met."

"No, no!" he laughs. "I mean sweeties—candies—*crispeddi di Riso alla Benedittina, susamele, 'nfasciatelle, nucatuli, nippitiddata, pignoccata.* Have you never tasted any of these?"

"Never."

The King summons food and drink. An array of thirty cakes and candies are set out on a tray. They drink Marsala. "My dear Princess," he says as they nibble, "if there is anything I may do for you you have only to—"

"There is one little thing."

"Name it!"

"My Equerry, Chevalier Pergami, a fine Italian family

—his sister is the Contessa Oldi?—very noble people—has just bought a Sicilian property—the Villa Franchina—near Taormina?—between Taormina and Messina?—a small property for holidays."

"Nice there," the King says.

"He has discovered that an amusing title accompanies ownership of the property—a title which merely requires certification by you."

"You wish official documents?"

"Of course."

"Well! We do a large commerce in these things, you know. It is not as easy as it seems."

"You have only to sign a paper."

"Aha! You see? You think that is all. Everyone thinks that at first. But a search must be made; great care taken. We have the responsibility of dealing with the past and future at the same time, you see. It is an expensive thing."

"How much?"

"Well! Generally, if such a request came to me from anyone else—but in this case we face a request from a member of the Household of the Princess of Wales—so—under the circumstances—"

"How much?"

"I would say—five thousand pounds?"

"Whaaaaat?"

"Oh, yes."

"My dear Ferdinand, I must say—"

"That would be for the *normal* request," he adds hastily. But—for your own Equerry—well! Surely a thousand pounds wouldn't be too much?"

"Fifty pounds."

"Fifty pounds?"

"All right. Fifty-five."

"This is utterly grotesque!"

"May I have the document now?"

"Yes," he says sullenly, wishing her to leave at soonest.

"Very good, Ferdinand. Fifty-five pounds to cover the cost of ink, paper and research. Please send for the form now so that you may sign it for me."

The royal party is to leave Palermo the next afternoon aboard the *Wendoon,* Captain McCarry, R.N., commanding. On the voyage to Palermo Captain Briggs had insisted that Pergami eat at the upper servants' table. Captain McCarry has been well briefed by Captain Briggs. When the Princess sends word that Pergami has been received into the Sicilian peerage by King Ferdinand IV and carries Letters Patent attesting so, and will therefore be dining at the Princess's table, Captain McCarry responds with a note requesting that Pergami dine by himself. McCarry is an autocrat, a fine English gentleman, and he can no more stomach dining with this man Briggs had told him was actually a barber than he could dine with one of his boatswains.

His suggestion is not well received.

Captain McCarry is to take the royal party across the Mediterranean to the Holy Land. Because of his delicate feeling, the Princess informs him that his services will be required only as far as Syracuse, on the south side of Sicily. It is an uncomfortable trip from Palermo. The Princess refuses to speak to the Captain. He presides morosely at one table with his officers. The Princess dines with the Barone della Franchina and his sister, the Contessa Oldi, at another table.

From Syracuse the royal party goes by muleback

across the mountains to Catania, through bandit country. The Barone brings the party through safely to the Palazzo Ursino. The Contessa Oldi returns to Italy. The Princess and the beautiful young man proceed to forget about the rest of the world. When they are exhausted by nearly perpetual love-making made possible by the local drinking water, the Princess orders the Barone to find them a sailing vessel to continue the voyage to Jerusalem.

Pergami finds a large trading polacre commanded by a Catanian named Fincari. By a stroke of luck they are able to hire the services of an English sea captain. Called Captain John Reese, he is actually the third member of The Milan Commission and winks at Pergami with his off eye as he comes aboard. Pergami tells the Princess. She is utterly delighted to be employing the man employed by her husband to spy upon her, and because she is giggling so much she tells Captain Reese she has liked jolly tars all her life because they make such fine bedfellows. Reese acknowledges this with a small bow and an anxious smile. That night she invites him to her rooms at the Palazzo Ursino and seduces him. Pergami walks in on them while it is going on, appears startled, does his best to leave, but looks directly into the policeman's face, creating a quandary for Reese as might regard his testimony against the Princess involving what had happened on the voyage to the Holy Land.

The Bey of Tunis receives the Princess and the Barone della Franchina in a blaze of Oriental color and magnificence. He gives Caroline a superb squadron of camel cavalry as her own male slaves, "to do with as you will," to accompany her on an extended expedition to last for nine days in the desert with silk tents, cushions, and a large quantity of the Bey's own Faithful Peace *bhang* and an equal amount of Haroun-al-Raschid *hasheesh.* It is decided after the first evening of smoking at the palace that the Barone della Franchina and Captain Reese are not to accompany the Princess into the desert with her twelve-man squadron of slaves. The Bey is more than hospitable. He arranges for two squads of female slaves to attend the two men, bringing with them an equal supply of good cheroots. The weed totally blanks out Captain Reese's memory. He tells Colonel Heller later, "We had these funny cheroots, then—blotto—I cannot remember a thing which happened before or after that on the entire cruise."

The Princess, not usually a smoker, lights up while on her white camel leaving the palace. When she returns from the expedition, Pergami tells her he has never seen a happier-looking woman. "Oh, Bartie!" she says. "I had a glorious time. And those slaves! I don't know when I'll ever be able to sit down again. I can hardly *pee!*"

Word of their arrival is sent ahead to Malta, through the Bey. When the royal party arrives there, the Barone della Franchina is elected a Knight of Malta. Henceforth, not only will he be able to wear the coveted Cross of the Order at the base of his cravat, but he is entitled to be addressed as Chevalier.

In order to insure his election it is necessary that Caroline advance him somewhat in military rank from *maresciallo d'allogio,* which is a corporal's rating, to the rank of full colonel. After the royal party leaves Malta, when the Knights open the confidential letter left behind by Captain Reese and learn the truth about the new knight, the Council of Knights is dissuaded only by the possibility of their own humiliation from expelling him.

From Malta, the polacre, re-christened the *Royal Charlotte,* sails to Athens, then up the Bosporus to Constantinople, then to Mytilene, Chios, Ephesus and Cyprus. Throughout the voyage Caroline sleeps in a tent on deck. The weather is hot and calm. The tent also encloses the Chevalier Barone, who always attends the Princess of Wales when she bathes in her cabin. Captain Reese, still a bit addled by *bhang*, for he has invested in a year's supply of it, attempts notes but almost all of these drift into fantasies. Frequently the Princess orders that the tent be closed "for fifteen minutes or so" in the daytime, and sportive noises are heard inside the tent. Often, the Princess kisses the Chevalier Barone while seated on his knee on the capstan.

At Jaffa, the royal party takes the pilgrim road to the Holy City. They travel by night to avoid the heat. They find Jerusalem on an early morning. It is under Turkish domination. They stay in a monastery but, tirelessly in the crippling heat, they visit the Holy Sepulchre, Mount Calvary, the Chamber of the Last Supper, the underground chapels and David's Tomb. To please the Princess, the dignitaries of the Christian church elect Chevalier Bartolomeo, Barone della Franchina, into the Knights of the Holy Sepulchre. To cap all the honors Pergami has had heaped upon him Caroline forms her own order: The Order of St. Caroline of Jerusalem and proclaims it upon parchments carrying a red and green seal:

BY THIS PRESENT, SUBSCRIBED BY THE HAND OF HER ROYAL HIGHNESS, THE PRINCESS OF WALES, AND BEARING HER SEAL, HER ROYAL HIGHNESS INSTITUTES AND CREATES A NEW ORDER, TO RECOMPENSE THE FAITHFUL KNIGHTS WHO HAVE HAD THE HONOR OF ACCOMPANYING HER TO THE HOLY LAND.

FIRST: THIS ORDER SHALL BE GIVEN AND WORN ONLY BY THOSE WHO HAVE ACCOMPANIED HER ROYAL HIGHNESS TO JERUSALEM, EXCEPT HER PHYSICIAN, DOTTORE MAXIMUS JUNGSTEIN, WHO, BY HIS NEED TO SERVE BOTANY AT HOME, COULD NOT FOLLOW HER.

SECOND: THE COLONEL, CHEVALIER BARTOLOMEO PERGAMI, BARONE DELLA FRANCHINA, KNIGHT OF MALTA, KNIGHT OF THE HOLY SEPULCHRE OF JERUSALEM, EQUERRY OF HER ROYAL HIGHNESS, SHALL BE GRAND MASTER OF THE ORDER AND HIS CHILDREN, MALES AS WELL AS FEMALES, SHALL SUCCEED HIM, AND SHALL HAVE THE HONOR TO WEAR THE SAME ORDER FROM GENERATION TO GENERATION FOREVER.

THIRD: THE GRAND MASTER SHALL WEAR THE CROSS ROUND HIS NECK; THE OTHER KNIGHTS SHALL BE OBLIGED TO WEAR IT AT THE BUTTONHOLE AT THE LEFT SIDE OF THEIR COATS.

FOURTH: THE ABOVE-MENTIONED ORDER CONSISTS OF A RED CROSS WITH THE MOTTO: *HONI SOIT QUI MAL Y PENSE* AND SHALL BE CALLED BY THE NAME OF ST. CAROLINE OF JERUSALEM. THE RIBBON SHALL BE LILAC AND SILVER.

CAROLINE

Princess of Wales

Two and a half months later the royal party is landed at Porto d'Anzio; Captain Reese still unfocused, still listening to a different entire orchestra. Under an escort of Papal Dragoons arranged by Lady Joyce Anglesong, they travel in carriages to Rome. "The Papal escort is not only to madden the Prince," Anglesong tells the Princess. "When your inevitable struggle begins in England, this will enlist the powerful body of English Roman Catholics on your side."

The Princess returns to the Villa d'Este, as she has re-
named the house at Lake Como. She chooses this name
because, according to genealogists, both the House of
Brunswick and the House of Hanover descended from a
certain Guelfo d'Este who left Germany for Italy in A.D.
1054. In her private apartments, the Princess takes great
pleasure in placing a large statue of Venus crowned by
Eros (attributed to Canova). It is surely the most beautiful
house in the most beautiful setting in Europe; totally restored and refurbished. She senses she will never be lonely
here because her Household consists of eighty people, over
sixty of whom live with her in the villa. She has eleven
carriages and forty-eight horses and a ship to voyage happily on the lake with a captain and a crew of eight.

When she returns from her pilgrimage to the Holy
Land, she finds a common circular letter sent out to all
British embassies to advise her of Princess Charlotte's
death, the only official word of it she ever receives. But, to
her joy, there is a letter from Malmesbury.

Constantinople

My dear Princess:

Because I know how greatly you can rejoice, my heart
falls now because I know how you have grieved upon
the death of your daughter. If I were only able to
assume some part of this burden! If there were only

some way I could have turned you in the maze which is
life which would have allowed the Prince to melt his
heart toward you so that you could have been able to
share your grief with the father of the dear girl you
have lost—but that is the vanity and arrogance of a man
who has thought about your life so much, wherever he
had been summoned to appear in this world. Always, I
have cherished fantasies of happiness for you and, while
they were only being enacted within my heart there was
no need to confront the reality of: what might have
been, can never be. Our lives march. Our memories
remain where they must, where there was gentleness
and charm and so much light.

Enter your grief and experience it, that you may shed
it at the time when it must be allowed to leave you.
Think of her as a happy, dear child—as I think of you
as a happy, loving young woman who saw the future
and rushed to meet it. That this future is now past
merely means that there is a future for you—and for all
of us.

Malmesbury.

To sauce up the days for the agents of The Milan
Commission who have been planted in her Household, the
Princess hangs pictures of the Barone della Franchina, in
his various robes of state, in every room of the villa and
upon all the plate in the dining room. Pergami is her tower
of strength. Anglesong reports to Henry Brougham, "He
is a remarkably good sort of a man." His brother, Louis,
becomes First Equerry; his sister, the Contessa Oldi,
is First Lady-in-Waiting; his mother superintends the
linen; his little daughter calls the Princess "Mama." The
Barone's bedroom connects with Caroline's.

The Princess is intensely happy with her domestic
life, but she is outraged to hear that the Regent is secretly
trying on various ideas for marrying as soon as The Milan
Commission provides the divorce for him. "It is preposter-

ous!" she tells Anglesong. "They offer him the daughter of
Victor Emmanuel, King of Sardinia. Sardinia! Because the
father is the great-grandson of Anne of Orleans, granddaughter of Charles I; a Stuart claimant to the throne. And
other brokers are trying to cook up a different match with
the Princess of Tours and Taxis."

"Metternich is at the bottom of that one," Lady Joyce
says.

"They are ghouls! Am I dead? They should know well
that he is never, never going to succeed in getting a divorce
from me. And if, by God, by some evil unforeseen machi-
nation that does happen—what of his true wife, Mrs.
Fitzherbert? You may be sure that I would be damned sure
that was raised again!"

By and large, worry is merely an affectation of the
Princess's. There is too much joy to be bothered with her
husband's problems. She is enthralled to have the famous
poet, Barnardo Bellini, who is much about her at the Villa
d'Este, to wander through the gardens with her, chanting
unrestrained lyrics about her beauty and her many won-
derments.

She becomes well-loved in every sense of the word by
the local peasantry because she overflows with generosity
and has so much interest in their beautiful brown children.
When the peasants of Cernobbio dance under a new moon
on festival nights, the animated Princess (who now also
signs herself Caroline d'Este) appears among them. Styles
of dancing loosen and the wine flows and the night goes on.
The Princess herself sets the pattern of the choreography,
taking on all comers as it were, giggling while couples
dance away into the obscurity of shadows, and barking
indelicate winey jokes when her Household argues that it
is time to go home.

The old King begins to die late in the summer of 1819.

The Whigs prepare their moves. Caroline begins with her obsession that she must claim her rights to be proclaimed Queen of England when the moment arrives. The Milan Commission is taken off its guard when it is told that the Princess and her suite have vanished from the Villa d'Este. The house and its outbuildings are locked; shutters are drawn. It is dreadful news for Colonel Heller, as it might possibly portend a sudden landing of the Princess in England, an event which the Whigs would most certainly combine with dangerous popular demonstrations in her favor. News flashes are rushed to London daily. Every British embassy and consulate on the Continent is ordered to search for her. Italy is scoured.

The Princess travels with Pergami under the name of Evalina Rosa Cacciare, using a "specially designed" passport which Lady Anglesong has procured from her cousin, Generale Melvini-Sestero. Lady Joyce has rushed to England to participate in the organization of the Princess's strike through the Whigs. The Princess is "recognized" in Parma because she insists upon alighting from her coach to listen to a man who sells vegetables from a barrow sing the entire part of Don Ottavio (a tenor betrothed to Donna Anna) in Mozart's *Don Giovanni*. He sings with the most glorious voice Caroline has ever heard. "There has never been a tenor like this!" she tells Pergami excitedly. "Why isn't he singing from the stages of the great opera houses of the world? Go! Ask him that, Bartie!"

The Barone is first to reach the singer's side while one-third of the city of Parma, hanging out of windows and surrounding the vegetable market, applauds wildly.

"The lady who weeps with joy at the beauty of your voice, in the carriage directly behind me," Pergami says to the barrow man, "is about to become the Queen of England."

The barrow man shrugs.

"She has bid me ask you why you are not singing at La Scala—and at all the other great theaters of the world."

The man answers. The worldly Pergami jaw drops. He returns to the Princess.

"Is it a hoax?" she asks. "Is he really the great Carpuccio Limon or one of the others?"

Pergami shakes his head.

"Then—why? Why is he singing here, instead of—out there?"

"Because," Pergami says slowly, "he said to me that he doesn't like to work at night. He told me the daytime is for singing. Night is for making love."

The Princess delivers a great whoop. She leaps out of the coach and sprints across the cobblestones of the marketplace, tugging at her purse. She throws her arms around the barrow man and kisses him with abandon. "If there were only time, you would make love tonight with the Queen of England!" She drops gold sovereigns into his hand, gives the crotch of his trousers a little squeeze, a little pat, then runs back to the carriage. The crowd roars its approval. Standing on the steps to the coach's door she shouts to them, smiling. "Ladies!" she yells in Italian. "Do this one thing for a woman who must hurry to meet her destiny." She raises her arm and points to the barrow man. "If that man can make love the way he can sing—why are you all just standing there?"

The crowd booms out its joy. The barrow man deserts his produce and begins to run. Pergami follows the Princess into the carriage.

A policeman named Colla, agent of Generale Melvini-Sestero, arranges for Lady Joyce to plant a horrendous piece of information on the desk of the one-eyed Count von Neipperg who passes it instantly to Nasalli, Governor of

Piacenza, who flings it away from himself to the British. The Prince-Regent sees instantly that it is clearly not a piece of information the Italians could have invented to prove their efficiency because it would have been impossible for them to have known its ramifications. The dispatch says:

> The young prince, William Austin, has many times declared openly that it is his fixed plan, when the time is deemed right, to return to England to contest his rights to the throne with his father.

The dispatch causes the Prince-Regent to believe that Colonel Heller is in the employ of the Whigs because the Regent knows Heller must have been hiding this information from him for some time. He summons Heller to England. They meet at Carlton House while Heller is still travel-stained.

"May I be allowed to suggest," Heller says, addressing the Regent, "that this is quite the wrong time for me to be away from Italy. I am directing a search for the Princess. We had established a pattern of movement which is quite characteristic."

"Heller?"

"Yes, Sir?"

"I have proof of your treachery."

"*Treachery?*"

"You have sold me to the Whigs."

"I? I—Franz Marx Heller, the man most loyal to you in the world, have sold you to the Whigs?" He cannot put it together. He strangles on his incomprehension.

"If you are not a traitor, you are the stupidest man in my service! Do you know the boy, Austin, is going to make his claim to the throne after his mother has been crowned?"

"No, Sir."

"What do you know then? You or your corrupt Commission, which has been spending England's money in Italy for three years—from Italy to the Middle East and back. What *do* you know then?"

Heller stands at attention. "We know we have built an airtight case against the Princess. When this case is set down before your Cabinet, there will not be a Minister who will not demand that the Princess be tried for adulterous, criminal conduct and flagrant misuse of funds."

"Never mind the misuse of funds."

"We have the case, Sir. She can hide, but if she sets foot in England, the record of what she has done with her body, her rank, and England's money will find her convicted, exiled forever, and denied the throne, beyond any question of a doubt. *This*, then, is what I know, Sir."

"All right! Now, I tell you this. If this case which you claim to have built over three years does not result in conviction and sentencing, I am going to strip you of your rank, have you given thirty lashes before the assembled German Legion, and then you will be sent back, penniless, to the most dripping, farthest north German forest to live in a goatherd's hut for the rest of your days. If you have bungled this, Heller, you have bungled your life."

8

Lady Anglesong waits bareheaded as the six-coach equipage of the Princess of Wales draws up at the Hotel du Côte
d'Or in Saulieu, France. When the Princess alights, Lady
Joyce holds out her slim wrists from her side and does her
best to curtsey. With a passionate, trembling voice she
says, "You are Queen!"

The King had died at thirty-two minutes past eight
o'clock on the evening of the 29th January. At fifty-seven,
the Prince-Regent is King; his wife, at fifty-one, the Queen
of England.

From the moment of the Proclamation of Accession
by the aged Garter King of Arms, the new King—im-
mobilized by the thought that the same proclamation has
made the woman he hates most in the world his Queen—
is stricken with pneumonia. Everyone gives up hope of his
recovery.

The Whigs pray for his recovery with deep earnestness. They have invested long years in Caroline. She is the
only lever they have to lift the King out of place among the
Tories into a government made for him by the Whigs.

When the King crawls out of his sickbed on February
14, the first feeble move he makes is toward the prayer
books in his library. He is looking for a precedent which
will support his determination to forbid Church congregations to pray for the well-being of his wife, and to exclude
her name and title from the liturgy, that list of royal names

included in all prayers by all Englishmen, asking God's blessing for them. He reasons that there is no quicker way to signal to the people that she is neither his Queen nor theirs.

The Archbishop of Canterbury does not concur in this; neither do some members of his cabinet. The King insists. He knows he has fallen upon the most credible stroke of his career. Lengthy deliberations are held until the government agrees that the King's wife should not be included in the liturgy and that she may not be crowned Queen. A memorandum of quite stunning length is produced which essentially makes these points: that although the government deprecates the conduct of "the Princess" as they carefully refer to her when writing to the King, they cannot recommend a divorce. They suggest instead that "the Princess" be given an additional allowance on the condition that she remain abroad, which they confidently expect she will do rather than face the evidence of The Milan Commission.

The King reads the memorandum "with much regret." His own lawyer, Sir Edward Masters, explains to him carefully that if a divorce action is taken up, the King could expect "every sort of charge" to be piled upon him by his wife's lawyers.

"I will face that gladly!" the King exclaims. "Gladly, gladly, if I can rid myself for all time of that unspeakable woman! And what of the evidence against *her*? By God, I have never seen anything quite so damning as that! When that fellow Pergami, whom Heller has all trussed up and ready to testify in an English court, tells his story, there is nothing she can say against me which can have the slightest weight. Hear me, Masters. Go you now to the Prime Minister and tell him I shall look for another government if we cannot agree to bring forward a Bill of Divorce."

A thunderous meeting is held. The discussion smokes with acrimony. The King orders the Prime Minister out of the room. He commands Wellington—*Wellington!*—to hold his tongue. When the Lord Chancellor says divorce is a matter of conscience, the King snarls, "My Lord, I know your conscience always interferes except where your interest is concerned."

Underlying the struggles over this apparent matter is the necessity of an enlarged Civil List which the King must have if his creditors are to be quieted. If he can gain extended powers to create additional peers and knights, if he can control more well-paying government posts to be handed to people to whom he owes money, he will be greatly relieved. But so far the government has refused to sanction such a bill.

No responsible minister can be persuaded to form or join a new government. "Damn all of you, then!" the King shrills. "I shall sack you all and throw the sack into the streets. The Whigs are standing waiting out there in the cold. There is no one unable to justify a Whig government."

"Except you, Sir," Lord Sissons says.

"Me?"

"The Whigs have spent seven years and a ton of money on the cause of the Princess. They are committed. They will not discard their most formidable weapon, Sir."

"By God, they would do so to get back into power!" A surge of elation sweeps over the King. He can have his Civil List and his divorce and see that his wife is betrayed all at one time.

"Oh, yes. To get to power. But when they come to power, they will pass so many reforms as to make you less a King," Sissons tells him. "Oh, yes. They will cut her very throat for you if you will meet all the terms they will present before they will do you the service of coming into power."

The King gives way. He takes what comfort there is from the cabinet's promise to institute proceedings for divorce should "the Princess" return to England.

9

With Anglesong, the Queen pushes on from Saulieu to the Channel. "Tell them any merchant ship or frigate will do for me," the Queen says as they roll along the French roads. "I will not insist upon the royal yacht. And tell them I will reside at the old Queen's house in Greenwich Park without any alterations or expense to the nation."

"And what else shall I tell them?"

"You may tell them that I take it in very bad part," Caroline says huskily, "that they have removed my name from the liturgy."

"The government is ready to offer you an additional fifty thousand pounds a year if you will relinquish the title of Queen or any other title indicating any relationship with the royal family."

"I cannot rescind being his cousin, can I, Anglesong? Or should I place a notice in a London paper saying that I resign as his cousin? I want my Georgie. My sweet, little Georgie-Porgie. I am Queen. Where is my darling King?"

The journey is broken at St. Omer, at the Channel, for a formal meeting with Lord Coomber, representing the King. Coomber owns Tory newspapers. The meeting is held in a low-ceilinged room on a dark, wet day. When the Queen enters, Lord Coomber begins to speak. She silences him. "You will speak only when I say I want to hear what you have to say, which will be never," Caroline says. "I have granted you the privilege of this meeting. That will save your face with your master. Tell him this: the Queen of the realm wishes to be informed through the First Minister to the King of the realm, for which reason or motive the Queen's name has been excluded from the liturgy."

Coomber attempts to answer. She cuts him off by turning away and leaving the room. Coomber, red-faced and panting with rage, strides out of the room. Anglesong joins the Queen.

"You have declared war," Anglesong says.

"No. That was declared twenty-four years ago," the Queen answers. "At about three days before I married him."

Anglesong performs her duty as the Whig Party's conscience: "As your political adviser, I entreat Your Majesty to reflect patiently upon the step about to be taken. Perhaps it would be far better to accept the generous annuity on the understanding that it would be granted without any renunciation of rank or title or right, and with a pledge from the government that you should be acknowledged and received abroad by all diplomatic agents according to your rank and station."

"Fortunately, I know you don't mean that, Anglesong."

"Nonetheless, Your Majesty, I must so state it."

"My answer is no."

"Then we are going to England?"

"If my husband is to be crowned, then I will be crowned."

"My duty also binds me to say that, if you return, you must do so secretly. A public exhibition could be harmful to the country's peace."

"I shall leave in five minutes for the drive to Calais," the Queen says. "There I shall board some ordinary packet steamer. If the English people choose to welcome me home, I cannot change that."

Lord Coomber sends a message to the King by waiting naval dispatch vessel. It foams with indignation.

It is impossible for me to paint for Your Majesty the insolence, the violence, and the precipitation of this woman's conduct. We have never seen anything so outrageous, so undignified, or so unamiable. She has assumed a tone and hauteur which is quite insufferable and nothing but the purest and least impeached innocence could justify. We have, at length, come to a final and ultimate issue. She has set the King's authority at defiance and it is now time for her to feel his vengeance and his power. Patience, forebearance, and moderation have had no effect upon her. I must now implore Your Majesty to exert all your firmness and resolution. The Queen has thrown down the gauntlet of defiance. The King must take it up.

10

The Queen embarks with Lady Anglesong and Willikin, age eighteen, upon the Channel packet boat, *Alain de Montreuil*. It is a rough crossing, so bad that the ship is kept offshore by the height of the waves outside Dover harbor and by contrary tides. But the crowds that gather at the sea-front are so vast that the shops have put up their shutters. Although there is a high wind and rough seas, Her Majesty orders the Captain to lower a boat because she is determined not to disappoint the people of Dover. As the ship's boat carries the royal party landward, the guns of the Dover fort break out in a royal salute. The Governor of Dover will suffer later for this observance of standing orders.

The Queen of England steps ashore in a wide black hat and a flowing lavender pelisse, as attractive and as forward-looking as any adventuress; then she is lost at the center of the surrounding mob of cheering men and weeping women, excited children, officers, sailors, shopkeepers, and soldiers. The noises are joyous. The body scents are strong. An avenue is broken through the crowd. The Queen swans through, gloriously pleased and wondrously triumphant, into Snargate Street and Wright's Hotel where an even greater crowd, more lustily cheering, awaits her. There are six brass bands. Shouted slogans and various short speaking parts have been assigned to paid members of the mob, all drawn from Lady Anglesong's stock company. The demonstrators have been well rehearsed in London by Whig political technicians. At the entrance to Wright's Hotel, the reliable bit player from County Limerick, Daisy Hanly, who has "done" the Queen twice already in popular demonstrations, falls to her knees sobbing and clutches Caroline around the knees. "T'ank God yer home saaafe, me gracious Queen!" she shouts. "An' duh English peepul will keep yuh safe from all harm from yer husband." Miss Hanly is led away weeping into a large yellow handkerchief as a platoon of kilted pipers shrills the Queen into the hotel with "The Laird's Doubloons." There, in the main front hall, a massed Welsh choir sends heavenward the massive pipe organ sounds of "Road to the Sea" (and other popular favorites). Anglesong signs to the Queen to stand listening to the end of it. It is an exhausting experience. Throughout the welcome, Sir Thomas Buckley's men are observing all details, which will be flown to their newspapers in London by pigeon. The tribute the nation is paying to their persecuted Queen is about to enter history.

After a short rest and some light refreshment the Queen attempts to nap while excited crowds rush back and forth beneath her window shouting and singing and repeating again and again the most popular slogan: "No Queen, No King."

In the late afternoon the carriages for the Queen draw up at the door of the hotel. The Queen and Lady Anglesong enter one carriage. Willikin rides, as though in high state, in the carriage that follows them. Instantly the horses are unharnessed and men take their places in the traces. Flowers are showered down upon her. Little babies are lifted up to be kissed. Church bells peal. It gets through to the much larger, unpaid portion of the enormous crowds that not only are they having a paid holiday and a thoroughly good time, but they are shouting and demonstrating on behalf of an *injured* Queen.

The men draw the carriage to the outskirts of the town where the horses are harnessed again.

Caroline spends the night at Canterbury, reaching the Fountain Hotel at nine o'clock. The mayor and members of the corporation are waiting for her, but the mayor's speech of welcome cannot be heard above the outcries of the crowd, which had been carried on ahead of the royal party in the afternoon so that the Whigs could be certain the Queen would have the mobs, noise, and applause.

The Queen's party, a procession that grows longer and longer, leaves for London, via Greenwich, the next morning on a perfect English day. Thousands line the way. The Whigs have shipped in quantities of copies of all three of Sir Thomas Buckley's newspapers, which spell out the excitement of the Queen's progress toward London. Two hundred and eleven babies are conceived on this day in southeast England, due to patriotism, only 61 percent being legitimate. Pickpockets make gross earnings of more than £2300.

At seven o'clock that evening, the Queen's open carriage crosses Westminster Bridge in London. She and Anglesong have been joined by Lady Jane Montant and the Contessa Gina Salvadore. The Queen wears a sombre mourning dress with an Elizabethan ruff out of respect for the loss of her uncle, King George III, and for the wattles at her throat. The second carriage contains Willikin, seated alone, taking the cheers easily, soberly. The third carriage is filled with Italian servants but no member of the Queen's Italian Household—neither the Chevalier Barone della Franchina nor his sister has come to England.

The streets are blocked with carts and carriages. Londoners have been professionally worked into the same state of happy hysteria as the people of Dover. The progress of the Queen's carriage is exceedingly slow but she bears this with great good humor. Sir Thomas Buckley's newspapers report:

> Her travelling equipage, mean and miserable by order of the King, her attendants apprehensive as if they had been warned to fear some reprisal unknown. But the majesty and glorious conveyance of the dignity of our Queen transformed the process into one which somehow combined the earnestness of the history of our nation with its resolution. Carriages, horsemen and running people followed and surrounded the Queen's coach all the way from Greenwich to Westminster. She was everywhere received with the greatest enthusiasm. What a great day this is for England!

When the disorderly procession turns into Pall Mall and comes to Carlton House, a solid line of scarlet uniforms stretches, bayonets fixed, three lines deep. It is an insult to the Queen that the soldiers are out, but the King is taking no chances. The mob boos and screams at the officers, but the sight of the bayonets keeps the rocks in their owners' hands. The Guards have no orders to the contrary so they present arms smartly as the Queen passes. A wild shout of approval goes up from the crowd. Men run among the soldiers, shaking hands, whispering which Whig-subsidized public houses to go to when they are off duty, where all drinks will be on the house in exchange for loyalty to the Queen.

The Queen's procession limps up St. James's Street, where the Queen bows and smiles to the men who are in the windows of White's Club. Her carriage moves slowly against the tides of flesh to Audley Street, to one of Lady

Anglesong's houses in London. The clamor forces the Queen to show herself again and again throughout the night while the wildly excited, militantly orchestrated crowd streams through the streets with blazing torches forcing all passers-by to shout "God Save the Queen!" and roaring, in cadenced unison, their support of "Queen Caroline and her son, King Austin." For two nights the whirling mass surges around the Anglesong house, occasionally withdrawing to break windows elsewhere or to overturn the coaches of people who are less enthusiastic in their support of her. The Duke of Wellington is caught in his carriage outside Apsley House. The mob packs in around him. The Duke stares contemptuously about him. Men catch at the horses' reins. A bass voice shouts out, "No foul play, m'Lud, but you must shout God Save the Queen." There is a snarl of approval from the crowd. "All right! Very well!" the Duke snorts. His voice goes up to a harsh shout. "God Save the Queen!" he cries out. "And may all your wives be like her!"

The hysteria ferments, reaching the government troops. Rumors of the frightening determination of the soldiery to support Caroline increase daily. Lady Anglesong uses little time for sleep. Each day she develops more effective mob ruses to stain and humiliate the King. Her work is done secretly, with Party funds, because of the certainty that only a fraction of the Whigs, the power tip of the Party spear, would countenance such artificially developed tactics. The rank and file of both parties believe that the Queen is being carried along on the river of popularity that has always carried her; a flood made up partly of her own attraction, the other part because the public despises the King. Most of all it is the Queen who believes this, because she doesn't understand that the hundreds who stand outside Carlton House and boo are a paid mob who then attract thousands of unpaid booers. The noise is horrendous. The demonstrators crowd in as close to Carlton House as the troops will permit them to go and shout, "Nero!"

The King withdraws to the Royal Lodge at Windsor Park. He is condemned as a coward who is afraid to show himself. The public feeling is beyond measure. Lord Kullers states that "The country is nearer to disaster than it has ever been since Charles I. If we live we shall see a Jacobin revolution more bloody than that of France."

It is terrifying. All over the United Kingdom there are protest meetings and all-out riots. Several times the troops are called upon to shoot, pouring more oil on the fire. Nevertheless, although the throne is tottering, the King will not turn back. He endures one shaking, tempestuous month of national passion. There can be no doubt that the drawn-out waiting and rioting help him, because such passions cannot remain at a fever pitch. One month sooner, had the trial of the Queen been held at the peak of the national feeling, the country might have exploded. England might have been plunged into a second Civil War.

§11

The King sends all the evidence collected by The Milan Commission to be laid on the center table at the House of Lords while in session, packed in a fat, green bag. Simultaneously, in both Houses, the King's message is read:

> The King, in consequence of the Queen's arrival, feels it necessary to communicate to this House certain documents relating to Her Majesty's conduct after her departure from this country. These documents he entrusts to the serious and immediate consideration of the House. The King has experienced a lively desire to avert, by every means which lay in his power, an obligation as painful to his people as to his own sentiments, but the latest step which the Queen has taken does not permit his hesitating any longer.
> The King feels the utmost confidence in making this communication, that the House will adopt that course of proceeding which the justice of the case and the honour and dignity of his crown require.

The Prime Minister, Lord Liverpool, opens the green bag, stating that he wishes to thank His Majesty for his communication and to assure His Majesty that their lordships would adopt that course of proceeding which justice and honor and dignity should appear to require. He will refer the papers in the green bag to a secret committee.

Lord Tinto Bennett, a Scots laird of Dallas, a reputed but unproven pirate, takes the floor saying, "Seeing no member near me disposed to question the noble lord, and with full permission of my humility, I feel most anxious to know from him whether Lord Coomber had instructions from ministers of the crown to call upon the Queen of England to lay down her right and title—a right held by the same constitutional securities as that of the King himself—for a bribe of fifty thousand pounds a year? I can never give credit to the statement that a British ministry, without the authority and consent of Parliament, would have dared to undertake such a filthy bribe, a filthy bribe not paid out of the pockets of the King himself, but to be paid for by the people of England who are labouring under the severest distresses. There are no words strong enough to convey an adequate impression of such a proposition. To call it treason to the monarchy might be considered extravagant, but I cannot consider it less."

UPROAR IN THE HOUSE OF LORDS

"When His Majesty called upon this House to interest themselves in that evidence in that green bag, he called upon them to become parties to a private persecution, a persecution in which the same person was the accuser, party, prosecutor, and procurer of evidence and might— in the event of a bill of attainder—also be the judge. Since the time of Henry VIII this House has not interfered with the Queens of England. Let them beware! Let this House not participate with a cabinet whose fifteen captive members have armed themselves against a single woman. Who is this fearsome woman, our Queen? Merely the daughter of the immortal Duke of Brunswick, the niece of the late King, the cousin and wife of His Majesty, and the mother of the lamented Princess Charlotte of Wales." Lord Bennett sits.

As though he has not been listening, the Prime Minister moves that a secret committee be appointed for examining the papers relating to the conduct of the Queen. Castlereagh seconds the motion. The Lord Chancellor takes the floor to say that a secret committee is intended to protect innocence. In fact what are grand juries but secret committees? It is the privilege of every subject, high or low, to have an open and public trial, but in this case, if there must be a trial, God forbid it should be public.

Henry Brougham reads the Queen's message in the House of Commons. Lord Winikus reads it in the House of Lords:

> The Queen thinks it necessary to inform both Houses that she has been induced to return to England in consequence of the measures pursued against her honour and her peace for some time by secret agents abroad and lately sanctioned by the conduct of the government at home. It is this day fourteen years since the first charges were brought against Her Majesty by secret committees conducting secret trials. Then—and upon every occasion during that long period—she has shown the utmost readiness to meet her accusers and to court the fullest inquiry into her conduct. She now also desires an open investigation in which she may see both the charges and the witnesses against her, a privilege not denied to the meanest subject of the realm. She relies with full confidence upon the integrity of the House of Commons and the House of Lords for defeating the only attempt she has reason to fear.

12

Enraged, the King presses Colonel Heller.

"How can she want an open trial? Why? *Why?* Doesn't she understand that Pergami will appear to testify against her?"

"Obviously not, Your Majesty. She probably believes the man is in love with her."

"Don't be disgusting! Just tell me that you are certain beyond the possibility of failure that Pergami will appear, in England, before the House of Lords, and will testify against her."

"He will appear. He will testify against her."

"Who else will testify?"

"We have twenty-seven witnesses, Your Majesty. There has never been such a case. It is totally incriminating. She is already convicted, Your Majesty. You are already divorced."

The King needs to be bled regularly and controlled with laudanum to calm him. It is explained to him patiently what the procedure of the government will be. Lord Liverpool says, "The government considers it legal and necessary to introduce a Bill of Pains & Penalties to be read in the House of Lords. It will accuse the Princess of having conducted herself toward Bartolomeo Pergami, a common army corporal, once a barber, with 'indecent and offensive familiarity and freedom.' It will state that she has carried on 'a licentious, disgraceful, and adulterous intercourse' with him and others, and it will seek to deprive her of the title, prerogatives, rights, privileges and pretensions of Queen Consort of this realm and to dissolve the marriage between Your Majesty and the Princess."

"But she must be found guilty!" the King says in a trembling voice.

"There can be no possibility, considering the evidence assembled, that she will not be convicted. Nonetheless, rather than risk such a public scandal, both interests must endeavor to reach a settlement."

"Lawyers!" the King croaks. "Lawyers! Lawyers!"

Lady Anglesong and Henry Brougham meet with the Duke of Wellington and Lord Castlereagh to endeavor to reach a settlement. It is a short meeting.

"The Queen," Lady Joyce says, "insists that her name be restored to the liturgy."

"On that point," Lord Castlereagh responds, "the King is as immovable as Carlton House itself."

The meeting for the purpose of reaching a settlement is over.

13

The House of Lords, in Abingdon Street leading into St. Margaret's Square, is a puny sort of building which lacks in size and lacks in sensuous, demonstrable splendor. The building is only 80 feet long, 40 feet wide, and 30 feet high; about like an old country church. The woolsack is at the far end, in front of the throne. Benches for members run along either side of it. Its richness of place, beyond an undeniable richness of spirit, is upheld by an extraordinary tapestry of the Armada hung under three semi-circular windows. Temporary galleries are built above the benches. Arrangements most necessary are made for the accommodation of her without whom none of the frantic rush and crush would have been needed—a woman in exclusively masculine surroundings. The retiring room normally set aside for use by the Chairman of Committees is held for her. She is to be permitted to bring one female companion.

On the west side, adjoining the building, are the quarters of the Black Rod and other officers of both Houses, known as Cotton Yard. Dormitories for more than two dozen Italian witnesses are established here. They are brought up the Thames to Parliament Stairs and whisked into a most cloistered existence with a lavish supply of ale; walled in as if for protection.

At a very early hour on Thursday morning, workmen complete timber fences thrown up from St. Margaret's

Church to the King's Bench Office on the one side, and on the upper extremity of Abingdon Street on the other, so as to enclose the entire area in front of the House of Lords and the whole line of approach, to keep it open for the movement of carriages of the peers to and from the principal entrance. Constables have been stationed in double strength at more than merely the key points. No one may pass after ten o'clock in the morning. A strong body of Foot Guards is posted at the King's Bench Office, the Record Office and Westminster Hall. All passages leading into Parliament Street are closed by heavy timber partitions. Gunboats defend the river side.

At eight o'clock, a troop of Life Guards rides into the Palace Yard and forms a line in front of Westminster Hall. Foot guards form under the piazza of the House of Lords where they pile their arms. Patrols of Life Guards are then thrown forward in the direction of Abingdon Street.

Dense crowds have taken up positions to see Her Majesty pass. At half-past eight the areas between St. James's Square and Parliament Palace Yard are occupied by more than ten thousand people. Windows and roofs are filled. Wagons packed with people at a shilling a head line St. James's Square, where the Queen will stay for the duration of the trial. Coaches pour in from all of the four streets that feed the square. By nine o'clock it is almost a solid human mass being explored by pickpockets.

At 9:37 A.M. Her Majesty's state carriage advances through this mass of bodies and noise, drawn by six caparisoned bay horses. The coachman, postillions and footmen are habited in rich costumes of scarlet and gold with purple velvet facings and black velvet caps of state—to the stitch the same equipage as that of His Majesty.

As Her Majesty enters the carriage the cry of "Hats

off!" rings throughout the square. Her Majesty descends
the grand staircase on the arm of Lord Francis Winikus,
Marquis of Idless, followed by Lady Joyce Anglesong. The
royal cavalcade sets forth amidst the most tremendous
pressure London has felt since the days of Charles I. There
is a waving of white handkerchiefs, towels, scarves and
even tablecloths. The cheering is deafening.

"I used to enjoy these occasions," Caroline says.
"There used to be so much more poignant pleasure in
ruining my husband."

"The feeling will return as the excitement grows,"
Lady Joyce says cheerfully. "You will have the old intense
pleasure out of it—all of it."

As the carriage approaches Carlton House the mob
seems unable to think of anything beyond whether or not
the sentinels will present arms as the Queen passes. When
the soldiers do acknowledge the Queen smartly, the uproar
of approval is hysterical.

At half-past ten the state coach passes into the Old
Palace Yard. The barriers break. People rush in behind the
carriages. Two women cling so close to the fore-horse of
Lord Winikus's carriage that they cannot be disengaged
from it. They scream with power when this is attempted.
The constables are carried away by the force of people
pouring in, thousands trampling each other yelling, "The
Queen! The Queen!"

Troops arrange themselves into a block around Her
Majesty. They form a lane through which she may pass.
They present arms. She enters the House with Black Rod
taking her right hand and Henry Brougham her left. He
wears a black silk gown and a long wig. The trial is already
in progress, as Lord Weldon took his place on the Woolsack at half-past eight. He was one of the Queen's friends

even during The Delicate Investigation. He is affection-
ately known as "Old Bags."

During a call-over of the roll of peers the Queen enters
the chamber wearing black sarsenet in mourning for the
passing of the Duchess of York. All peers stand to gaze
upon the Queen's full white veil, which falls decorously
over her bosom. Henry Brougham is the Queen's Attorney-General. Thomas Denham is her Solicitor-General.

The Prime Minister, Lord Liverpool, introduces a Bill
of Pains & Penalties. Such a bill is an act of Parliament for
punishing a person without resort to legal trial. It is not a
judicial act although in its procedure it may closely resemble a legal trial. As with any other bill it must be passed
by Sovereign, Lords, and Commons. The justification for
a bill of pains and penalties is that it can be used where
proofs of wrongdoing are unlikely to secure a conviction
under the law. Many people, not only the partisans of the
Queen, hold that a bill of pains and penalties is an extreme,
unconstitutional, and justly unpopular measure. Therefore Liverpool's bill firmly confines the issue to Bartolomeo Pergami, whose relations with the Queen are described as "a most unbecoming and degrading intimacy,"
"a licentious, disgraceful, and adulterous intercourse," and
"scandalous, disgraceful and vicious conduct." The Bill
enacts that "Her Majesty, Caroline Amelia Elizabeth shall
be deprived of the title of Queen" and that the marriage
between her and the King "shall be for ever, wholly dis-
solved, annulled and made void." Lady Joyce Anglesong
has said publicly of it: "The degradation this procedure
brings is not merely at home, but abroad. To complete the
picture, the peers of England—the representatives of noble
families and descendants of heroic ancestors—the pillars of
the state—are sent to pry into foul clothesbags and to pore

over the contents of chamber utensils. Is such the legitimate duty of a peer of Parliament? Is this the mode in which the lawmakers of the greatest country of the world should be employed?"

The second part of the Bill, which divorces the King from the Queen, is highly controversial. Possibly, the King has dreams of a second marriage that will produce more children. But all the evidence of his life with his wife provokes the public conviction that he wants surcease from the awful conflict which she represents to him. Whatever the reason, the inclusion of the divorce clause is a mistake because it antagonizes many of the bench, of the bishops, and some of the strongest supporters of the Crown, who still display a deep, abiding faith in a commonwealth resting on church and state.

Brougham rises to object to the principle of the Bill. "I put it to you that this most distinguished assembly sits here to listen to what has become nothing more than a Bill of Divorce. As such could it not go before normal courts if he who has, for the past twenty-five years, been casting heavy stones is without guilt? But he has chosen injustice once again as he has throughout the life of this oppressed woman, by using this distinguished House as his catspaw by causing it to frame this unspeakable Bill of Pains and Penalties. If this Bill should become a law may it not, one of these days perhaps, be provocative of the greatest calamity which can befall a nation—of a Civil War resulting from a dispute as to the succession to the Crown?"

When Brougham finishes his opening address, the Queen leaves the chamber while Brougham calls her opponents' intentions "unfounded and foul" when they say that the King does not appear because it does not suit his high character and station, that he is a consenting, not a complaining party.

In the Withdrawing Room with Anglesong, the Queen is bleak. "The prices we pay to revenge useless acts, Anglesong!" she says bitterly. "I had to hold down my ragged nervousness to keep my dignity out there, I tell you. I wanted to tremble, but I held fast."

"See them for what they are!" Anglesong says harshly. "Only a few hundred men who are playing at justifying themselves. Let them strut and thunder like the silly roosters they are. We are organized. The work was done in Italy. You are to fear nothing, Your Majesty."

"I have never feared to be a clown when I chose to be a clown, but I despise being made into a clown for Georgie."

14

"Is Pergami in Cotton Yard?" the King asks Heller. "Has he arrived with the other witnesses?"

"Not yet."

"What in damnation does that mean?"

"He did not arrive with the other witnesses. He has not come yet."

"When will he come?"

"I would say that is a question for the Prosecutor, Sir."

"I want to know why you are so uncertain about Pergami and when he will be used in that trial."

"They have kept me engaged, Sir. They have needed me to prepare all the other witnesses, Your Majesty. I have been in Cotton Yard for seventeen hours every day since they arrived."

"Are they ready? Do they understand what to do down to the last sentence?"

"They know what they must say better than they know their own names."

"Go to the Attorney-General. Tell him specifically that I have commanded you to learn from him when Pergami is to arrive and when Pergami will testify."

As the days of the trial go by, the Queen takes time each day to ride in an open carriage in the parks and in the most central areas of the city. She is cheered wherever she goes. Each morning before they leave for the trial, Anglesong arranges for a different deputation of citizens to come to St. James's Square to address her with honoring petitions, supporting her. These are published widely in Sir Thomas Buckley's newspapers: The Ladies of South London (11,000 signatures); The Mechanics' Guild (61,000 signatures); the Taxed Carters' Guild (31,000 signatures). The Lord Mayor of London and his Council are persuaded to call. "Justice Eludes Our Queen," is Buckley's ringing leader (in return for the promise that, when the Whigs come to power, he will be the government's choice for election as Chairman of the International Tennis Committee, a "world-wide" body which meets in Oslo once a year). This moving appeal for truth and justice is reprinted in the Whig newspapers throughout the United Kingdom and ultimately in key cities of Europe. It mourns that the lovely Queen is inexorably being ground down by the cruel power of her husband's lust to stand alone at the helm of state, to share the shallow vanity of a great nation's loyalty with no one.

The editorial diverts the King for well over a week from his Pergami preoccupation. Insensate with rage, the King orders a many-level investigation of Buckley seeking evidence sufficient to bring the press lord to trial for "flagrant abuse of his King" in the manner in which the King dealt with the Hunt brothers.

It is the one light moment in the bad period for the Queen, she is so delighted by the King's consuming, self-crippling rage as it is reported to her twice a day. "I tell you, Anglesong," she says wiping the tears of laughter from her eyes, "they are going to have to bring Georgie before Parliament and try him for mopery."

"It is just the be*ginn*ing!" Anglesong exults. "Next week Buckley will actually unhinge your husband's mind!"

"Oh, no! Tell me! Tell me! I cannot wait."

"Next week the newspapers will ring out like trumpets establishing that everything every witness for the prosecution is testifying is only hearsay evidence. Buckley is going to demand to know when is the government going to produce the only legally acceptable testimony from the only witness whom the government witnesses say has 'violated you with your permission.' "

"Bartie?"

"Yes. Where and when will Pergami appear before the House of Lords, Buckley will ask again and again until there is a veritable pile of broken bodies around the King. He will have gone quite mad."

The Attorney-General for the Crown reads a statement in deposition from the Queen.

> I arrived at Milan on the 8th October 1814. The Austrian government received me very well, Milan being a part of the Hapsburg empire. Count Ghisiliare, Chamberlain to the Emperor, attended me everywhere. I told him it was my intention to settle in Italy for a few years. The Count then proposed that I should have a person who understood the arrangement of a large family—how to keep it in a proper style of elegance and at the same time with economy. I desired the Count to look out for such a person. He did so and recommended me to Mr. Pergami. My people thought it would be best to have Mr. Pergami thoroughly investigated and this personal investigation was undertaken by Generale Aleamalia Melvini-Sestero, chief of the Italian Secret Service, who reported that Mr. Pergami was a man with an outstanding army record who possessed unassailable abilities with which to undertake the duties to which he would be assigned in my Household. Mr. Pergami accepted our offers. He undertook work which was inferior to that to which he was accustomed on the understanding that, should a vacancy occur in my

establishment, I would then promote him to higher station. He became my courier but he was a superior kind of courier, more like an ecuyer whose province it is to keep near the royal carriage by way of protection and had nothing to do with posting horses. A courier de cabinet holds the rank of colonel in the army and that was the situation which Mr. Pergami held in my Household, a rank accepted without question by the council of the ancient and distinguished order of the Knights of Malta who elected him to become a Chevalier of their order.

Lady Joyce Anglesong, who has enormous prestige with all members of the assembly, is called to testify. The attention given her is total. She states: "Chevalier Bartolomeo Pergami, Baron della Franchina, is a superior person. I think of him as a straightforward, remarkably good sort of man. I had cause to observe him closely whenever I visited the Queen in Italy. He assumed nothing. He was entirely occupied with the matters which came before him. He had a great deal to do and was very active. People liked him—except the few who envied his situation. He may not be a man of true education—he is a soldier, after all—but he understands figures very well and oversees everything down to the payment of a single shilling. His grandfather was a physician. His sister is a countess. Chevalier Pergami was aide-de-camp to General Pino and was at the battle of St. Petersburg."

The Attorney-General for the Crown then calls up a succession of twenty-four witnesses for the prosecution who repeat over and over again what they almost had seen concerning Pergami's relations with the Queen, but most certainly had had such things reported to them by people who should know about those things. Their testimony is all of a piece. A typical example is the testimony of Theodore Majocchi whose words reveal to the House what three years of diligent investigation by The Milan Commission had uncovered for an expenditure of £112,521 of the country's money.

Majocchi states that he first knew Pergami in 1813 when they were both serving under General Pino and that Pergami was the general's *valet de chambre.* He says Pergami had gotten him a job as livery servant to the Princess of Wales. He is asked to describe the sleeping arrangements of Pergami and the Princess.

"Pergami's room was separated from hers by a small corridor and a cabinet," he testifies. "Twice, when Pergami hurt his leg, he asked me to sleep in the cabinet and I saw the Princess come through after midnight on her way to Pergami's bedroom."

An hour is spent with the witness in the House securing minute descriptions of sleeping arrangements as the Princess and Pergami travel from place to place. Majocchi establishes that there was always a way to move undetected from one bedroom to another. Majocchi says he often made the beds and that Pergami's bed was seldom occupied.

By the fifth day the Attorney-General for the Crown is asking such desperate questions as: "Do you remember at any time examining the contents of the carriages in which the Princess and Pergami rode and finding a bottle in it?"

"I found one bottle."

"What was in the bottle—for what purpose was the bottle used?"

"It was used for Pergami to make water in."

Henry Brougham begins his cross-examination innocently. "Did you leave General Pino's service on account of killing a horse?"

"No."

"You have never killed a horse?"

"Never."

"After you left the employ of the Princess were you then employed by the British ambassador at Vienna?"

"Yes."

"Sir Charles Chapman?"

"Yes."

"When did you first see the British ambassador?"

"I did not see him. I saw his secretary."

"What was his name?"

"Colonel Reese."

"Colonel John Reese?"

"No, sir. John Reese was his brother; Captain Reese. He was in Milan."

"Did you travel from Vienna to Milan to visit Captain John Reese?"

"Yes."

"What induced you to leave your excellent post at the British Embassy in Vienna to visit Captain Reese in Milan?"

"He wanted to speak to me."

"Do you go everywhere and anywhere whenever anybody comes to you and says, 'Captain Reese wants to speak to you?' Is it not true that you had been urged to take a leave of absence from the British Embassy in Vienna by Sir Charles Chapman, formerly one of the three ranking members of The Milan Commission—the *infamous and very costly* Milan Commission—in order that you could meet Captain John Reese, then one of the two ranking heads of the infamous, costly Milan Commission?"

"Yes, sir."

"Who paid you to make the journey and who paid for your expenses?"

"Captain Reese."

"What did Captain Reese want from you—all the way from Vienna to Milan?"

"Information."

"Information about what or whom?"

"The Princess of Wales."

"Is it not true that you have it backwards, that Captain Reese gave you information about the Princess of Wales and ordered you to learn it by heart, then to make the information which he provided your testimony in this court?"

"Yes."

UPROAR IN THE HOUSE OF LORDS

Brougham lifts a newspaper from a table. "This is the *Gazette Universelle* of Vienna. I enter it as an exhibit of evidence. I will read only a part of the story aloud and ask you to confirm it or deny it." Brougham reads from the newspaper:

The Gazette of the Court of Vienna and The Austrian Observer have published, on the part of the English ambassador, a contradiction of an article contained in The Gazette Universelle relative to some witnesses against the Queen of England. These are the incontrovertible facts: Theodore Majocchi, formerly a stable boy in the service of the Princess of Wales during her residence in Como and Milan, arrived in Vienna in 1819. He stopped at the Faubourg de Weiden at the Inn of the Three Crowns. According to his own avowal he has received from the English Ministry, supplies and indemnities. He has also received promises of pensions for life for himself and his family. The so-called facts which Theodore Majocchi agreed to testify against the Queen of England are very grave and will cover her with shame. Theodore Majocchi has declared that his pensions are paid to him monthly in Milan by Captain John Reese. The Gazette Universelle derived these facts from Theodore Majocchi and from his family.

If these facts are false, the English ministry will have recourse to law against this newspaper and Majocchi.

Brougham faces the entire House, turning slowly as he speaks. "My Lords, I have done with this witness except for one question." He turns again to Majocchi. "Have you or have you not received supplies and indemnities, appointments and pensions from this English government as stated in the *Gazette Universelle?*"

"Yes. I have been paid by the English government to do what is described in the *Gazette Universelle.*"

"I have no further questions," Brougham says. "In a common case I should certainly be satisfied with this examination. And In this case I see no reason to question this man further."

After Majocchi's testimony, the Queen leaves the court. Slumped in her Withdrawing Room she is so pale and haggard that the paint on her face stands out like the paint on a puppet's head. Lady Joyce is shocked by this change. "Your Majesty! You are ill!"

The Queen answers in a weak, still voice. "I don't know why Majocchi should affect me this way. We designed what he was there to do. But somehow Majocchi makes me see everything so differently."

"You must not do that," Lady Anglesong answers firmly. "There is only one view here. Your purpose is to shame your husband and to protect your Crown. The government's purpose—your husband's purpose—is to disgrace you, to divorce you, and to deny you the Crown in order to keep their power. The Whig purpose is to topple the Tories."

"I know," the Queen says, "but if I could only sleep." She is dazed. Her eyes are as bright as glass. The strain has been intense and she looks so bad that Anglesong wonders how she will get the Queen out of the building without attracting unwelcome attention.

"The Delicate Investigation was much worse than this, but I was so much younger. I was stronger, and I didn't believe I would ever grow weak." The Queen lifts herself to her feet and stands swaying. Her face is tragic. Lady Anglesong pushes open the folding doors to the great staircase. Holding the Queen by the arm, as the Queen clutches the balustrade, Anglesong leads gently, pausing often, in their descent while the Queen shudders badly.

"I had to punish him to repay him," the Queen says harshly. "But what a waste it has been of my own life, Anglesong. I have punished myself. I am coming to the end of all of it and I see that he has defeated me."

15

At 9:00 A.M. on the day after the Majocchi testimony the King meets with his Attorney-General, Lord Edward Masters, the Prime Minister, Lord Liverpool, and Colonel Franz Heller, at Carlton House. He wastes no time.

"We saw a shocking dereliction of circumstances yesterday in the House of Lords," he says. "I have been ill all the night because of it, but I should think the Tory Party feels much more ill."

"Brougham is diabolically clever," Heller says.

"Is he?" the King shrills. "Is he diabolically clever enough to refute the direct testimony of one Bartolomeo Pergami who was planted by this government as a paid spy in the bed of the Princess of Wales? Whom this government has had—in their own words—trussed up for the past three years of dutiful monthly meetings and depositions to prepare him for this moment? *When will my Attorney-General and my Prime Minister produce Pergami before the House of Lords?*"

Silence.

A terrible anxiety decomposes the King's face. "What has happened?" the King cries. "When? When will you produce Pergami?"

The Prime Minister answers slowly. "Pergami has disappeared, Your Majesty. But before disappearing he informed Captain Reese in Milan that he has no intention of coming to England to testify, and that if he were abducted he would not only reveal that fact in court but he would refute every charge made against the Queen by every government hearsay witness."

The King collapses, his legs having turned to water. He slumps on the small of his back upon a sofa, staring blankly at some disgusting vision. "We have had to administer His Majesty's government," Lord Liverpool says in self-justification. "All the Whigs have had to do is to administer His Majesty's destruction in order to place their client upon the throne."

The King vomits. The three men stand at attention in a semi-circle around him while his monstrous gobbets cover the carpet and sofa. The King rests at last, falling backward with his eyes closed. "Summon the Captain of the Guard," he says weakly. No one moves.

"*Guard!*" the King screams.

"Sah!" The materialized Guards Captain shouts, saluting, clicking his heels, standing at resounding attention.

"Arrest that man," the King says waving feebly at Colonel Heller.

"Your Majesty!" Heller exclaims with pain.

"You are going to be stripped of rank, pay and privileges and flogged before the German Legion." The King is looking at Heller with such loathing that the other men instantly share the identical sensation that the King believes he is looking at himself, and sentencing himself to disgrace and punishment. "When you have been flogged you will be sent to prison in Hanover where you will be flogged every year on this date." The King inhales deeply to put force behind his sound. "Take him away!" he wails.

Brougham brings forward character witnesses for the Queen: Lord Malmesbury, recalled from Constantinople;

Lord Winikus, the astute collector of priceless furniture; Lady Alexandra Wells, Princess Charlotte's companion; Lady Jane Montant and Lady Joyce Anglesong. All are fiercely loyal and impressive. The essence of their testimony is that they had not seen anything improper at any time across twenty-five years of friendship with the Queen and that therefore she is not an immoral person. This testimony of English witnesses of highest reputation flies dramatically in the face of opposition foreign witnesses of a menial class, seventeen of whom have openly admitted to being bribed by the government. Further, Brougham's uncannily skillful cross-examinations are so couched as to deliver the menial foreigners as "hired spies," creating deep doubt and distaste about them. The Defense rests its case, but more than all the brilliant work and oratory by Henry Brougham it is the solid and unavoidable matter of the divorce clause in the Bill which proves to be the salvation of the Queen.

Debate rages in the House for five days.

16

The third and last reading of the Bill of Pains & Penalties takes place on the 10th November, three months after the start of the trial.

The astonishment of sudden self-knowledge has crippled the Queen's mind and assaults her health. Her hair has gone gray. Her face is a ravaged battlefield on which the heavy wheeltracks of an artillery of paint and powder make grotesque marks. Her hands tremble. Her voice quavers. She tells Anglesong she cannot sleep at night because she sees Death wedged under the grate of a cold fire.

The vote on the Bill is taken. The majority, held by those favoring the Bill, drops to nine. The government has lost nineteen votes. Lord Liverpool gets to his feet laboriously. He follows the accepted parliamentary procedure. "If, upon the third reading of the Bill, the majority had been the same as upon the second, I should have considered it my duty to send the Bill to the House of Commons. After today's vote I consider that inexpedient and I propose that the Bill be adjourned to this day six months."

He has declared the Bill to be dead.

The signal is passed to the mob outside. London goes into an hysteria of joy; the King is irrefutably exposed as a tyrant, badly defeated by British justice. The glorious exultation of the people is beyond all description.

But—within days—this same public comes starkly

face to face with the realization that the country is in a worse state of affairs than existed before the trial started. The thrilling enthusiasms turn to feelings of bitterness, to a growing hatred of King and Queen alike. The King has not been betrayed, they reason dimly in a great, mindless reflex; the Queen has not been betrayed. On the very evidence, the people are betrayed.

§17§

The Queen, from circumstances being obliged to remain in England, requests the King will be pleased to command those ladies of first rank His Majesty may think the post proper in these realms, to attend the Queen on the day of the Coronation, of which Her Majesty is informed is now fixed, and also to name such ladies which will be requested to bear her train on that day.

The Queen, being particularly anxious to submit to the good taste of His Majesty, most earnestly entreats the King to inform the Queen in what dress the King wishes the Queen to appear, on that day, at the Coronation,

Caroline R

Caroline is in earnest. She knows that the King has been assembling precedents to show that more English Queens have not been crowned along with their husbands than have been crowned; that the matter is not one of claim, but of privilege, which the King is determined not to grant.

Caroline sits, lonely and desolate at Brandenburg House, writing letter after letter to the King, becoming less and less, and then still less a figure of interest to the English people as they begin to prepare themselves for the glories of His Majesty's coronation.

In May 1821 a royal proclamation is issued from Carlton House declaring "His Majesty's pleasure touching his royal coronation" and nominating commissioners to hear and determine the petitions and claims of those persons who, "by ancient customs and usages, as also in regard of divers tenures of sundry manors, lands, and other hereditaments, were bound to perform certain service on the day of the coronation."

The Queen, although His Majesty's Ministers have given her no official advices concerning a coronation, writes to the Prime Minister demanding to be present at the ceremony. The government replies: "His Majesty, having determined that the Queen should form no part of the ceremonial of his coronation, it was his royal pleasure that the Queen should not be allowed to attend the said ceremony."

On the 9th June a second proclamation is issued naming Thursday, 19th July, for the performance of the coronation ceremony. Henry Brougham forces the House of Commons into a debate demanding its support of Her Majesty's legal right to be crowned. It is decided that her counsel, in support of her petition to attend the coronation as Queen, should be heard before the Privy Council.

The Privy Council meeting at the Cockpit, Whitehall, at ten o'clock the following morning to hear counsel faces a greatly crowded Council Chamber. A long memorandum from the Queen is read which protests her right to be crowned. Henry Brougham rises. He examines the history of the coronation ceremony because the coronation is the creature of precedent and rests upon practice rather than principle. "If it shall be found that the custom of crowning the Queens Consort has been uniform and uninterrupted, the right will be established in the largest sense."

The Queen's full, indulged, and corrupted face is different than Anglesong has ever seen it. Its expression is shattered. The eyes retreat, burning with a fire of sleeplessness. She twists her fingers together, each finger attempting to hold another down so that none will tremble. Her voice is cracked, hoarse. "They will talk and talk, but nothing will change," she says. "The King is the greatest lawyer because he has ruled that I am not to be crowned and they will all talk until sunrise or until they find some reason why that must be so."

"If you were a man they would not do any of this," Anglesong says. "You are a woman so you are a victim."

The Queen laughs gutturally; without pleasure. "If I were a man I not only wouldn't be Queen, but worse I might be married to someone like me."

"Nonetheless the laws are made to fold over men like golden armor."

"My husband is only male, he is not a man. But, I am a Brunswicker! I shall not be denied the coronation I have paid for with all of my foolish life."

Brougham moves ponderously forward through Canute, son of Sweyn Forkbeard, to Edward the Confessor and William the Conqueror; to Stephen of the House of Blois, through Henrys, Richards, and Edwards of the Houses of Plantagenet, Lancaster, York and Tudor; on into the Houses of Stuart and Orange to the Houses of Hanover and Brunswick. Thus, of the eighteen married kings from the Conquest to the reign of Henry VII inclusive, not one was crowned that had not the coronation of a consort celebrated. Fifteen coronations were celebrated for the sole purpose of crowning Queens Consort. All coronations followed this order:

> The consecration of the King, after which followeth the consecration of the Queen, who, with honour, shall be

anointed by the Bishop with the oil of holy ointment, and in the Church with due honour and regal state shall be blessed and consecrated for the partnership of the royal bed; who also shall be ornamented with a ring for the completion of faith, and for the glory of the eternal State, with a crown.

Twenty-one days are consumed by the arguments of the Queen's counsels. On the 8th July the King's counsel advances their rebuttals which, in essence, are: the Queen has no legal right to enjoy the ceremony of coronation. It is a right which is altogether derivative and permissive; they maintain that the single ground upon which the Queen makes claim rests merely on usage. "However, if it is proved that the usage is not original but derivative then there is an end at once to the claim."

The Privy Council rules, and so advises the King, that the Queen is not to be crowned nor will it be necessary to invite her to his coronation.

Caroline had shown uncanny insight; the King indeed was the greatest lawyer in the land.

She becomes deeply frightened.

18

By pressing to collect payment for many carefully executed favors she has patiently granted over the years, Lady Anglesong comes into possession of the official account of all monies expended on any proceedings respecting the Queen from the year 1817. She has this account presented to the House of Lords where it is ordered to be released to the newspaper press of the United Kingdom. The expenditures demanded by the King for the continuing persecution of his wife amount to £177,870. 18. 0.

The English people are askew with dismay. One hundred and seventy thousand pounds of their money has been spent by a man trying to get rid of his wife. But Anglesong goes too far. She gives Sir Thomas Buckley the listing of all expenditures for The Delicate Investigation of twelve years before. The sum spent by the King to expose his wife now comes to £214,638! The repeated theme in the Buckley newspapers is that these expenditures were "derogatory to the honour of the crown and injurious to the best interests of empire." But the public reads something vastly more invidious in these figures. For the first time the public can see the clear outlines of two mortal enemies. People begin to ask each other about the Queen's innocence, which they had supported so long. The King's desperate actions against her, which they had seen as wicked, unjust and unnecessary, appear in new perspective as those of a King who has been plagued by a corrupt and licentious woman for twenty-six years and has frantically devoted time, effort and great wealth to expose her as the monster. The massive reasoning against Caroline is that they have all choked on twenty-five years of black, billowing smoke and now, all at once, they feel the heat of the conflagration it has concealed. To those taking readings for the Whig Party throughout the kingdom it is confirmed that the Queen is fast becoming a millstone around the Party's neck. The Whigs equivocate, but the Tories quickly grasp this opportunity. Because they insist, the King is seen in public more often amid admiring, cheering paid crowds. He is seen at the opera, at theaters, in Rotten Row, in hospital wards, in open carriages all over the city always accompanied by "the admirers" and followed by journalists from Tory newspapers. The small parts actress, Daisy Hanly, the Limerick player, tackles him at the knees before a large crowd outside Carlton House. "Our king! Our king!" she sobs. "The overburdened savior of our people!" He does not kick her because the situation's effect is, fortunately, explained to him before he comes through the door.

The King begins to cultivate Sir Thomas Buckley (who is in despair over the Whigs' return to power in time to place him at the top rung of international tennis). He dines with the King and Lord Liverpool at Carlton House.

"Buckley, I would like to consult with you if I may," the King says. "Increasingly I am overcome with the conviction that what our people need is some gracious propulsion into exercise which would bring them health as well as grace of form and movement."

"I see, Sir," Buckley answers, not having a clue as to what the King is talking about.

"I am thinking in the shape of advanced, really important international tennis competition, Buckley. I am told you have interest in this."

"I do!" Buckley lights, he leaps to his feet, he rubs his

hands together until the King becomes curious to see if smoke will rise from them. "If I may say so, I am really a *very good* tennis player of long standing and an *indefatigable* friend of tennis. It is a *glorious* sport which can fulfill this nation!"

"Splendid, Buckley. What would you think if I were to sponsor a British World Rank Tennis Association—with you guiding all of its affairs at the very top, of course—to set tournament standards internationally and to encourage the public's interest in the game?"

"Why—I would say that would be a stroke of incalculable strength, Your Majesty."

"And I would present the Lord Buckley Cup to a winner each year. That might sustain interest."

"*Lord* Buckley's Cup?"

"That is sound, Your Majesty," Lord Liverpool says. "The introduction of such a cup wants *rank*. It wants a *peer*, if I may say so, Buckley, with no intention of denigrating your station as a knight."

"It is settled then," the King says. "For the sake of the sport we love and the people we serve you must agree to accept a peerage whilst you also agree to chair our new British World Rank Tennis Association and permit its silver cup to be named for you."

"I—I most humbly accept, Your Majesty. I cannot express my gratitude strongly enough."

"I thank *you*, milord."

"Oh, yes," the Prime Minister says. "We were badly seized up about finding an expert here. All thanks must go to you, milord."

19

William Austin is an unquestionably banal young man of nineteen whose concentration on the mirror, foppery, and mopery, in that order, is his genius. He calls the Queen "Mama" when they are alone or with Anglesong or Mrs. Keifetz. Everyone in the Household still calls him Willikin. The Queen dotes on him as much as she did when he was an infant and would be carried, bawling and soiled, to annoy his mother's guests at dinner parties in Montague House. He has accompanied Caroline whenever she moved house to wherever she goes. He has traveled through many countries and met many brilliant or distinguished people but nothing, absolutely nothing, has rubbed off on him.

His tutors have explained to the Queen that he is approximately five and a half years behind the average boy of his age in education and aptitudes, but the Queen tells Lady Anglesong that she would rather have a sweet and amiable young man about the house than some *bébé savant*. "Very few men in court life impressed me as being very bright," the Queen says as she said a hundred times when she was Princess of Wales. "My God, do you remember the husband of Lady Jersey? Willikin is a mental marvel compared to him. How about that Sir John Douglas? One might as well waltz with a tombstone, you know. Willikin will spend his whole life at the court and I would say he knows quite enough, thank you—he knows to be sweet and charming and kind and never, never obtrusive."

He is a good boy; an obedient boy, and he never gives anyone trouble, offense or bother despite the fact that rumors have convinced him that he has the strongest claim to succession to the throne. He and the Queen take tea together every day no matter where they are, and frequently he asks her about his becoming king one day, bland little sounds from his adorably empty little face.

"You really wouldn't want to be king, Willikin," Caroline advises him dotingly. "You have seen your king. Do you know a greater mess than that? He is bloated and spotted and purple and wheezing mostly because his father was a king and this one wanted to be king himself. It tilted his mind. It has ruined his health. No, no," she always says, one way or another, at these sessions, "you will only let them believe you can be king, but you will never allow that to happen. If they think you can be king if you choose, you will always be treated as one and live a long, very comfortable life without the problems."

Lady Joyce Anglesong attends the Whig policy meeting chaired by Earl Grey and attended by Henry Brougham and Sir Martin Gabel and Lord Winikus to discuss the matter of Party support for the Queen during the period immediately preceding and immediately following the coronation.

"As we anticipated," Lord Grey says, "the pendulum of public opinion which has for so long swung in our favor is now, by some mathematical law of averages, swinging against us. Therefore it is the feeling within the leadership of this Party that we would do best not to press things for the moment. Before the coronation the King—as preposterous as this sounds—will become a popular figure because the public will be undergoing a spiritual experience, a transcendental uplifting for the entire nation. You will agree, I am sure, that we would be foolhardy to fly in the face of this present experience and this new wave of feeling."

"Lord Grey?"

"Yes, Lady Anglesong?"

"Are you proposing that we abandon the Queen?"

"No."

"Then I am not sure I understand what you mean."

"I am proposing, and Party discipline is endorsing, that we withdraw from our position of seeming to further the Queen's ambition to be crowned or, indeed, of offering her any chance of feeling that she should expect that we believe we can assist her in that matter."

"Is she to be told that, my Lord?"

"Only if she demands action from us. Otherwise let us see as little of her as can be managed until the coronation is well out of the way and this whole disadvantageous time is passed, until we can judge whether we will need her again."

"I have used her more than any of you," Anglesong says, "so I cannot leave her now. She is ill and she is frightened."

"If you must support her as your friend, then, of course, you must," Lord Grey says. "But you will be doing so entirely without the support of the Whig press. Without our street mobs. Without Party funds and support."

At noon Monday, the carriages carrying the same Whig hierarchy draw up at Brandenburg House. They attend the Queen in a meeting called urgently by Lord Grey. Lady Anglesong is with the Queen when they arrive. No time is lost.

"For a number of years, Your Majesty," Henry Brougham begins, "we have been your sole counsel and protection against the ravening intentions of the King. We have thought for you as if we were, each of us, thinking not for himself but for a sister, a mother—or, if I may be permitted to say so, a dear wife. In two days, the King will be crowned at Westminster Abbey. Throughout London, at this moment, large bills have been plastered across the town which say that the Queen will certainly attend the coronation and will be at the Abbey as early as six o'clock Wednesday morning. These notices have been read by thousands. The numbers of people who will remain on the street until morning in the hope of witnessing an untoward drama at the coronation will grow to tens of thousands."

"I can go on believing as long as they believe in me," the Queen says.

"Mr. Brougham in no way meant to imply that they will believe in you, Your Majesty," Sir Martin Gabel says. "In sadness, we are here because we see it the other way and are alarmed for you."

"What other way?"

"There has been a severe and most perceptible change in the climate of public opinion, Your Majesty," Earl Grey says. "The very masses who, such a short time ago, were so vociferously your partisans have shifted for mysterious reasons unknown to them or to us, but their entire affection, as of this moment, hangs most precariously in the balance, as it were. If there is one untoward incident they can—all of them—swing entirely over on the side of the King."

"Impossible!"

"Oh, it is possible, Your Majesty," Lord Winikus of

Idless says. "These are the sands upon which history was built."

"What could happen?" the Queen says with fright and anxiety. "What is this untoward incident which will set the fuse to them, then?"

"We have come here, Your Majesty," Earl Grey continues with his beautiful voice, "to urge you to remain within this house throughout the coronation and for those days afterward in which the country will be in its state of religious ecstasy demanding that they worship their King because he has just been consecrated to God and to them."

Brougham comes in urgently. "We ask you, not for any reason of ruling by His Majesty's Privy Council, or because of the iron lust of the King to put you down and to keep you down, but because it will do harm—perhaps irreparable harm—to all that we have jointly striven for across all these years."

"Oh, no!" The Queen weeps into her hands. "Oh, my God, oh, no!"

They wait for her to recover herself; each man staring at her. The Queen puts her head back upon the sofa, as if she were resting, her eyes closed. "Am I to reach the safety of the door of a burning building to turn back?" she asks herself and only herself aloud with a hoarse voice. "Am I to outswim the sharks, outrun the carnivores, be poised to strike off the snake's head yet turn away from it?" She opens her eyes. "You saw me come here as a young girl. You know every stripe of the lash across my back. You watched his power grind me down for twenty-six years; then at five seconds to the very hour which will bring us both to triumph, after twenty-six years of seeing me play the clown and smile like a fool when my soul cried out to me to scream with pain—are you now telling me blandly

that all of it, every agonizing day of those twenty-six years
was nothing but a matter of incidental political opportunity and Party policy and that, to me, it should never have
been anything more than that? That is a monstrous lie. It
has not been what you would make it now, it has been my
life. It has been the destruction of my child. It has been an
impossible weight upon my dignity which, because of
what he has done to me, has almost rotted away. I have
lived through the whole gambit and I am dying from it, my
Lords. It is his life wagered against my life and nothing
you can say will turn me away from the gates of a heaven
such as that!"

"You must turn away!" Brougham cries.

Lord Grey stares into her eyes with sadness. "You
know the King," he says, and there is fear for her in his
voice. "He has held his appetites for your destruction at
bay through all those years you have marked. You were
saved because he dared not defy the people. But, if you
were to succeed in what you intend to try to do, it would
not only be the hatred or worse, the indifference of the
people I would fear but—" He halts suddenly. "That is all
I shall say. I will not speak treason."

The Queen sits up quite straight. She looks better,
invigorated perhaps by the crisis she has overcome. "I will
be fair," she says. "You have much at stake. You see what
you want to attain as being the next hundred years for
England. I could have felt for that once, but no more. But
I will be fair. I will agree to put this to a judge."

"A judge?" Winikus says.

"What judge?" Gabel asks.

"Lady Anglesong is a part of your collective ambition.
I will abide by her judgment."

The men are silent. The clock ticks more loudly than

before. The men stand. They face the Queen. Lord Grey
nods to Anglesong, standing beside the hearth at the
Queen's right hand.

"Her Majesty must grasp what history leaves her,"
Anglesong says slowly and with grating pain. "She must
be crowned tomorrow."

"Does that fix your decision, Your Majesty?" Lord
Grey asks the Queen.

The Queen nods gravely. "It does."

"In that event, please understand that you will need
to proceed without Party support. We are obliged to withdraw the friendliness of our newspapers and the enthusiasms of our street partisans. I greatly fear, Madam,
that you will face something you have never seen before."
He bows. The men bow. The Queen stands. The men leave
her with Anglesong.

"The way is now clear for something or other," the
Queen says. "Please send word to Lord Malmesbury, An-
glesong. Tell him I must see him." She laughs harshly.
"Before I die."

The Queen writes a letter to His Majesty:

The Queen, out of circumstances which will at once be
apparent to the King, requests that His Majesty be
pleased to instruct those responsible, now that it seems
indicated that the Queen's presence is not immediately
found necessary to attend His Majesty at his coronation,
to issue a valid invitation to William Austin to attend
the coronation in her place. With the realization that the
Abbey is small and that places within it at coronation
will be oversubscribed, the Queen wishes to offer her
understanding to say that should the King wish her to
attend this great ceremony she sees no need to ask the
King to issue invitation for individual places for both
the Queen and William Austin. The Queen knows she

makes it clear to the King that it must be one or the other.

Caroline R

The King does not acknowledge receipt of the letter nor is the letter returned unopened, but William Austin disappears in the night. When the Queen awakens after the nap her physicians have insisted she take early each evening, she becomes cross because Willikin does not attend her at tea as he has always done for many years. She sends for him. The servant says he is not in his room. The Queen commands that the staff search the house for him. He is not in the house, the Queen is told, as the arrival of Malmesbury is announced.

The Queen does not wait to receive him, she hastens to greet him, meeting him at the top of the stairs.

"Malmesbury! Malmesbury!" is all she can say, weeping at the joy and comfort of seeing him once again. She flings her arms around his body and crushes her head to his chest. "So many years, so many years! Oh, my friend! My dear, my dear, how happy you make me by coming here today."

"You honor me, Your Majesty," Malmesbury says huskily. Moisture appears in his eyes.

She takes him by the hand and leads him into her sitting room. "Where have you been this time? Tell me all about everything which has happened to you."

"Wherever it was," he says, "they only changed the name of the city. It is always just another court."

"With all its hardships?"

"With all of its complexities."

They sit down side by side upon a sofa. He is sixty-eight years old; no longer portly. His hair is white but ardor fills his spirit. He looks transparent with the fatigue of decades of conspiring among nations.

"Something which you have always given me has brought you to me, my dear Malmesbury," the Queen says. "I need you badly. Willikin has disappeared."

"The boy—your—your protégé?"

"Not a boy anymore. He has vanished. He has never spent a night in his life outside my houses, but he is gone."

"For how long?"

"Since yesterday afternoon."

"Perhaps he has had some slight accident. He is undoubtedly safe in some hospital and you will be told shortly."

"No. He is the Queen's protégé, as everyone understands. There would not be such delay." Her head begins to shake as if in a tic. Her body trembles violently. With a dim, hollow voice, as Malmesbury holds her hand, the Queen tells him what she had written to the King that afternoon. Malmesbury is alarmed. "But, why, Your Majesty?" he asks her. "It is a bad time to pour more fright upon the King's deepest fear."

"I must be crowned with him!" the Queen says in a sharp cry. She buries her face in her hands.

Malmesbury looks indignant. "He would not dare to harm the boy!" he says. But his eyes, above her sunken head, seem to see otherwise.

20

Malmesbury requests that the King receive him. Malmesbury has been the King's counsellor and friend since the King's boyhood. It is a busy time, but he invites Malmesbury into his study at Carlton House.

"You've been away such a long time, my dear fellow," he says. "Moscow, Vienna, Paris and Constantinople and ever deftly effective."

"Thank you, Your Majesty."

"Your message said this is to be an urgent meeting, Malmesbury. What of that?"

"The young man, William Austin, has disappeared, Sir. He vanished from Brandenburg House while the Queen slept."

The King's face moves into a deeper shade of purple. "What of it?"

"The Queen is ill with worry."

"The Queen is ill. Full stop. Here, you, Malmesbury." He strides across to a desk drawer. He takes up the Queen's letter. "Read that choice piece of blackmail if you will, my Lord."

Malmesbury reads. "It is poorly conceived, Your Majesty. But it is a childish thing. You can see that the Queen, so distraught because she is not to be crowned with you—"

"With me or without me!"

"The letter is a clearly infantile manifestation of defiance, Sir. It is a clumsy and, I fear, a silly threat wholly without meaning, Your Majesty."

"Malmesbury, you have not watched her become transformed from a little German girl made out of cheese into a corrupt and malevolent creature who is so twisted by her ambition that she would willingly overthrow this throne and set the people against each other. This ranting about William Austin is no new threat, nor is it a childish act. Time and time again she has warned—oh, so subtly— how she would get this throne for her bastard even during the life of our own daughter. She means every word in that letter and rather than permit that snivelling little bastard contest to become the King, I have acted to dispose of it forever."

"Dispose, Your Majesty?"

"My people took him yesterday afternoon."

"Where is he, Sir?"

"He is in a madhouse where he will remain until he dies. I depend upon you to inform the Queen of that."

21

The King's robes for the coronation are of astonishing splendor. There is a crimson velvet train ornamented with golden stars. It is twenty-seven feet long, four and a half times his own length. He will wear an enormous black Spanish hat from which leap sprays of dyed ostrich feathers and a tall heron's plume. He will wear an ermine collar and ermine-trimmed robes. His dress costs the State £24,000. His coronation will cost £243,000. He is fat, deeply paunched and pouched, with a baggy face of spotted brown on purple. His thighs are so wide and so tight under his trousers that he walks as if he were carrying a bowling ball between them just above the knees. He pants and sweats at the movement of his rehearsal with the garments. But his eyes, like two open-broke hen's eggs, carry gleams of joy and triumph. He has defeated her. He knows he has defeated her. How sweet the thought is to him, as if an ancient alchemist after eighty years of trying has at last transformed the basest metal into purest gold.

He stands panting among his brothers, his pudgy arms extended outward from his sides because of the cushions of fat, wearing that enormous, plumed and grotesque hat and exclaims to them, of his coronation, "It will be an unforgettable experience for history!"

For months, architects, builders, painters, upholsterers and joiners have been at work in Westminster Abbey and Westminster Hall. Tiers of crimson cloth-covered benches, boxes and galleries are ranged beneath the western windows of the Abbey to look down upon the nave. Seats have been provided in the choir and in the north and south transept. Boxes for the royal family, the press and for foreign ministers have been built in the sanctuary.

The coronation banquet will be held in the adjoining Westminster Hall, now totally transformed. Its stone flags have been covered with a new wooden floor, which has been covered with blue cloth. Tiers of seats rise above it against the cloth-draped walls. The dais for the King and the royal dukes is at the far end of the hall; across its whole length stretch dining tables and chairs for the distinguished guests.

A raised, covered wall of vivid blue carpet leads from the Abbey to the Hall. This is destined to be the last coronation banquet ever to be held in England.

Once the King has settled himself in his appointed place, the meal will be brought to him by a procession of Household officials, gentlemen pensioners, and, on horseback, by the Lord High Constable, the Lord High Steward, and the Deputy Earl Marshal. Then a white charger rented from Astley's Circus will gallop into the Hall bearing the direct descendant of the Champion of King Richard II in full armor, the helmet on his head adorned with a white plume, to fling the gauntlet down in front of the royal dais, challenging any and all to impugn His Majesty's title.

There will be soups and salmon, turbot, and trout; venison and veal, mutton and beef; braised ham and savory pies; daubed geese and braised capon; lobster and crayfish; cold roast fowl, and roast lamb. There are dishes of piled pastries, jellies and creams; nearly five hundred sauce boats.

On the 18th July 1821, the King, the King's robes, and the King's enormous, plumed black hat are transferred to the Speaker's House at Westminster, but the ceremony of the coronation actually commences with the military occupation of London. At eleven minutes after midnight the troops that have been collected in the city are put into motion and, before one o'clock in the morning, a body of four thousand infantry have assembled in St. James's Park. This soldiery is immediately filed off in detachments to make secure the entrances into the town and to take up commanding positions in the principal streets.

Fifteen hundred men occupy the platform in the Palace Yard. Two companies of grenadiers are posted at Westminster Abbey. The 1st and 4th Life Guards, the Royal Horse Guards, the 2nd Dragoons, 9th Lancers, 10th Royal Hussars, and the 14th Light Dragoons keep up a chain of communications between the different posts. All military postings are completed before 2:00 A.M.

At 4:00 A.M. a considerable crowd assembles about Anglesong House in South Audley Street where Her Majesty waits. The crowd is so large it spills off around the corner into Hill Street. Men climb the brick wall and, sitting at the top, announce all happenings to the crowd.

"They're bringing up the horses to the door!"

"The door is opening!"

"Here she comes!"

At eight minutes after five the gate is thrown open. The Queen's coach of state, drawn by six bay horses, rolls out into South Audley Street. Lady Anglesong and Lord Malmesbury sit in the coach opposite the Queen. It is a rare sight: a leading Whig counsel and a leading Tory diplomatist attend a Queen who has been abandoned by both parties.

As the state coach moves out, Her Majesty looks shaken. She acknowledges the cheers with heavy dignity. The crowds run silently along beside and behind her coach. Her eyes are deeply wounded. "What will happen to poor Willikin?" she has asked a dozen times that morning, no longer listening to the answers.

Malmesbury decides that if he tells the Queen the truth of what has happened to William Austin, it will preoccupy her entirely throughout the cruel day ahead. Perhaps it will permit her to move more easily and mechanically through the maze of frustrations and hostility which is going to face her at Westminster Abbey.

"Your Majesty, I have had certain conversations last evening concerning the young man, William Austin."

She stares at him in the seat in front of her, her expression helpless with entreaty.

"He is safe," Malmesbury says.

"Safe? But where is he?"

Malmesbury clears his throat. He leans backward upon his life of experience in bringing bad news as if he were a comforting cushion. "Your Majesty, what I am going to tell you is but a matter of moment—"

"Say it to me!"

"He has been put into an institution—temporarily. I have no doubt it is some plot of Colonel Heller's to hold him for some exotic ransom he has devised."

"An institution? Do you mean a madhouse, Malmesbury?"

The Earl does not answer but his gaze affirms this.

"A madhouse?" the Queen says dazedly. "Willikin's mind is not strong enough to survive a madhouse. He joins his little world wherever he is and, if he is among the mad, he will go mad. What am I to do? What will I do?"

Lady Anglesong reaches over to touch the Queen's hand for just a second. "It is only a temporary thing," she says softly.

"Decidedly, yes," Malmesbury says. "Only temporary."

"But what if there is no way to make it temporary?" the Queen says in a terrified voice. "What then?"

"Your Royal Highness," Lady Anglesong tells her, "in that case, the first act by the Whig Party when it comes to power will be to free Willikin from wherever the King has put him."

But the Queen cannot know that the Whigs will not regain power for nearly eleven years. By the time they are able to rush to Willikin's aid, he will have died in the madhouse.

.   The route to Westminster Abbey is through Great Stanhope Street, Park Lane, Hyde Park Corner, through Green Park and St. James's Park to Bird Cage Walk, then by Storey Gate along Prince's Street to Dean's Yard. As they approach their destination the crowds have multiplied enormously. All along the route the soldiers present arms as Her Majesty passes, but the tone of the shouting of the mob has changed from that of the old days. There are no longer even silent, ominous mobs running beside the coach. The Whig claques have vanished as if they never were. They have been replaced with harshly hostile Tory-hired street voices that scream jeers and insults at the Queen; people who pound on the walls of the coach and spit upon it to earn the going rates.

The coach rolls to Dean's Yard Gate of the Abbey where they are told that the entrance for persons of rank to the coronation is near the Poet's Corner of the building.

Malmesbury directs the coach to drive there.

"Do you hear what the people are shouting at me?" the Queen asks Anglesong, greatly confused.

"No, Your Majesty, and neither do you."

The coachman follows the line of the platform to New Palace Yard but there is no further thoroughfare. He drives opposite the Westminster Hall Gate and stops. Lord Malmesbury alights stiff-jointedly to inquire for means to get through to the Abbey. He is shown an open gate leading to the Speaker's House where His Majesty is then waiting. Malmesbury goes back to the coach.

"I think we should alight here, Your Majesty," he says. The Queen gets down from the coach. She is weeping; the mob has shocked her deeply; she is frightened for Willikin; she tries to think only of willing herself into the Abbey to force them to lead her forward to be crowned with her husband.

With Anglesong and Malmesbury on either side of the Queen they struggle to make their way through the jostling passage. They reach the steps where persons having peers' tickets are permitted to ascend. The Queen mounts the steps alone, her head high. Her two loyal friends follow. Before she can reach the entrance, soldiers are drawn across the passage. As pale as snow, the Queen leans heavily on Malmesbury's arthritic arm. An officer advances asking for their tickets.

"This is your Queen," Malmesbury says. The officer salutes. He signals to the soldiers to allow the royal party to pass. They cross the platform and descend the other side. The Queen moves stolidly forward through the dense crowd; nine constables have moved in front of her and hold the mob away from her on all sides. They lead the way toward a passageway leading to the kitchens. Malmesbury stops the procession. "One moment, please!" he says loudly. "Her Majesty's desire is not to go into the Hall. She wishes to enter the Abbey."

Without a question, the constables change direction. The Queen is conducted through an opening in a covered way. At the entrance, Malmesbury demands admission for the Queen.

"I am sorry, milord," the doorkeeper says, "but my most profound orders are to admit no person without a peer's ticket."

"Did you ever hear of a Queen being asked for a ticket? This is your *Queen!*"

"My indelible orders are to admit no exceptions, milord. I have been drilled to know my orders."

"Once more I say to you that this is your Queen. Do you refuse her admission?"

"I am your Queen," Caroline says shakily to the doorkeeper. "I desire to pass."

It is an agony for the doorkeeper but he stands firm. "My orders could not have been more peremptory, Your Majesty. I cannot suffer you to pass without a ticket."

"I have a ticket," Malmesbury says.

"Produce it and I will permit you to pass."

"Will you enter the Abbey alone, Your Majesty?" Malmesbury asks. The Queen hesitates.

"Have preparations been made inside for Her Majesty's arrival?"

"None, milord."

"Then I am to understand that you refuse your Queen admittance to Westminster Abbey."

"I will admit her with that ticket, milord. But not without a ticket.

"I am the Queen of England," Caroline says. "I will not go unattended."

"You must not," Malmesbury says.

"Far more important than the temporary matter of your attendants, Your Majesty, is that you witness this coronation inside Westminster Abbey," Lady Anglesong states harshly. "We have already counted the cost."

"No. I would not know where to go or what to do. I would be far less than a Queen in English eyes were I to become lost in the crowd like some waif."

"We will return to the coach," Malmesbury says flatly.

People standing at the door laugh at them vulgarly. Her Majesty stares them down.

"If you will give me your card, sir," the elderly Malmesbury says to the foremost of the men, "I will deal with you tomorrow." The men walk away into the mob. Her Majesty is badly jostled by a crowd of fashionably dressed women approaching the gate with tickets in their hands. They take no notice of her whatever. The mob follows the Queen, hooting at her, making the rudest noises and laughing metallically. Daisy Hanly, the bit actress who has made royalty her specialty, blocks the Queen's way and spits at her feet. "Yer nuttin' but a little hoor," she shrills into Caroline's face. "Why don't yiz go back where yiz came from?" Lady Anglesong kicks Hanly in the ankle with all force. As the actress hops, grasping her injured ankle, Lady Anglesong strikes her across the face with her parasol, knocking her down. The Queen steps over the woman daintily and makes for the coach.

"This is a paid Tory claque!" Anglesong snarls at Malmesbury.

"You should know, Madam," he says.

The Queen leans back in the coach, her eyes closed. She is elegantly dressed in a muslin slip on a petticoat of silver brocade. She wears a small purple scarf and a splendid diamond bandeau around her head. The crowd has surrounded the coach, jeering. "Take me home, please," Caroline says.

As the coach rolls away from Westminster Abbey, the Queen's rusted voice struggles its way through the silence. "I won all the battles but I lost the war," she says. "We win what we can. There is comfort. What has Georgie won? He is old and rotting and nearly insane. He is purple and swollen and diseased. I helped to hasten that." Her eyes fill with tears. "History will think he and I were fighting for the affections of the people, as if we were politicians. But we know. We were fighting visions of each other. I could have loved him if he had been kind to me." She cuts a sob. "He could have been kind to me if I had loved him. That was the true battle both of us lost. It is grotesque, but I could have loved him. Think of that! My God! I could have *loved* him!"

When her physicians are summoned as soon as she reaches Brandenburg House, within the hour, they bleed Caroline immediately. She lies alone in a darkened room. Afternoons become nights as four days go past without Caroline taking food.

Very late on the fifth night or early one morning, still very dark, with only a candle guttering near her, Malmesbury wakens her. She stares up at him blankly.

"The King is here," he says.

"The King?" she whispers, knowing she must be dreaming. "Georgie?" She says the name as she has always said it, "Chortchie."

"He is beside you," Malmesbury says and fades into the darkness out of the room.

The old, broken woman on the bed turns her head to face the wreck of time who sits beside her bed. He glares at her with hatred.

"By God, you're a dumpy, mottled witch," he says, the candle fluttering light across his decayed face.

"It is twenty-six years later, Chortchie," she answers, trying on an appalling smile. "Why?"

"Why what? If you mean why twenty-six years, that is a good question."

"Why are you here?"

"Because you are dying and I am not."

She laughs painfully. "Oh, yes, you are, Chortchie."

"I am here because you must tell me something before you die."

She coughs. When she finishes coughing she wipes blood from her lips. "Ask."

"Who is William Austin?"

She groans. "Oh, God! How could you have done *that?*"

"Who is William Austin? I must know!"

"There is something I must know."

"What?"

"Who was Charlotte's father?"

"Ernest. Who is William Austin?"

Her breathing is very shallow. "Your brother."

"Never mind my brother. I have named my brother as Charlotte's father; now tell me who Austin is, damn you!"

"William Austin is your brother."

"My *brother?*" His voice breaks.

"William Austin is your father's son." She begins to cough again.

The King stands up and stares down at her. "You bitch! You silly, silly, *silly* bitch!" He strikes at her blanket, futilely, with his hat, snaps away from her and runs out of the room.

Thirteen days thereafter, on August 7 at twenty-five minutes past ten at night, Caroline dies at Brandenburg House. Her will directs that she be buried in Brunswick.

23

The King commands that the Queen's body be removed from England not later than Tuesday, four days away. The ships in the Thames run their flags at half-mast. Many shops close. No official day of mourning is proclaimed.

The Queen's body is wrapped in seere cloth by Her Majesty's Apothecary and his assistants in the presence of Lord Weiler. The body is placed in a shell of cedar wood. The cedar shell is placed inside an exterior coffin. There is no lying-in-state. Desperately, Lady Anglesong writes to the Prime Minister to plead with him to show humanity by extending the heartless haste which has been ordered to put the Queen's body out of England.

Your government knows English history and English customs. A monarch of England has died in England and all respect, ceremony, honour, and memory must be paid to her who was the Queen of England. Is she to be sneaked away to our coast, then shipped out as if she were a bolt of goods consigned to the German market? How can you, an Englishman of long memory and long standing, permit such an outrage to be shown to your Queen?

Allow me, my Lord, to put another question to you—why is there this so-called guard of honour appointed to attend the Queen's funeral, which honour was never given to her in life? If such is persisted in I can see much mischief and, I fear, bloodshed. No claques will control this funeral. The Queen will pass through the ranks of English people who loved her and they will take up positions to defend the outrages which the King is doing to her memory. The people have been Her Majesty's only friends. Suffer them to pay tribute to their beloved and injured Queen without being interrupted by the military. I have attended Her Majesty for twenty-six years through immense crowds and not a single incident has ever occurred.

Why, my Lord, is this corpse to be carried far off and away from the direct road through the City of London where the Lord Mayor and his Council hope to pay their Queen their distinguished respects? Is this government now deliberately trying to agitate the people? For Heaven's sake, revoke this sentence; the evil of it exceeds all calculation.

Further I will ask you why the funeral of the Queen of England should be so much more hurried than that of your Lordship's late wife?

> Yr. humble servant,
>
> Joyce Anglesong

Brandenburg House

Lord Liverpool sends Lady Anglesong his regrets that he has since received renewed commands from the King to continue to act in conformity with the orders given. The funeral must proceed from Brandenburg House Tuesday morning with a military guard of honor.

Lady Anglesong is unable to reach Sir Thomas Buckley because he is "deeply involved" with plans for an All-Ireland Tennis Competition and is "conferring with tennis officials" in Kilmoganny, County Kilkenny. No other newspaper will publish her letter to the Prime Minister either.

Her Majesty's remains are to be taken out of Brandenburg House at seven o'clock Tuesday morning in a hearse drawn by eight black horses. The funeral procession is to be preceded by the Knight Marshal's men on horseback carrying black staves. This is to be followed by the state coach of her late Majesty which will convey Lady Anglesong and Lord Malmesbury together with the Cushion and the Crown. Carriages with any mourners wishing to follow the casket to the coast will follow. The procession will be escorted by a squadron of the Royal Regiment of Horse Guards with a standard. They will be relieved at Romford by a like guard of the 4th Light Dragoons. Similar reliefs will take place at Chelmsford and Colchester. When the funeral reaches Chelmsford, the remains will be placed in a church under military guard during the night.

"Disgraceful!" Lady Anglesong yells as she balls up the piece of paper and flings it into the undertaker's face. "You are a toad to agree to bury a Queen of England in such a fashion!"

By Her Majesty's will simple identification is to be the only inscription placed on her coffin. HERE LIES CAROLINE OF BRUNSWICK, INJURED QUEEN OF ENGLAND. His Majesty's Government ignores the Queen's last request. The King orders the attachment of a different plaque to the coffin top.

Depositum
Serenissimae Principesse
CAROLINE AMELIE ELIZABETH
Dei Gratia Reginae Consortis
Augustissimi Potentissiami Monarchae
GEORGI QUARTI
Dei Gratia Britanniarium Regis Fedei
Defensoria Regis Hanoverae ac Brunsvici
Ac Luneburgi Ducis
Obit VII die mensie Augusti
Anno Domini MDCCCXXI
Aetatis Suae LIV

At 5:30 A.M. the undertaker, an oily mask named John Bryson, presents himself to Lady Anglesong, the Queen's executor. At 6:00 A.M. precisely a squadron of the Oxford Blues arrive from their barracks in Regent's Park. They ride up the avenue from the lodge and form a line in front of the house. The helmets of the officers are half-covered with black crepe. Bryson informs Lady Anglesong that he is ready to proceed with the funeral.

Anglesong makes a formal announcement in the presence of Lord Malmesbury, the Duchess Van Itallie, Lady Jane Montant, the Contessa Salvadore, and the Margravine Schrader as witnesses. "I enter my protest against the removal of Her Majesty's body in right of the legal power which is invested in me by her late Majesty, as executor. Proper arrangements for the funeral of a Queen of England could not be made in the few swift hours allotted to funeral preparations by the King. Proper arrangement for the long journey of the body of the Queen of England and its voyage by sea upon the ships of a great maritime power have not been made because time has not been allowed for it. I command that the body not be removed until the arrangements suitable to the rank and dignity of the deceased are made."

Anglesong's short cropped hair is grizzled with gray. She wears spectacles. Her square shoulders bulge with indignation through her coat. She wheels like a drill sergeant and leaves the room, the witnesses following her. As soon as they are gone, Bryson summons his carpenter, produces the government's elaborate gold plaque, and orders that the carpenter. screw it upon the coffin after removing the plaque ordered by Caroline's will.

The funeral procession is a shabby affair. Even the cavalry horses seem to be rented for the day from some failing livery stable. The horses struggling to pull the hearse are bony and listless. The carriages for the mourners are badly in need of paint and springs and squeak noisily; Bryson is a cunning man with a farthing.

The procession requires eleven and a half hours to cross London, a journey of about nine miles. Outriders seem to be reporting to Mr. Bryson's carriage about where the crowds are assembling across London to say farewell to their Queen. Bryson attempts to route the cortège around these crowds but soon enough the mob catches on that they are being cheated. Several ugly riots are recorded. Four civilians and two soldiers are killed. Sixty-one people and forty soldiers are wounded. Roadways are blocked with wagons and carts. Iron fences are ripped up and their pikes used as weapons. Stones are hurled. Great outrage is expressed against the King's brutal conduct toward his dead wife.

The procession arrives at Chelmsford at dawn on Wednesday, twenty-two hours after its non-stop departure from Brandenburg House. The handful of mourners are told that they may sleep for a while, but Lady Anglesong goes into the church to see the coffin. She discovers that the Queen's requested plaque has been removed. She summons a carpenter, has the King's plaque taken off and a new plaque bearing the Queen's inscription screwed into the coffin top. Mr. Bryson sends a dispatch rider to London for instructions from the Prime Minister. When Lady Anglesong awakens to the tolling of church bells and to the blast of bugles of the 4th Dragoons playing the Dead March from *Saul*, she hastens to take her place in the procession to find the Queen's plaque gone and the King's plaque once more screwed into its place. Bryson looks at her from his place beside the driver in the hearse and gives her his turd-eater's smile. The funeral leaves at once, half-hoping to leave Lady Anglesong behind. The royal coach needs to travel at double speed to overtake the procession on its swift way to Harwich. After a two-hour ride they come to Doverport, a hamlet on a hilltop where the sea opens to their view.

Far out on the Channel off the Lagnard Fort they see the *Glasgow*, the frigate that is to carry the royal coffin to Germany, surrounded by six smaller vessels, which will sail as an escort. At Doverport the funeral is met by a detachment of the 86th; 150 men with a stand of colors and a band. Dense collections of people line the road that goes down the slope past the fort.

Bryson's greasy hearse leads the way into Harwich. Twenty-five cavalry of the 4th Dragoons follow. Inside the royal coach, Lady Anglesong clutches the Cushion and the Crown upon her lap, the crown a tawdry bauble decorated with white beads strung round in a manner that would have disgraced a Sunday School theatrical.

At the quay, Malmesbury hands out the Cushion and the Crown to Bryson, then clambers out and down with painful slowness. Painfully he reaches up and, still more painfully, hands Lady Anglesong down. When, at last, they are standing on the quay, they see twelve bearers *running* with the coffin out along the far jetty, which is fifty yards away. The Cushion and the Crown, held by a sprinting messenger, pursue the coffin.

"I am ordered by the King's command to state that this is as far as you may go," Bryson says with his gagging west country dialect.

"May you and all your family be buried in this same cowardly way," Anglesong says. She and Malmesbury drive off in the royal coach, directing the driver to take them to the top of the hill. As they drive away the slings are slipped under the unpalled coffin and the jetty crane swings it aboard the barge of the *Glasgow*. Six of the long boats from the escorting vessels tow the barge off as the first minute gun is fired from the fort. Twelve laborers and a nondescript from the Chamberlain's office pay last homage to the departed Queen of England.

From the top of the hill, Anglesong and Malmesbury watch the *Glasgow* and her escort grow smaller and smaller. They stare, remembering.

"I loved her," Malmesbury says.

Anglesong breaks. She turns to face Lord Malmesbury, her hands reach out to him for support, her head falling upon his frail chest. "Oh, my God, Lord Malmesbury," she sobs. "How long and how much I loved her as well."

However bizarre the facts of the life of Amelia Elizabeth Caroline, Princess of Brunswick-Wolfenbüttel, she did indeed suffer to marry George IV of England to live unhappily ever after. She was born on May 17, 1768. She had many gifts and skills as a musician, toymaker, sculptress and developer of children. She was the daughter of the greatest martial figure among lifetime professional soldiers of northern Europe, Charles William Ferdinand, Duke of Brunswick. Her mother was the favorite sister of George III and the enemy of his wife, Queen Charlotte. Caroline's husband was her first cousin; George III, her uncle. She was related by blood and by marriage to the great, reigning houses of Europe: the Hohenzollern, the Romanoff, and the Hapsburg. With her uncle, her mother, and her husband she carried the taint of porphyria in her blood, a disease which produces mental imbalance and sudden collapse. It was a legacy from Sophia, Electress of Hanover, granddaughter of James I of the English House of Stuart. The Hanoverians, represented by these Georges, inherited the English throne through these Stuart lines.

Chosen by her uncle, thwarting the will of Queen Charlotte, Caroline married the Prince of Wales on April 8, 1795, for political reasons of her father's, desperate money reasons of her husband's. The royal couple separated in 1796. Caroline lived in retirement until 1813, having had one child. She traveled abroad notoriously in the years between 1813 and 1820. She returned to England as Queen on July 5, 1820, was accused of adultery and tried before the House of Lords in August that year. She died August 7, 1821, and was buried in Brunswick. Several characters introduced into this novel are fictional; and three situations. The rest is starkest history as it was lived.

Richard Condon
Kilmoganny, Ireland
13th October 1976